# THE EARTHSTONE

## FRANCESCA TYER

*The Earthstone* © Francesca Tyer 2023

The right of Francesca Tyer to be identified as the Author of the work has been asserted by her in accordance with the Copyright, Designs and Patents Act 1988.

All rights reserved in all media. No part of this publication may be reproduced, stored in a retrieval system, or transmitted in any form or by any means, electronic, mechanical, recording, photocopying, the Internet or otherwise, without the prior written permission from the author, nor be otherwise circulated in any form of binding or cover other than that in which it is published and without a similar condition being imposed on the subsequent purchaser.

Printed and bound in Great Britain by Clays Ltd, St Ives plc

Authors Reach
www.authorsreach.com

ISBN: 978-1-7392469-4-5

All characters and events featured in this publication are purely fictitious and any resemblance to any person, place, organisation/company, living or dead, is entirely coincidental and unintentional.

# Prologue

THE sky was the colour of cracked ice. It was not the pale blush of dawn nor the deeper shade of twilight but the semblance of something man made. A bluish haze hung just below the clouds which streaked across the sky in imperfect lines. Though the air was still, it crackled with an uneasy tension. It was the kind of atmosphere created by restless people. Those who are drawn like magnets to a crowd and thrive on expectation and secrecy.

Waiting in hushed silence under the icy sky were many such people. They stood close together, like penguins huddling to keep warm in the depths of an Antarctic winter. Every one of them was dressed in black, their faces concealed by deep hoods. Even without these hoods however, they would have remained anonymous, their features carefully covered with unsmiling silver masks.

The people stood in a multi-layered semicircle around one curve of a great earthen basin. Once it had been a lake but the water had dried up many centuries ago, leaving this pit behind. Years of drought had cracked the reddish earth, the fissures branching out in all directions like swollen veins. As the people stood waiting, a low hum began somewhere at the back of the group. A single voice which was then joined by a second and a third. The sound passed like a wave through the crowd, swelling as new voices joined the force. No words were spoken and the sound rose and fell between three semitones in a minor third.

The voices were greedy, desperate even and the chanting became more and more frantic. As the sound reached its peak, fully flourished like the head of some hideous flower, a figure appeared at the edge of the basin. The chant faded into a unanimous gasp and the people then fell silent. Some dropped to their knees but others stayed standing as the mysterious figure swept towards them. Like those in the crowd, the stranger's face was hidden beneath a deep hood. Dressed all in black, there was no way to distinguish them from the masses, save for the bluish light carried in one palm. The crowd stood rapt, waiting with breathless anticipation. Silence presided a moment longer before it was broken by a single voice.

'You come to see if I am real.'

The crowd gasped again as the figure raised a hand and whipped back its hood. A woman stood before them, jet black hair falling in waves over her shoulders. She too wore a mask but it only covered half her face. At least, it appeared to be a mask, but the lacy silver patterning almost looked like it was part of her skin. Her eyes were dark green and so deep that they were impossible to define. The people in the crowd had indeed come to see if this woman was real. They had all heard rumours of an enchantress who possessed a power unlike any other before her. Not just an enchantress but a Dark Mistress, the first woman to take on the power of the Dark Masters who had passed before her.

'If you come to honour me, why do so many of you still stand before me?' the woman whispered. Her lips did not move but her voice filled the basin like the whisper of wind in the trees. 'Kneel and you too will be honoured. Kneel and you will bear witness to the making of history.'

Those in the crowd knew they were here for more than one reason. They were here to be tested, to see if they were worthy enough to join the cause. What this cause was, they didn't yet know. Before those still standing had the chance to kneel, the woman swept her hand through the air, left to right in a great arc. The people fell like dominoes at her will, heads bent towards the earth.

'Much better,' she hissed. 'If I am to welcome you into the cause, you must show your dedication and respect. As you well know, I have gathered you all here for a reason. Today we make history. Today we take all the false promises of the past and create a new world. Many in Emryth have forgotten that there is more than one way to think and feel. More than just the light. There is great power to be found in the shadows, an ancient power that many have chosen to forget.'

Her eyes raked over the crowd. The one or two people who had dared to look up dipped their heads once more.

'There are some among you who are truly worthy to join me. If you wish to turn away, now is your chance.' She paused expectantly, waiting to see if anyone dared move. 'All desperate to be honoured,' she whispered. 'It is the human way.'

As her voice trailed away, another came from the crowd. The tone was confident, spoken by one who seemed not to fear her.

'How do we know that what you offer is real? How do we know this ancient power exists?'

The woman's eyes flashed dangerously and fixed themselves upon the brazen speaker. 'Step forward so that I may see you better,' she commanded.

Slowly, but with head held high, the speaker stepped from

between the throngs. The heavy gait suggested that it was a man. The woman laughed as he knelt on the ground before her. She raised her hand and a bolt of lightning split the icy sky. It shot downward and struck the man directly in the chest. He shrieked in pain but did not fall. The lightning burnt him where he knelt, running through his veins like molten gold until he became no more than a pile of ash.

'Who else?' the woman demanded.

No one answered her. She raised her hand again and the ashy mound spun into a whirlwind before her. With a flick of her wrist, she sent it hurtling towards the crowd. It showered upon all those standing in the first few rows but no one flinched.

'Tonight, all those who join me are part of a great task.' The woman touched her fingers together and light sparked between them. 'Long ago, the Dark Master Jasper claimed to have found a power that could surpass all others. In his search to become the most powerful being that ever lived, he stumbled across another world.' A fresh gasp ran through the crowd but the woman ignored it. 'This world lay across time from our own. It was much the same but with one key difference. It was a world without magic.'

This information proved too much for one person at the back of the crowd who keeled over in a dead faint. The woman saw this occurrence but did not react as many thought she might. She simply carried on speaking.

'Jasper believed that if he could claim power over this other world, he could make himself immortal. He dedicated his life to finding a way to break down the barrier between worlds, a barrier some people believed to have been forged across many millennia. If the worlds were once joined together, it has not yet been proved. While Jasper made progress, he never achieved his goals for one reason and one alone: Arvad the Wanderer. The legend of Arvad states that he created four crystals that when combined, had the power to make a man immortal. Not only that, but they had the ability to destroy the light once and for all. These crystals and their power somehow strengthened the gateway between the worlds, making it almost impossible to penetrate the barrier without them.'

As the woman spoke, a shadowy figure appeared at her side. Then came another and another until a whole row of cloaked strangers stood in a semi-circle around her, their bodies wavering uncertainly in the cold blue light.

'Tonight, we achieve what Jasper never could,' the woman continued, her voice rising. 'We enter this other world: Earth.' She waved a hand at the figures standing around her. 'These individuals are already of my blood. They share my thoughts, my purpose, my poison. Once they were like you, ordinary people. I changed them, gave them new power. They are now Shadows, thriving in the dark and weakening in the light. They are here to test you.'

The Shadows began to filter amongst the crowd. They raised their hands as one and a vast sheen of light burst forth over the hushed people. The light was the same cold blue as the sky, hazy yet electrifying. Several individuals began to scream. They clutched at their throats as the light closed in around them, suffocating them one by one. More voices joined them, the sound filling the basin, louder than the chanting had been but equally unsettling. Just as swiftly as these voices had swelled however, they began to diminish, as all around the basin life was snuffed out.

When the sheen of light faded at last, only ten people had been spared. As they knelt on the dry red earth, awaiting their fate, ten bolts of lightning shot from the sky. There was the smell of burning flesh as the searing beams struck the ten survivors. In a matter of moments, their bodies became piles of gritty ash. Something moved where each of them had been. Smoke rose from the ash piles, swirling upwards to form ten translucent pillars. The fumes shifted and changed until they took on shadowy human forms.

'Welcome, Shadows.' The woman stepped towards these newly birthed beings with outstretched arms. 'You are the worthy ones,' she crooned. 'Now you too are of my blood. I ask you to stand in a circle around me and join hands.'

The newly born Shadows did as she commanded. They joined hands with their dark-hearted kin to form a wide circle around her. Blue light filtered around their ghostly fingers, binding them together. In the centre of the circle, the woman opened her palms to reveal a crystal resting in each: one white, the other black. It was from these crystals that the icy light emanated. Now uncovered, the sky glowed brighter and brighter until it was almost blinding. The air began to shiver, like a snake casting off its skin, and the Shadows trembled with it.

'Tonight the world changes,' the woman whispered. 'The darkness rises again and the age of the Belladonna begins.'

Her voice was drowned out by an unbearable crashing sound and everything went dark.

∞

In a brightly lit corridor on the third floor of a hospital building, a man was pacing back and forth between the bare white walls. His expression suggested that he wished to be patient but his restless movements gave his true feelings away. The corridor was silent, too silent for a maternity ward. A midwife had told him that his wife was the only woman even close to birth that night but so far no infant cry had rung through the ward. The midwife had sought to comfort him but her words had instead rendered him incapable of anything but pacing. He couldn't even bear to sit by his wife's side, despite her begging for him to stay.

As he strode towards the window at the far end of the corridor, the strip light above him flickered. He stopped for a moment to consider it. It flickered again, then dimmed, the yellow-white bulb turning an odd shade of blue. The man was not superstitious; he was editor-in-chief of an important newspaper for goodness sake! He published serious stories for serious readers and was a firm believer in science, facts and logic. Yet somehow the flickering light made him uneasy. Perhaps because it matched the uncertain rhythm of his heart.

He stopped by the window, his eyes fixed on the door at the far end of the corridor. From the other side, screams of pain drifted towards him. He wanted to block out the sound but found himself frozen. As if in some dream, he then heard a child's cry. It sounded far away and yet he knew it came from behind the door. He took a step towards it but the corridor suddenly went dark. In fact, all the lights inside the hospital and in the streets outside the window flickered and went out.

Inside the delivery room, at the end of the hospital bed, the bright red lines of the digital clock froze at ten to twelve.

# Chapter 1

JAMES Fynch opened his eyes. He was trembling, though he wasn't sure why for his evening doze had been dreamless. His throat felt tight and he pressed it gently, half expecting it to be bruised, though again he wasn't sure why. A memory hovered at the edges of his consciousness, one that he couldn't quite grasp. He had almost caught it at the point of waking but it had all too quickly slipped away.

Perhaps it was the voice outside the window that had unsettled him. Even though he couldn't make out the words, he knew what was being said. The speaker stood in the same spot every day from dawn until dusk, murmuring words of mutiny to anyone who would listen. He was not the only speaker either. There were others, scattered across the Arisselian streets, luring in vulnerable listeners with their charmed voices. As yet, no one had dared to try and stop them.

The voice droned on and on, slithering through the air in search of unsuspecting listeners. Though the speaker's tone was dull and unimpressionable, the steady rhythm of his speech was strangely irresistible. The words were almost indistinguishable, delivered like a low chant, but this hardly mattered to the speaker or his listeners. All charm belonged not to the words or meanings but to their mysterious deliverer.

Disentangling himself from his bedding, James rolled off his bed and stumbled over to the window. A sliver of evening light gleamed through a gap in the curtains which he now pulled aside. The speaker stood in the street below, just a few steps away from the door of the Night Inn, dressed in a long black cloak. A group of people were clustered around him, listening greedily to his words. Curiosity overriding his better judgement, James pushed his bedroom window open and leaned outside to listen.

'Lies,' the speaker rasped. 'All lies. They say you are safe, that this is the age of peace, but these are falsehoods.'

'How do you know?' a deep-voiced listener asked. 'How do you know they are lying?'

'How do I know?' The speaker laughed softly. 'People are dying. Not just in the south but all over the world. The darkness is rising once again and it is stronger than ever before.'

'The Circle wouldn't let that happen,' another listener declared. 'They defeated the darkness once before, for good. There has been peace for seven hundred years.'

'The Circle is weak,' the speaker replied scornfully. 'Open your eyes! There is darkness everywhere and still you don't see it. Yes, their forces were once defeated, but never for good. Darkness has bubbled under the surface for centuries and now rises again to end the age of peace. The power of the north is dwindling and the centre of the world will soon lie in the south, in Tenbrisen.'

'How is it that you know this too?' The deep-voiced listener spoke again. 'Are you one of them?'

Before the speaker had a chance to reply, a new voice piped up.

'What of the boy?'

James froze. He had listened to these speeches several times before but they had only ever referred to unrest in the west and south and to the rising darkness. The speakers were advocates of neither dark nor light, but of the truth and rebellion against corrupted governments. To his memory, there had never been any talk of a boy.

'There is no boy,' the speaker spat. 'There is no saviour coming to your rescue. You are alone and must build your own armies to fight against those who seek to control you.'

James shivered, even though the evening air was warm. None of the listeners seemed to understand that they too were being manipulated. The government, the darkness and these speakers were all the same, seeking to indoctrinate those weaker than themselves. The gullible masses, Will had called them. Yet the crowd still listened, completely entranced, as the voice droned on.

'Where is this rumoured boy you speak of? Will he put down his toys and save us all? I think not.'

The crowd laughed. It was not the easy laughter shared by friends over beer and wine. It was a tense, uneasy sound, uttered by those who are no longer certain of their own beliefs. Tired faces turned towards the speaker, doubtful and yet too fearful to question otherwise. James shivered again. Outbursts like this had become all too common in Arissel. The overground city was no longer lifeless, but a place where speakers and listeners walked freely. Some even managed to slip into the Underground City where they were forbidden to go, but again no one dared stop them.

James was about to pull away from the window when the speaker suddenly looked up. His face was covered with a thin silver mask, beneath which a pair of dark eyes glittered. James hurriedly withdrew but the speaker's gaze followed him. Even with the curtains drawn between them, those dark eyes penetrated the fabric, daring him to reveal himself. Leaving the window open, James hurried back to his bed. Reaching under the crumpled pillow, his fingers met the smooth surround of the gold clock. He drew it out carefully, feeling the second hand pulse like a tiny heart against his skin. He had grown so accustomed to its presence that he hardly noticed the ticking sound anymore. The clock came everywhere with him, partly to keep it safe but also because its presence provided him with a sense of comfort. It offered a way back to his world, the only way he knew.

Ever since Albert had told him about the quartz bound within the mechanisms of the clock, he'd been especially careful with it. Part of him feared that, like his phone, which also contained traces of quartz, the clock somehow connected him to the darkness. Turning the timepiece over in his hands, he let his fingers explore the familiar curves of the rounded frame and the irregular edges of the dials. For the hundredth time since his return to Arissel from Muir, the little fishing village on the Davo coast, his thoughts turned to the clockmaker. It was odd how much the old man seemed to know but never quite said. On the three occasions James had met him, he'd spoken of the clock as if he'd known about its powers, though he had never revealed its secrets.

As James turned the clock over in his hands, its base caught the evening light still seeping through the gap in the curtains. The usually smooth base was interrupted by a small scratch and he frowned. He was certain there had never been a mark there before; the clock always looked bright and smooth, despite being an antique. Crossing over to the window again, he held the object up to the light. To his surprise, he saw that the metal wasn't scratched at all but etched with a row of letters, the strokes so tiny that they were unreadable. He almost wished he had his phone to take a zoomed in photo with but this desire quickly dissipated. He wondered if the letters spelt out the name of the clock's maker but before he could properly consider this, a knock sounded at his door. Slipping the timepiece into his pocket, he hurried to answer.

'Are they out there again?'

Will stood in the landing, dressed in shorts and a t-shirt with his cloak flung carelessly over one arm. He stepped past James who stood holding the door open for him and went to peer out of the window.

'Just one,' James replied, his voice still croaky from sleep.

'You shouldn't listen to them,' Will reproved. He peeled aside the curtains and looked down to where the speaker still stood. 'We'll have to go the back way to avoid the crowd.'

'The back way to where?'

A great shout suddenly rose from the street. James joined Will by the window and they looked down at the crowd below. Two of the listeners had broken into a fight. One launched a fist at the other but this weak attempt was countered with a burst of light. Another flash quickly followed but this one wasn't the result of magic. It was instead the glint of a knife. The assailant lifted the blade and plunged it into his rival's chest. His victim crumpled to the ground, blood pouring from the wound onto the cobblestones. All too quickly, the onlookers melted away, leaving the body to turn cold in the street.

'This kind of thing is going to keep happening.' Will turned to James with pursed lips. 'Come on, we should go. We said we'd meet Arthur and Rai before the festival starts and we're already running late.'

James tore his eyes away from the body. 'Right,' he replied vaguely. 'The festival. Let me just grab my cloak.'

The street behind the inn was quiet when they slipped out onto it several minutes later. They made their way quickly towards the Underground City, seeing no one along the way. There was only one person lingering outside the city gate when they arrived. On seeing James and Will however, the stranger darted through the gate and vanished into the tunnel beyond. The boys hurriedly followed, trying to make up the time they'd lost watching the fight outside the Night Inn. Reaching the end of the tunnel, they stopped for a moment to admire the transformation taking place in the Underground City.

Thousands of orbs floated in the cavernous space above them. There were more than usual, working together to exile any shadows which might otherwise have dared to linger. The air vibrated with sound, an intense hum like that of bees in a disturbed hive. Rich scents also permeated the space: spices, animal skins, cakes, raw meat and cinnamon punch. There were perfumes too, drenching the air yet still unable to mask the unavoidable stench of people. This swirling sensory pool reminded James of Christmas fairs back at home in Kent, only here everything was intensified by the compacted space.

'Festival day is always mad,' Will warned with a grin. 'Come on.'

He slipped between two food stalls and James followed. Will hadn't told him much about the festival. He had simply referred to it as the Festival of Light, an Arisselian tradition that had taken place on the same day each year since the city was first built. When that was exactly, James didn't know. As he followed Will through the thickening throngs, he couldn't help smiling to himself. He had become used to the busy underground streets, having spent almost every day here since their return from Muir. For the first time in his life, he felt like he really belonged somewhere. His own world, his parents, a life without magic all felt like a dream.

This evening, the underground streets were busier than usual. People swarmed about him and Will like flies, crowding about the stalls and stuffing themselves with food and drink. He kept his head down with his hood pulled low over his eyes, fearful that he might be recognised. Few people in Arissel really knew him but many looked at him as if they did. It was as Albert had said, the first time they'd come to Arissel: people could sense the absence of magic. Even though his wrist bore a symbol and he had been able to conjure magic for some time now, he still carried traces of his world.

The courtyard outside Elliad's Library was surprisingly quiet when they reached it. Arthur and Aralia were waiting for them, perched on the stone seat which surrounded the central fountain. Both were reading but looked up as Will and James approached.

'Been waiting long?' Will enquired, reaching the fountain in two strides.

Aralia shook her head, her long blonde plait swinging over one shoulder. 'Not long at all, but it looks like the festival is about to begin so you're just in time.'

The courtyard had been decorated with hundreds of candles. They were as yet unlit, placed in every available nook and cranny. They ran all along the walls and up the library steps, waiting to fulfil their purpose.

'How d'we know when it starts?' James asked.

His words were drowned out by an air splitting crack. The cave was suddenly illuminated by a shower of sparks that fizzled between the orbs like shooting stars. A great cheer arose and the candles in the courtyard sprang to life of their own accord.

'That's how you know,' Will grinned. 'Now we can celebrate. For one night and one night only, we're free.' He spread his arms out theatrically and a coin fell from his sleeve, bouncing onto the cobbles with a dull clink. His smile widened. 'Drink, anyone? It's on me. I forgot my mum gave me some money.'

After receiving nods of approval, he wandered away to find some refreshments. Almost every night since their return to Arissel, James, Will, Arthur and Aralia had been committed to long training sessions with Dina, Kaedon and Oede. As soon as it was dark, they crept out of the city and into the Ari Forest where they could work without disturbance. From Kaedon, they had learnt navigation, including how to read complex nautical charts. Oede had taught them essential combat skills, using both physical strength and magic, his quick feet making him an impossible opponent. Dina meanwhile had worked with them on marksmanship, using daggers to find the bullseye in the centre of target rings she'd etched onto the trees. The companions had learnt a lot but the relentless nature of their training was making them restless.

Watching the light wavering across the courtyard, James' gaze came to rest on a figure lurking near the library steps. They were leaning against the left newel post and facing the fountain. Like most people in Arissel, the figure was dressed in a long black cloak with a wide hood concealing their features. Though he couldn't be sure, James felt the stranger's eyes upon him. He wondered what purpose they had in watching him so intently. Trying to smile as if he hadn't noticed the observer, he sat down beside Arthur and spoke in a low voice.

'We're being watched,' he hissed. Arthur made a sound as if he hadn't really heard. 'We're being *watched*!' James repeated, a little louder this time.

Aralia's head snapped up. 'Where? Who by?'

'Try not to make it obvious,' James whispered, 'but they're standing by the library steps.'

'There's no one there,' Arthur said bluntly. 'We're the only people in the courtyard.'

Glancing towards the library again, James saw that the stranger had vanished. He was about to speak again when he saw a movement on the other side of the library steps. Hovering beneath the eaves of another building stood the same figure. He knew it was the same person from the way they stood, right leg slightly bent, carrying their weight. Now however the hood had been pushed back to reveal the soft features of a young woman. Her eyes were far from soft however and her gaze pierced through him from across the courtyard. As he watched her, she began walking towards him. He was suddenly struck by the feeling that he'd met her somewhere before.

# Chapter 2

JAMES stood up hurriedly, no longer trying to hide the fact that he'd noticed the stranger. Stepping backwards, he bumped into Will who had appeared behind him. The full jug his friend was carrying spilled over, splashing the cobblestones with crimson juice.

'Whoa,' Will exclaimed, steadying himself. 'These drinks weren't cheap.'

'Sorry!' James apologised. 'Look, I know you've just bought us drinks but we have to leave. Now.'

Will raised his eyebrows questioningly. 'Why? What's happened? We've only just arrived.'

'Look, over there.' Arthur set down the cup Will handed him and pointed across the courtyard.

A group of people had appeared at the edge of the courtyard. Each held an orb in their right hand and stood facing away from the fountain. Above their heads, three flickering flames hovered.

'Who are they?' Aralia asked in a hushed voice. 'Where did they suddenly appear from?'

'This can't be good,' Will cut across her. 'You were right, James; we should probably go.'

He downed the juice he'd poured for himself in one gulp and set his cup down on the stone bench. A great shout arose from the other side of the courtyard. The group of people raised their right hands and one by one the orbs they held burst into flame. Without any hesitation, their bearers flung the balls of fire towards the library. Though the library was built from stone, the orbs were not formed of ordinary fire and the steps began to burn. The small flames flourished into a great blaze, encouraged by the arsonists who gathered up the candles set around the courtyard and added them to the inferno.

'Come on,' Will urged, 'follow me. I know a way out.'

He led the way across the courtyard and slipped into an alleyway on the other side. It was long and narrow and devoid of people. When this alley came to an end, they joined another and another, heading towards the heart of the Underground City.

'I didn't know there were all these backstreets,' James remarked.

'There's a whole labyrinth back here if you know where to look,' Will replied with a nervous glance over his shoulder. 'Shops, cafes, a bank. There's even a small school on the other side for those who don't have tutors or go to the academy in Idessa. This end of the city isn't as pleasant as the other. People don't tend to come here if they can help it.'

'Why's that?' Arthur asked.

'It's where people come to trade in illegal goods. There are laws against it happening but the city authorities never do anything about it. Come on, the sooner we leave this part behind, the better.'

It didn't take them long to reach the tunnel leading out of the Underground City. It was the only route in and out of the city and on busy days, easily became overcrowded. They had to fight against the noisy throngs pushing their way into the already packed cavern. The newcomers were evidently unaware of the disruption in the library courtyard. Even the stallholders who had been here for hours were oblivious.

'James!'

Hearing someone call his name, James spun around. Scanning the colourful crowd, he spotted a familiar, red-haired figure pushing her way towards him.

'Dina!' he exclaimed. 'What're you doing here?'

She stopped in front of him and placed her inked hands on her hips. 'Looking for you! All of you. I'm afraid I need you all to come with me.'

Will's face fell. 'Come with you? Where? We thought you weren't going to be here for the festival. You weren't meant to come back from Idessa until tomorrow.'

Dina nodded and her hooped earrings glittered. 'Plans change,' she said dryly. 'It wasn't my choice, believe me. Now come on, follow me and quickly.' Pushing her way past the companions, she entered the city tunnel.

'Where are we going?' Will pressed. He kept close behind her as she forged a path between the throngs.

'I can't tell you right now.' Her voice sounded strained and the patches beneath her eyes were dark with worry.

'Are Kaedon and Oede back too?' Aralia asked.

Dina came to a standstill and spun around. Her hair swung to one side, revealing the usually hidden butterfly tattoo on her neck. 'Will you all just stop asking questions, please?' she snapped. Seeing Aralia's taken aback expression, she softened a little. 'Look, I need you to collect your things and meet me in the forest as soon as you can. You know the place. That's all I can say for now. Just promise me you'll come as quickly as you can?'

'Yes, we'll do as you ask,' Aralia meekly agreed and pursed her lips at Will.

Above ground again, Dina parted ways with them and hurried off into the evening gloom. Arthur and Aralia split off too, heading back to their lodgings just outside the city. Their City Passes had been approved that morning and they were due to move into the Night Inn in just a few days. With their group now diminished, Will and James also hurried away. The streets were clear and they reached the Night Inn without interruption. The body had been removed from the street outside the front door but the blood had dried in uneven lines between the cobblestones.

With little time to waste, the boys hurried upstairs to collect their things. It didn't take long as their travel bags had been packed and ready for months, just in case. James had borrowed a rucksack from Will as his old bag was no longer fit for use. In just five minutes, they were ready and reconvened by the back door. Neither of them spoke as they made their way along the streets towards the city gates. They usually crept through the hidden door in the city wall to reach the forest but tonight the main gates stood open, welcoming visitors from neighbouring towns and villages to the Festival of Light. Though there were guards standing watch, they paid little attention to James and Will as they slipped past.

It was dark amongst the trees but they knew the way and crept panther-like through the undergrowth. It did not take long to reach the clearing where they usually trained. Arthur and Aralia were already there, standing beneath the light of an orb. Dina, Kaedon and Oede were also present, occupied with saddling five ferastia. The animals stood close together, their silvery, reptilian skins liquified by the dancing light. These horse-like creatures could travel long distances at high speed and although James had ridden one before, he felt a knot of anticipation settling in his stomach. As he stepped into the clearing, his gaze fell upon another figure who stood amongst the trees. Though the stranger's back was turned towards him, he instinctively knew who it was.

'Albert.'

On hearing his name, Albert turned around and stepped into the light. His body was not faint as James had come to expect based on previous encounters, but as real and solid as the surrounding trees. His gingery hair peeked from beneath his hood and the stubble on his chin and cheeks had grown into a healthy beard.

'We're all here,' he said without introduction. His eyes flickered from one face to another before coming to rest on James. 'I have summoned you all here for a reason. Darkness is spreading across all corners of this earth. The Belladonna has advanced more quickly than anyone could ever have imagined. Her powers continue to grow and she will not rest until she has assumed absolute power over all.'

'These are rumours, are they not?' Kaedon interjected. He too stepped into the light, brushing his shaggy hair back so that his single earring was for a moment exposed. 'The people of Arissel and Idessa say that there is little to fear. Even the academics say as much.'

'The people are wrong,' Albert countered. 'They do not know what they say. As for the academics, they only believe what they think to be true. The Belladonna is gathering an army in the south, an army of Laithe. Several troops have been dispatched from Arvora and are heading south as we speak.'

'You've mentioned the Laithe before,' Arthur recalled. 'What are they?'

'Sad creatures, born from the souls of those who still cling to life. Those who suffered unhappiness or sickness and cannot let go of this realm for the next.'

'Ghosts, then,' Will suggested.

'In some ways, yes, but in others, no,' Albert replied vaguely. 'These creatures have been poisoned with darkness. They cannot be killed with physical weapons or with magic. In fact, no one knows how they can be killed. It is both their strength and their weakness.'

His words cast a spell over the forest. James felt their impression settling on his skin like melting ice.

'How is their indestructability a weakness?' he asked.

Albert turned his gaze onto the surrounding trees. 'Immortality breeds arrogance.'

'An indestructible army.' Kaedon gripped the dagger at his belt. 'An army no one can survive against.'

Albert nodded, his usually serene features marred by a frown. 'Neither the Laithe nor the Shadows will strike without her command. She is waiting.'

James suppressed a shiver. 'Waiting for what?'

'For you to make your next move.'

Unable to speak for a moment, James simply stared at Albert whose unsmiling gaze was now fixed upon him.

'It is becoming increasingly evident that the Belladonna will not seek out the crystals herself,' Albert continued. 'In fact, her interest in them seems to be waning, though her reasons are not clear. Her interest in you however suffers no such decline. For this reason, we must leave Arissel tonight. I thought we could wait longer but there is unrest in the city and it is not safe.'

'They were setting the library on fire,' Aralia remarked. 'Who would do such a thing?'

'Those who listen to the speakers who stand in the streets.' Oede spoke for the first time since their arrival but did not step forth from the shadows. 'They nurse a hatred for authority. Here, in Idessa, across Camil and no doubt beyond.'

'There was someone else in the Underground City,' James said. 'A young woman. She was watching us but disappeared when the protest began.'

'Ah yes, the ancient Festival of Light,' Albert recalled. 'I am sorry you'll be missing it but there will be other years.'

Glancing around the clearing, James became aware of a new presence lurking just beyond the light. A girl stood in the shadows, watching them. Realising she had been seen, she stepped into the clearing. Her boyish face was instantly illuminated and her brown shoulder length hair gleamed golden. Staring at her, James suddenly realised she was the young woman from the Underground City. She was not as old as he'd thought, his own age perhaps, though he couldn't be sure. Once again, he couldn't shake off the feeling that he'd met her before.

'I'm afraid it was Tala watching you in the city,' Albert announced, a little brightness returning to his voice. 'I sent her to find you and I'm terribly sorry if she made you uneasy.'

*Tala.* James had heard that name before and his memory of her came rushing back. She looked different to the last time he'd seen her, sitting on the street in Idessa with her cropped hair and grubby face. In fact, she was almost unrecognisable apart from her expression, characterised by a calm secretiveness that he had not so easily forgotten.

'I know you!' Will exclaimed before James could say anything. 'You're the girl without a symbol.' His tone carried the same judgement as it had once before, when they'd come across Tala as a starving child in Idessa.

'If that's how you choose to remember me, then I suppose

I am,' Tala replied coolly.

'You look so...' Will stopped speaking, suddenly aware of what he'd been about to say.

'Different?' Tala finished for him. 'People change and grow up you know. You look different too.'

Will opened his mouth to retort but Albert cut him off. 'We should go. The ferastia are growing restless and we have a way to travel. It isn't safe for us to linger in the Ari Forest either.'

'It's not safe anywhere at the moment,' James said under his breath.

'You still haven't told us where we're going,' Will objected.

Albert didn't reply. Instead, he wandered over to the ferastia and swung himself onto the back of the smallest beast. Will glanced at James, his expression doubtful. This hadn't been part of their plan. They had decided to wait until the day after the Festival of Light before leaving again. They had packed their bags and mapped out their route in anticipation of their next journey.

The plan had been to search for the remaining gifts and crystals on the southern continent. They knew they needed to find the Quartet Keepers, those who knew the rest of Arvad's tale. With so many rumours stemming from the south, it seemed like a good place to start. The crystals were not their only motive, however. They wanted to see the place where the Belladonna's central armies were rumoured to be. Mellia, in Tenbrisen. The speakers in the Arisselian streets often spoke of this place; it made their listeners afraid.

Albert's intervention had now interrupted this plan but it would be alright, James told himself. Leaving Arissel had always been part of the agenda, only they had hoped to do it alone without Albert or even Oede, Kaedon and Dina. Right now however, there was nothing they could do but go with it. There were five ferastia altogether. With Albert already mounted, everyone else divided themselves between the four remaining beasts. Kaedon and Oede took one, Arthur and Aralia another. James gestured for Will to join him but too late as Dina swung herself into the saddle behind him.

'It looks like you're with me,' Tala said to Will, a hint of displeasure in her voice.

He looked at her with equal distaste but left with no other choice, pulled himself into the saddle behind her. As soon as everyone was settled, Albert patted his ferastia. It began to walk and the other animals followed its lead. The shadows in the Ari Forest were beginning to lengthen, the last light of the summer evening fading away above the trees. James glanced over his shoulder at Tala but her eyes were masked by the gathering gloom.

'You want to know what I'm doing here.'

Her voice startled him, sounding somewhere deep in his mind. She had spoken to him like this once before, in Idessa. She had told him her name then but had already known who he was.

'Who are you?' he asked. 'Who are you really I mean?' His tone was curious rather than demanding and he hoped she knew that.

'Are you sure you don't know?'

James felt faintly irritated by this question. 'Why would I ask if I already knew?'

It was a strange feeling to speak and listen with his mind. A bit like talking to yourself, he had once explained to Will. The speaker had to find a way into the listener's mind, a similar sensation to that of searching for an elusive memory or word.

'You are curious about me because you know there is something to be curious about,' Tala responded.

James closed his eyes. Even though Tala had stopped speaking, he felt a thought pushing its way into his mind from hers. He held still until he was able to grasp it and his eyes flickered open again.

'Is it true?' he asked. 'I've wondered about it before but I couldn't be sure.' He waited for her to reply and when she did not, he continued. 'How long have you known? Why didn't you say something before, in Idessa?'

'I've known for some time now,' she said at last. 'I didn't tell you because it wasn't the right time and Albert didn't wish me to.'

'Albert knows?' James couldn't hide his surprise. His thoughts turned to Aralia and he wondered if Albert knew about her too. As if reading his mind, Tala spoke again.

'Aralia is one of my sisters. I know that too. Now you see why it was inevitable that we should meet a second time.'

Before James could answer her, an eerie howl sounded somewhere deep in the forest. It echoed through the trees; the cry of some prowling beast. James felt the hairs on his neck stand to attention and looked towards Albert. The Twelfth Messenger's voice sounded tense in the darkness.

'The Lowane,' he said. 'The moon wolves have found us.'

# Chapter 3

THE howl came again, a ghostly echo slinking through the trees. It sounded closer than before, as if the creature that had uttered it was advancing towards them.

'What are the Lowane doing out here?' Will asked when the howling finally ceased. 'I didn't think they came this far south, especially in summer. It doesn't make sense.'

James shuddered to remember their last encounter with a Lowane, deep in the forest where the firestone had been set free from the Chinjoka dragon egg. The creature had been fierce, guided by sight, instinct and intuition alone as its other core senses were muted.

'They've been migrating further south for several months now,' Kaedon began. 'The residents of Idessa even claim to have seen them prowling outside the town walls at night.'

'It is a sign,' Oede added in a low voice, 'a sign that the darkness spreading.'

'Are they running from it?' Arthur asked.

Oede shook his head. 'They serve it.'

The ferastia came to a sudden halt and Albert's voice sounded.

'When the natural patterns of the world are disrupted, it means something evil is at work. The signs are always the same. The presence of the Lowane in the Ari Forest is another reason why we cannot linger here. Where they go, the darkness follows and will continue to spread until…'

His words trailed away as another howl echoed through the trees. He did not return to his sentence and nudged his ferastia into walking again. The forest fell silent for a time, disturbed only by the gentle clopping of hooves. The minutes stretched out alongside the shadows until the Ari Forest was pitch dark. Only when their pace began to slow did Albert bring the animals to a halt with a gentle 'whoa'.

'Even the ferastia have limits to their eyesight,' he remarked. 'We don't have long until first light so we'll rest until then. We should reach the edge of the Ari Forest before the sun is fully awake.' An orb formed in his hand and he sent it floating above his head.

'Surely it's risky to create a light?' Will glanced anxiously upwards. 'Won't the Lowane be able to see it?'

'It is only temporary,' Albert reassured. 'We must light a fire. They are afraid of fire.'

Dismounting after Dina, James saw they had stopped in a small clearing. Two ramshackle huts stood to their left, tucked between the trees. The walls were in ruins and the roofs caved, leaving the rooms below partially open to the trees and sky. There were no remaining windows or doors; the buildings were shells of their former selves. Ivy crept over the stonework, digging into the cracks which gaped like open wounds.

'What is this place?' Arthur asked, daring to break the eerie silence.

'They're old Keepers huts.' Will brushed his fingers along one crumbling wall, releasing a stream of stony dust.

'Keepers of what?' James peered over one of the outer walls. It was too dark to distinguish one part of the ruin from the next.

'The forest of course.' Will wiped his hands on his cloak. 'In the old days, Keepers used to be stationed every few miles in huts just like these to keep watch over the forest.'

'For poachers?' James glanced over his shoulder, half expecting to see someone lurking amongst the trees.

'Poachers, invaders, spies. All kinds of people. Anyone who posed a threat to the forest and the people who lived here. I've seen huts like these before, but only on the other side of the forest. I found them once while playing hide-and-seek. I got lost and thought I'd have to camp out in the forest all night but luckily my dad found me.'

James nodded, noting the confidence with which Will spoke of his dad. His friend had come to accept the fact that he might never know what had happened to his father. It was this act of acceptance that had given him the freedom to reference his dad in everyday conversations without pain or discomfort.

In the wavering light cast from Albert's orb, James saw that he was standing on a stone slab that must once have been part of a doorway. It still served as a weak divide between two small rooms, if they could even be called that. A strip of broken roof covered the back half of both spaces but the front half of each was open to the sky. Stepping into the room to his right, James saw that the earthy floor was scattered with the remains of someone else's fire.

'It's a little eerie, isn't it,' Aralia commented as she entered behind him.

James nodded and slung his bag into a dark corner. He then followed Aralia back out into the clearing where Oede and Kaedon had begun building a fire. The flames burned low in their stone surround and no smoke rose from the blackening wood. A tell-tale sign that the fire had not been lit by natural means. Three large logs lay around the fire; makeshift seats on which Dina, Arthur and Tala were already perched. James, Aralia and Will joined them, squashing up to leave room for Kaedon and Oede. There was no sign of Albert, but James had learnt not to question his absences.

'The huts are haunted you know.' Will held his hands over the slow flames.

'You can't get us that easily.' Arthur rolled his eyes in mock dismissal. 'Eerie, maybe, but not haunted.'

'It's true,' Will insisted. 'Arisselian children are told all kinds of legends about the Ari Forest.'

'The truth is in the word *legend*,' Dina remarked with a wry smile.

Brushing ash from his hands, Kaedon came to sit beside her. 'Well, go on then,' he encouraged, looking at Will. 'You've offered up the bait so now you have to tell us one.'

'I hoped you'd say that!' Will grinned and sat forward so that he could rest his elbows on his knees. 'Long ago, in a time before Arissel and Idessa were built, a group of travellers found themselves at the edge of the Ari Forest. It was not as cold here as it was in the north and there were berries to forage and animals to hunt all year round. The travellers built huts out of sticks and were able to live here quite happily.'

He paused to take the mug of tea Oede handed him. After a quick sip, he continued.

'One day, a group of powerful men came to the forest. They had been sent by their master from the capital, which in those days was in Mallin. They gave orders for many acres of trees to be felled and built a great city in the centre of the forest. The city, Arissel, became the new capital of the north and was, for a long time, the centre of the world. It's why so many people speak Camil,' he added, looking at James.

'People would travel to Arissel just to see the Grand Master.'

'A role now divided into Regional Heads,' Dina interjected, also for James' benefit.

Will nodded and continued speaking in his best storyteller voice. 'When the order to cut down the trees was first given, the Keepers stood their ground. Angered by this, the city founders had them all killed. It wasn't a secret assassination but a bloody massacre. A display of power where men, women, children and even animals were murdered. New huts were built, this time from stone, and new Keepers were appointed. Their task was not to care for the forest however but to find and kill anyone who posed a threat to the city. On their first night, as they lay asleep in their beds, the new Keepers heard screaming.'

Will paused for effect and glanced at Tala across the fire.

'What happened?' she asked. 'Did they see ghosts?'

Will grinned. 'The Keepers rushed out into the forest but there was no one there. Each night they heard the same screams and sometimes even the whining of ferastia. They ran outside every time but the forest was always empty. One by one they went mad and hanged themselves. The Grand Master kept sending new Keepers to replace them but it was always the same. Those who lived in Arissel said the huts were cursed and refused to enter the forest. Eventually, the Keepers became extinct but the legend of the Ari Forest lives on.'

'A good story,' Kaedon acknowledged as Will fell silent. 'Let's hope the ghosts have now been laid to rest.'

'I guess we'll find out,' Will said under his breath and winked at James.

Dina pursed her lips and stood up. 'We should try and get some sleep. It's not long now until we ride again.'

She, Kaedon and Oede disappeared into one hut and

James, Will, Arthur, Aralia and Tala crammed into the other. There was still no sign of Albert but no one mentioned his absence. James sat down next to his discarded bag while Will and Arthur settled themselves around him. Aralia and Tala disappeared into the adjoining room, clearly displeased by their sleeping arrangement but left with no other choice. Silence soon fell over the clearing. No more howls rang through the forest and the companions fell quickly asleep.

James awoke feeling stiff and shivery. The sky above the hut was still dark and apart from the sound of breathing, everything lay quiet. He stood up and crept over to the slabbed stone doorway. To his right, he could just make out the sleeping forms of Aralia and Tala, lying in opposite corners of their crumbling room. Passing silently out into the clearing, he saw that the fire was still alight. A figure sat beside it, hunched close to the flames. Blinking sleep from his eyes, James realised it was Albert. His head was uncovered and his hair glowed golden in the firelight. Not wanting to intrude but too wakeful to return to the hut, James approached the fire.

'I find I can't sleep on nights like this,' Albert said without turning around. 'I prefer to walk or sit quietly and think.'

James sat down on the opposite side of the fire and held his hands out to the cooling flames.

'Darkness stirs,' Albert murmured, seamlessly changing the topic. 'Its presence makes me restless. Nothing like this has occurred for centuries. No one alive today remembers anything even close to this.' He raised his eyes but his gaze fell past James. 'There were always those who sought to conjure and control the darkness, but none like the Belladonna.'

James remained silent but watched Albert closely over the flames. His wrist lay uncovered and for the first time James saw his symbol. The mark was unlike any he'd seen before. There was no circle emblazoned on his skin but rather an equilateral triangle with twelve equally spaced lines emanating from its centre. These lines did not grow within the skin itself but were drawn on with golden ink.

'The mark of the Twelve Messengers,' Albert disclosed, noting James' curiosity. 'I am the twelfth, but this you already know.' He pulled his sleeve over the symbol and fell silent.

'How is it that the Belladonna is more powerful than those before her?' James asked, finally bringing himself to speak. 'Where does her power come from?'

Albert sighed and folded his hands in his lap. 'In the days of Arvad, the Dark Master Jasper built many great armies as a show of his power. He gathered men around him and spread his darkness through battle and hardship. He too tried to break into your world, as you well know.'

'Why didn't he succeed?'

'No one knows for certain but the barrier between worlds was stronger then. Your world has weakened its own defences through modern invention.'

'Technology, you mean.'

Albert inclined his head. 'The Belladonna is different because her power doesn't come from this world alone. Though she cannot enter your world in physical form, she is already much closer to it than Jasper ever was. She spreads like an invisible poison to which there is no simple antidote.'

'If all this is true, why does no one believe it?'

'She is waiting to strike and when she does, the world as we know it will change irreparably. The general populace does not believe there is anything to be afraid of because governments around the world tell them as much. Even the Circle, the centre of interregional power, tells them so. They, like all other leading bodies, refuse to acknowledge anything that might render them guilty.'

'Guilty of what?'

'Of not acting sooner. Those in positions of high power choose to ignore the evidence piling up around them. They are the ones the speakers in the Arisselian streets seek to condemn. They imagine that if the people really knew what was happening, they would be condemned for not smothering the darkness while it was still weak. I suspect some of them are in fact feeding it.'

James nodded slowly. 'D'you think if they'd tried to smother the darkness, they would have succeeded?'

'No, I imagine not,' Albert replied. 'The Belladonna is far stronger than they ever were and has been since the beginning. It just shows you how little truth there is in any of it.'

'Why can't people like you, the Messengers that is, spread the real truth?'

James knew from listening to the interactions between speakers and listeners in the Arisselian streets that people were unwilling to lose faith in their governments. Theories about the rising darkness, without real proof, would fall on deaf ears. Even so, the people still lingered in the streets, listening greedily to the stirrings of rebellion.

'People are unable to see the darkness that spreads around them,' Albert said. 'The closer it comes and the darker it gets; the less people are able to see it. After all, when everything is dark, it is impossible to distinguish one shadow from the next. There are some in this world who seek darkness and others who seek light, but the vast majority are blind to both. In time, people will have to make a choice and many will choose unwisely. To follow the light takes great courage. It is far simpler to allow oneself to be consumed by darkness.' He looked at James as if really seeing him for the first time. 'On this journey, James, there will be many challenges. Do you understand that?'

James nodded, slightly stung by the message Albert sought to impress. Of course he knew. He and his friends had overcome many dangers and understood the gravity of their task.

'I know you are strong and have overcome much on your own,' Albert said as if reading his thoughts, 'but this time it is different. The Belladonna is more powerful than anyone ever imagined.'

'Where are we going?' James asked, his gaze turning to the fire. 'Where are you taking us?'

Albert unfolded and refolded his hands. 'To a safe place on the borders of Jantra. You see, the Belladonna cannot find the crystals alone, nor break into your world without your help. She needs you and once her hunt for you has begun, there will be no stopping her.'

'If she is so powerful, why hasn't she found me yet?'

Albert thought carefully before answering. 'Evil works in mysterious ways. The Belladonna will have her reasons I'm sure, reasons the rest of us may never understand.'

James knew there was more that Albert wasn't telling him. A greater reason why the Belladonna had not found him, why she had so far only sent those like Kedran in her stead. She hovered at the edges of his consciousness; a dark presence not yet fully formed. Either she was biding her time or concealing her weakness. Raising his eyes, he saw that Albert was still watching him and wondered if the Messenger was again trying to read his thoughts.

'It is almost first light,' Albert gently reminded. 'You

should get some rest before we ride.'

Wanting to ask more questions, but knowing the conversation was over, James stood. Albert did not look at him again and he wandered back towards his hut. At the entrance, he paused and looked back over his shoulder. Albert remained by the fire as the flames sank to embers. Concealed by the darkness, James then heard him speak.

'He is still too young to know all. The world is stirring. She is preparing for war.'

# Chapter 4

JAMES stood paralysed. He knew that the darkness was rising. Knew too that there were battles to be lost and won. But war? He had never truly believed there would be a war. It had been a possibility but certainly not a reality. Large scale conflict was something he'd been lucky enough to live without, only ever reading about it in history books or watching stories on the news.

Concealed by darkness, he waited expectantly for Albert to speak again. The Messenger sat by the fire in solitary silence, his shadow shrinking beside him as the last fiery embers petered out. Knowing it was pointless to linger any longer, James went back inside the hut. He lay down in his cold corner, mind racing with everything Albert had disclosed. He had only just settled himself again when a howl sounded out in the forest. It was not a distant wail but the resounding cry of a creature lurking somewhere close by. The cry came again and again, creating layers of mournful sound.

'It's come closer.' Will's voice sounded in the darkness.

'I think there's more than one,' Arthur joined.

A bulky shape appeared in the doorway, making them all jump.

'Get up,' Kaedon's voice barked. 'The Lowane are closing in on us. We must go.'

The boys leapt to their feet and grabbed their bags before

following him outside. The forest was still swamped in shadow but the sky above the treetops had lightened a little in anticipation of the dawn. Albert was waiting by the ferastia, calming them as the Lowane continued to howl. He ushered everyone to mount before climbing into his own saddle.

'I didn't think the Lowane would come this close,' he admitted. 'We must hurry to reach the edge of the forest before they cut us off. They are unlikely to follow us beyond the trees, especially after dawn.'

He dug his heels into his ferastia's side and it leapt forward, equally keen to leave the forest behind. The trees thinned out as they rode and the light seeping through the forest grew brighter. One by one the shadows withdrew, making the surroundings seem less menacing. The ferastia travelled quickly but did not run despite the decreasing distance between themselves and the Lowane.

'Can't we make the ferastia go faster?' Aralia asked in a tremulous voice. 'The Lowane are closing in on us.'

'The speed of the Lowane matches that of the ferastia,' Albert calmly replied. 'The beasts may not be able to hear or smell us but they can still see and feel. They can trace the vibrations of running hooves. A steady pace makes it harder for them to track us.'

He was interrupted by another howl, this time so close that James half expected the beast to leap out in front of them. It remained elusive however, running where the early light could not reach. Another cry came from the other side of their path, a warning that the hunt was on. James felt his ferastia shudder beneath him. Before he could offer it any reassurance, the creature lowered its head and broke into a run. Unseated by this change of pace, James grabbed onto the reigns so tightly that the leather burnt his palms.

'Hold on tight!' he shouted to Will who was sitting behind him on the double saddle. He tugged on the reigns, trying to slow the ferastia down, but the creature simply ran faster.

Daring to look over his shoulder, James saw the blurry shapes of the other ferastia close behind, all stirred into the same frenzy by the relentless howling. It was as he turned his head back again that he saw the blurred outline of a Lowane blocking the path just ahead. There was no time to react. The ferastia screamed and pulled away from the path. In the same moment, the Lowane pounced. Its claws sank into the ferastia's side and the creature screamed again. Everything was a blur of hooves, teeth and blood.

'We have to fight it off,' Will shouted. He raised his hand but another beam of light shot past him and struck the Lowane directly in the chest. The animal crumpled to the ground, its yellow eyes rolling.

'Keep riding!' Albert's voice sounded behind them. 'We don't have much time.'

Already the Lowane was trying to stand up again. Despite its wounds, the ferastia carrying James and Will began to run again. It showed no signs of pain as it bore them onwards. Suddenly, the air changed. The shadows vanished as the pale light of dawn took hold. James saw they were no longer caged in by trees but riding across an open stretch of grassland. The vegetation was sparse and the grass was brown from the long drought that had plagued Camil for months. Feeling more at ease, the ferastia began to slow. Glancing over his shoulder, James thought he saw two Lowane slinking back into the forest.

'We should keep going,' Oede advised as the ferastia he and Kaedon were riding also slowed. 'The dawn can't protect us from everything. What the shadows hide, the daylight reveals.'

'We'll have to stop for a moment.' Will's voice caught in his throat. 'Our ferastia is wounded.'

'Wounded?' Kaedon dismounted and hurried over to inspect the ailing beast.

Will and James joined him on the ground. The wound wasn't deep but it was raw. The ferastia's silvery flesh had been torn in several places, the edges of each gash ragged and swollen. Will pressed his hands around the largest wound and the animal shuddered.

'Rai, d'you have anything in your bag that could help?' he asked desperately.

Aralia also dismounted. Her plait had come loose and the runaway strands formed a static halo about her head. She began rummaging in her bag for something that could help but a word from Albert stopped her.

'Don't,' he said. 'You will not be able to help the poor creature. The teeth of the Lowane carry a poison to which there is no antidote.'

Will kept his hands pressed to the animal's side. 'Poisoned spasms. I didn't know there was no antidote.'

'Will it die then?' Tala asked.

She slithered to the ground and placed her hands on the animal's nose. It sniffed her gently before its legs buckled and it sank into the grass. The other ferastia came to stand around the weakening animal, whinnying to see its pain.

'We have to stay with it,' Will insisted, 'at least until the end.'

Albert inclined his head. 'Very well. It won't be long.'

The ferastia began to shudder uncontrollably. The tremors were small at first but grew in strength until its whole body was consumed with them. Foam dribbled from its mouth and then the beast lay still.

'He was a good beast,' Albert stated. 'His name was Tobikuma, meaning flying cloud.'

Will took his hands from Tobikuma's side and stood up. He offered one hand to Tala who still sat cradling the animal's head. James wondered if this gesture was a peace offering, a sign that his friend was able to overlook the fact that Tala was 'cursed'.

As Will and Tala stepped away from Tobikuma, Albert cast a stream of light over the animal's fleshy carcass. It began to disintegrate before their eyes, returning to the earth from which it had come. Albert said nothing. He quietly remounted his own steed and gestured for Tala to join him. James took Tala's former place in front of Arthur and Will squeezed on with Aralia and Dina. With Albert in the lead again, they began to ride across the sundried landscape, leaving the forest and its shadows behind them.

No one spoke for a long while. Dawn turned to morning and the sun climbed higher, spreading its oppressive heat across the landscape. The companions sipped water and pulled up their hoods but nothing helped to cool them down. Intent on reaching their destination, Albert didn't once stop to suggest they should rest. As morning turned to afternoon, the heat intensified. Streams of sweat ran down their faces and dried in salty streaks on their already parched skin.

'When did it get so hot?' Will grumbled, shaking the last drops of water from his gourd.

Hearing this complaint, Albert reigned in his ferastia and wheeled it around. Sweat beaded on his freckled brow but he appeared relatively unflustered.

'I know you are all tired,' he acknowledged, 'but it is vital that we reach our destination without delay. We have already made good progress and are on track to arrive before dark. However, as the day is so hot, I will allow for a short rest under those trees just ahead.'

The trees were scrawny and provided little shade from the scorching sun. It was a relief however to dismount and stretch their aching legs. Unused to long stretches in a saddle, James felt his muscles cramping. He wandered restlessly between the trees, trying to loosen them. Sensing someone behind him, he turned to find Tala watching him. Her hair, like Aralia's, had formed a frizzy halo about her face which sparkled with perspiration. She held her hand out to him. A pile of dried leaves lay on her palm, grey and crinkled in the sunlight.

'What are those?' he asked suspiciously.

'Leaves from the Acca tree. Take one and chew on it. It will help with the saddle-soreness.'

Surprised but grateful, James took a leaf and held it up to inspect it. Its grey-green skin was waxy and threaded with purple veins. He tentatively placed the leaf between his teeth and began to chew. It disintegrated easily, turning to a fine powder on his tongue. From the corner of his eye, he saw Aralia watching him coldly. She still believed Tala was cursed for not having a symbol. James ignored this look and thanked Tala for her medicinal offering.

The sun was still high in the sky when Albert called for them to mount again. They set off into the slow heat of the afternoon, a little less tired but still overheated and sore. The landscape had also begun to feel the effects of the sun; the grass scorched and the ground cracked and hard. Everything lay still, waiting for the cool of evening. It was almost twilight when a sharp whistle split the air, bringing the ferastia to a halt. It was not a human sound but the piercing cry of an animal whistle.

'Night Watchers,' Albert announced. 'They should not be about this early in the evening. We'll have to go through the copse just ahead to avoid being seen.'

Understanding the urgency of the situation, the ferastia trotted towards the copse. The low hanging branches provided little cover but there were enough early evening shadows to partially hide them. Streaks of soft pink light crossed the sky as if put there by a painter's brush. There were no clouds, just the clear twilight air spattered with tinges of the setting sun. Coming to a standstill between the trees, Albert held up a hand for silence. Travellers and beasts held still, listening intently. The whistle sounded again and a light appeared in the near distance. It bobbed towards them, a fiery pendulum swaying from side to side in regular motion.

The bulky shape of a man appeared, close to the outer line of trees. He stopped to peer through the gathering shadows, his breath heavy with exertion. Something on the ground caught his attention and he held his light low to the stubbled grass. James feared he might have seen a footprint or hoof impression but the man straightened up again with a huff. Evidently satisfied with his inspection, he cast one more glance between the trees before wandering away into the twilight.

'We move,' Albert commanded as soon as the man was out of earshot. 'Through the copse where we can't be seen. There may well be others.'

'Who are the Night Watchers?' James asked as the ferastia began to walk again.

'Another breed of her followers,' Albert replied. 'People ordered to keep watch for suspicious travellers, those who might pose a threat to her cause. Those like us.'

'How do they know who poses a threat and who doesn't?'

James pressed.

'I don't believe they do. They are a brutal breed who take pleasure from condemning guilty and innocent alike.'

The ferastia passed quickly through the copse. On the other side, the landscape changed. Where the ground had been flat, it now bubbled into small, grassy mounds. These spread out as far as the eye could see, like a giant sheet of green-brown bubble wrap. To the right of the copse, the ground swept upwards into a peak, a canine tooth amongst stubby molars. Beyond this peaked slope, the land fell away into a valley or ravine. It was towards this slope that Albert rode, his posture softening as if all urgency had suddenly dissipated.

By the time they reached the base of the incline, the last rays of setting sun had vanished from the horizon. Albert dismounted and gestured for everyone else to do the same. Looking at the slope in awe, James noticed a set of steps dug into the uneven ground. In wetter months, they might have been hidden beneath the grass, but the long drought now left them exposed. They were made from uneven logs, pressed into the earth in an uneven formation. Most were rotten and black, suggesting they had been here for a long time. The steps wound their way across the slope to the farthest edge where they disappeared.

Still offering no explanation as to what they were doing here, Albert dismounted and ventured onto the first step. He began to climb and everyone else hurried to follow. What had looked like the edge of the slope from below now turned out to be an unexpected ridge. Beyond it, the ground continued to curve towards a second ridge. Rather than follow this curve, the steps came to an end. They were replaced by an earthy tunnel that led up to a wooden door.

'Where are we?' James asked, stopping behind Albert. 'What is this place?'

Albert didn't reply. He simply raised his fist to the door and knocked.

# Chapter 5

THE door slowly opened and a young man appeared behind it. He was dressed in a floor length blue toga with a matching cloak and his black hair was braided across the middle of his scalp. His face was adorned with tattoos, small black dots arching where his eyebrows should have been. Despite the fierce expression these gave him, his face lit up when he smiled.

'Greetings, Messenger,' he began. 'We have been expecting you. I trust you had a safe journey.' His voice was lightly accented though he spoke perfect Camil.

'A few obstacles but we made it here nonetheless,' Albert replied, also smiling.

The young man stood aside to let his guests past. Following Albert inside, James saw they had entered a short, dark hallway. A single orb hovered against the ceiling, reflecting soft light off the earthen walls. The air smelt of petrichor, earthy and damp.

'Where are we?' James whispered to Albert as they proceeded down the hallway. 'Surely you can tell us now.'

'You have entered the Minha Mound.' It was the young man who spoke. He wove his way to the front of their group and came to a standstill beside Albert. 'A brotherhood of learned men live here. There are twenty of us at present.'

'Is it a monastery?' James asked curiously.

The young man smiled. 'It is a temple. The men here call each other Brothers. My name is Brother Menid.' He paused to smooth down his toga. 'Now, you must be tired and hungry, so please follow me.'

At the end of the hallway, he pulled aside a curtain to reveal a set of descending stairs. Albert stood aside to let James go first, still saying nothing. The staircase was dark but a faint light glowed somewhere at the bottom. The light was hazy, as if engulfed by steam. At the bottom of the stairs, James was confronted by two doorways. The light was coming from the doorway to his right and without hesitation, he stepped through. He found himself in a small, square room. Clouds of steam drifted outwards from a stone basin in the centre. Though the steam was thick, it did not drift outside the chamber, lingering within like an enchanted tropical mist.

'The water is drawn from warm underground springs,' Brother Menid announced from somewhere behind him. 'You must cleanse yourselves. When you are finished, you should return to the hallway where I will meet you. There are two Spring rooms, so you may divide yourselves accordingly.'

James couldn't see their host through the steam but he heard footsteps retreating upstairs. Approaching the basin, he ran his fingers through the water. It was warm and cupping both hands, he splashed some over his salt-crusted face. There was no privacy in here so he, Will, Arthur, Kaedon and Oede simply washed as best they could while Dina, Aralia and Tala disappeared into the adjoining room. Clean clothes had been laid out for each of them on the stone bench at the back of the room. Baggy linen trousers, cotton shirts and crisply ironed cloaks. All were the same shade as Brother Menid's tunic.

Their host was waiting in the main hallway as promised. He greeted them all with a nod before turning to open a door on the opposite side of the hallway. A cool gust of air rushed in, ruffling the light fabric of their clothes. Brother Menid stood aside to let his guests pass through before closing the door behind him. The companions found themselves standing at the edge of a beautiful garden. A pebbled path ran between the temple door and a pavilion on the far side. Other pathways branched out from it, laid between wild grass lawns. Each path was lined with hovering orbs and their light turned the garden golden.

'Please make your way towards the pavilion,' Brother Menid instructed. 'Your host, Father Eldon, is waiting for you to join him. He is fasting but he wishes to greet his guests.'

The pavilion stood within a circle of birch trees. It was built from a series of curved archways and slim wooden pillars. The roof was also curved and had been designed with a hole in the centre so that the sky could still be seen above it. In the centre of the pavilion, a young man sat cross-legged on a cushion, his unlined face raised to the night sky. His eyes were closed but he opened them as his guests approached.

'Welcome,' he greeted them. 'Welcome to the Minha Mound. I am Father Eldon and I am honoured to share the home of my Brothers with you.'

He was dressed in a dark blue tunic and his hair, like Brother Menid's, was plaited on top of his head. His face was also peppered with tattoos, the black dots inked in almond shapes around his eyes. A set of small keys hung around his neck and they clinked every time he moved.

'Come and sit with me,' he urged, gesturing to the cushions spread all around him. 'I would not have you stand when you are tired. You must be hungry too. We will eat.'

He clapped his hands and five men appeared in the pavilion arches. Each one carried a platter of food which they laid down between the cushions. The aroma of fresh herbs filled the air, making James' stomach rumble. Father Eldon gestured for his guests to join him and this time they obeyed.

'Replenish yourselves,' he offered. 'The food we eat here is simple but we grow and make most of it ourselves.'

Unable to resist any longer, Will made the first move. He took a chunk of bread from one of the platters and sank his teeth into it. It crunched pleasantly; an invitation for the rest of them to tuck in. There was no meat or cheese but the meal was plentiful. Crusty bread, steamed vegetables and bowls of grain mixed with oil and herbs. Piling a slice of bread with rice and discs of an unfamiliar purple vegetable, James took a great bite. Fresh parsley and basil filled his mouth and he closed his eyes, savouring the flavours. Father Eldon did not eat but poured himself a mug of water and drank thirstily. James wondered how long he'd been fasting for. He looked thin and sickly in the half-light, making it difficult to tell how old he really was.

'You wonder how old I am.' Father Eldon turned to look at James. 'I am not much older than you. My predecessor died young and so I took his place. Only those who bear the Eldon birthmark may become a Father.' He raised his left hand to reveal a misshapen red mark on his wrist. 'The name Eldon means sacred father.'

'Are you able to tell us why we are here?' James asked after a respectful pause.

The young man smiled. 'The Messenger Albert asked me to keep you safe here. I gave him my word that I would protect you. All of you.'

'Protect us from what exactly?' Will mumbled through a mouthful.

Father Eldon continued to smile. 'I do not know. In this place we offer protection to whoever finds themselves at our door. We do not ask questions.'

'Where *is* Albert, by the way?' James looked around the pavilion, half expecting the Messenger to suddenly appear. 'I haven't seen him since we arrived.'

'Your companion has his own business to attend to. He will return when the time is right.'

Before James could find the right words, Aralia spoke. 'When the time is right? Did Albert really say that? Are we just supposed to stay here until he comes back?'

James wondered why Dina, Kaedon and Oede didn't join in the conversation but sat listening quietly, their expressions unreadable.

'I hope you will find it comfortable here,' Father Eldon said patiently. 'We are simple people but we are happy to share what we have with those who stay with us. We grow our own food and rarely wander beyond our walls. It is how we keep ourselves hidden from so many.' He turned his gaze upon the garden and held it there.

'How is there a garden here?' Tala asked curiously. 'It doesn't seem like the most natural place.'

'The garden rests on an angled ledge which juts out from the main slope,' Father Eldon explained. 'There is a thick layer of rock below us which then drops away into a ravine. The way the peak is angled above the garden provides it with some shelter. You can't see it in the dark but you will tomorrow. Our plants have adapted to thrive here. Now,' he continued in a changed voice, 'I must leave you in the care of Brother Menid. He will show you to your rooms.'

He stood up and without another word, wandered away towards the temple. The companions stared after him, unanswered questions resting on each of their lips.

'What d'we do now?' Will asked as soon as their host was out of earshot. 'We can't just sit around here waiting for Albert to come back.'

'That's exactly what we can and must do,' Dina said sharply. 'Albert has our best interests at heart; it would be wise to trust him.'

James knew she was right about trusting Albert but it made no sense to hide here like fugitives when out in the real world the Belladonna was preparing for war.

'You knew he was bringing us here, didn't you?' He looked carefully into Dina's eyes, half expecting to be burnt by their green fire.

Dina nodded. 'We had to know.'

James held back a retort, knowing better than to argue with her. She had a fierce temper and he had no desire to unleash it. Dina pursed her lips but did not speak again.

'Greetings.'

An unfamiliar voice sounded and a man appeared in one of the pavilion archways. He looked much like Brother Menid, only his hair was tied in two plaits rather than one.

'Greetings,' he repeated and offered a low bow. 'My name is Brother Hagal and I am to take you to your rooms. Brother Menid has been detained. Please, follow me.'

Rising from their cushions, the companions followed Brother Hagal back down the pavilion path to the temple. He carried a bunch of keys at his waist which clinked dully as he walked. Inside the temple again, he led them through a curtained doorway and up a steep flight of steps. At the top, a small, white-painted room spread out before them. The space was comprised of three solid walls and a fourth set with glass doors covered with gauzy curtains. Six mattresses were laid on the floor with a folded blanket at the foot of each. The room was otherwise empty.

'You may rest here until dawn,' Brother Hagal instructed. 'If you step out onto the terrace, you will find the entrance to another room where the women may sleep. You will eat at sunrise and fast during the day until the evening meal. You must not wander about unchaperoned between sunset and sunrise. Entry to the garden is forbidden before dawn, with or without a chaperone, but at all other times you may wander about it freely.'

Having said his piece, Brother Hagal left the room without so much as a goodnight. As soon as he'd gone, James flung himself down on one of the mattresses. It was thin but comfortable enough and he closed his eyes as his friends sorted themselves out around him. He wished he could speak to Will, Arthur and Aralia alone but knew this would not be possible before morning. Kaedon and Oede showed no signs of leaving or falling asleep and Dina had left with Tala and Aralia to find their room.

The minutes ticked by and eventually the room fell still. One by one, Will, Arthur, Kaedon and Oede fell asleep. Even though his eyes were closed, James did not feel tired. A deep sense of urgency settled in his chest, a sensation he couldn't easily ignore. Too restless to simply lie still, he left his bed and padded over to the glass doors. They had been left unlatched and he slipped silently through. He found himself standing on a long stone terrace, hemmed in by a balustrade. Beyond this barrier, the night sky glittered with thousands of stars. Daring to look over the edge at the bottomless darkness, he imagined there was no terrace beneath him. He was floating in the sky itself, a lone star far from home.

In the stillness of the night, he became aware of the clock ticking against his chest. The steady rhythm of the minute hand working its way around the numberless face. He took it from his shirt pocket and turned it over in his hands. He hadn't yet told his friends about the markings on its base. There just hadn't been time. However, he also knew that they would disapprove of the plan that had gradually been forming in his mind. A plan which relied upon him returning to his world, to Silver Street and the mysterious clock shop. He felt sure that the clockmaker would know what the markings meant.

It would be easy, he thought, to simply turn the dials and enter his world once more. Their cold circumferences rested beneath his fingers, daring him to try. He let his index finger brush against one and then the other. The hour hand stuttered as he disturbed it. Undecided, he held his breath and listened to the stillness of the night. It was the same feeling, he imagined, of waiting to abseil down a cliff but not quite daring. The decision was too great; it was no use dwelling on it or choosing too quickly. Both led him to the same point of uncertainty.

He squeezed his eyes shut and suddenly it was happening. The dials moved beneath his fingers and the clock hands came to rest at ten to twelve.

## Chapter 6

JAMES waited but nothing happened. There was no dark tunnel pulling him into the depths of space and time, nor the swirling mists of No Man's Land. There was nothing but the cool night air and star spattered sky. The clock continued to tick in his hands and he shook it, wondering if the mechanisms had somehow become stuck. Still nothing happened.

Trying to ignore the dread weighted in his stomach, he turned the hour hand full circle until it came to rest at ten to twelve once more. It was no use. The glass doors, the terrace, the balustrade: all were there just as before. He lowered himself to the floor, the cold stone seeping through his clothes. For the first time in several months, he felt afraid. The clock was his only passage home, a link between this world and his own. Without it, he might never see his parents again or the house on Greenwood Avenue where he'd grown up. It had never felt much like a home and yet it was where he'd spent most of his life.

Too tired to function any more, he let the clock fall into his lap and closed his eyes. A white mist crept into his dreams. Standing within the swirling cloud, he listened for the voice he knew would come.

'You sought me out.' She sounded far away; her words muffled by the distance between them.

'Sylvia.' James stated her name, testing its truth. He could not see her but he felt her presence all around him. 'You appeared in my dream.'

'You are not dreaming,' Sylvia said. 'Your subconscious has merely entered another dimension.'

'What does that mean?'

'The subconscious mind is far more aware of itself than most people realise. Sometimes it asks the questions that the conscious mind cannot. You sought me out, whether you intended to or not.'

The mist parted and she appeared before him, little more than a ghost. Even as she walked towards him, he could only just make out her eyes.

'The clock,' James began. 'I turned the dials as I've done before only it didn't work. It didn't take me back to my world.'

'The barrier between worlds is thinning,' Sylvia murmured. 'As time passes, it will become harder for you to cross between.'

'If it's thinning, then surely it will become easier to move between worlds,' James responded. 'Isn't that what the Belladonna wants? To change the laws of the universe so that she can enter my world too.'

Sylvia held his gaze. 'Each time someone passes between worlds, the barrier weakens. It is the way. Every attempt and success cause small fractures in the fabric of the universe.'

James stared at her, not wanting to believe her yet knowing she was right. 'It will become harder to cross between,' he finished, 'until I can no longer cross at all.'

'It is the way,' Sylvia repeated. Her form began to fade until he could no longer see her. 'Think carefully before you try to pass between the worlds again. You never know when a crossing might be your last.'

James woke up with a start. He blinked as early sunlight flooded his retinas, temporarily blinding him. He felt around in his lap for the clock and was relieved to find it still resting there. The hands were as he had left them, hovering at ten minutes to twelve. Shaking off the remnants of sleep, he slipped the timepiece into his pocket and stood up. Night had turned to dawn and the landscape beyond the terrace was steeped in pale light. Leaning over the balustrade, James couldn't help but gasp. Below the terrace, the ground simply disappeared. There was nothing between the stone he stood upon and a deep ravine far below.

Daring to lean a little further, he realised he could see a section of the temple garden. The pavilion was concealed beyond a cluster of trees but he could see the path they'd walked along the evening before. The garden, like the terrace, was hemmed in by a balustrade. Father Eldon had said the garden rested on an angled ledge and James could now see what he'd meant. Beyond the balustrade, the rocky ground gave way, leaving the garden partially suspended.

As he raked his eyes over the scene, he spotted a lone figure standing amidst a clump of trees. He thought for a moment it was Father Eldon, but the man's grey hair and light blue tunic suggested he was one of the Brothers. James remembered Brother Hagal's warning that the garden was prohibited before dawn. Perhaps the dawn hours had already passed, he thought to himself. The sun, though pale, was already level with the terrace, its light spilling onto the grey stone. Its rays carried some warmth, though not yet enough to heat the morning air.

'Beautiful, isn't it?'

A voice startled him. Turning, he saw Tala walking along

the terrace towards him. She was dressed in a loose white shirt and trousers, the fabric crumpled from sleep. The same night clothes had been laid at the end of his own mattress but he'd been too fatigued to change.

He greeted Tala with a nod as she approached but said nothing. Sylvia's voice still haunted his thoughts, making him feel unsettled.

'You're up early,' Tala continued. 'I thought I'd be the first.' She shook out her hair and began plaiting it into two short braids.

'I couldn't sleep,' James said.

A movement at the far end of the terrace caught his eye. He thought he saw Aralia standing there but before he even had time to acknowledge her, she had vanished.

'Albert has our best interests at heart, you know,' Tala remarked, breaking his thoughts again. 'He wouldn't have left us here without good reason.'

James nodded vaguely. He wondered why Tala felt the need to defend the Messenger. Albert was a good man but he had a habit of disappearing without explanation.

'There is going to be a war.' He watched for Tala's reaction but she continued to plait her hair with deliberate calmness.

'If there is going to be a war, isn't it better that we're prepared for it?'

The flatness of her tone surprised James. He looked over the balustrade at the garden again. The mysterious Brother had vanished.

'It's past dawn,' he observed after a brief silence. 'We should eat.'

He slipped back through the glass doors into the first bedroom. Will and Arthur were just getting up but there was no sign of Kaedon or Oede.

'Hey, no girls allowed,' Will said indignantly. His eyes moved past James to where Tala stood in the doorway.

She smiled and crossed the room to the top of the stairs. Whether she noticed Will's half-dressed state or not was impossible to say.

'Where are the others?' James asked.

'Already gone down for breakfast,' Will replied in a muffled voice as he pulled his shirt over his head.

As soon as they were ready, the boys hurried downstairs. They could hear Dina's voice coming through a curtained doorway to their left and stepped through. They found themselves in a small, earth-walled room. Breakfast had been laid out on the floor between piles of brightly coloured cushions. Platters of bread and fruit and jugs of steaming herbal tea. Dina, Kaedon, Oede, Aralia and Tala were already present, sitting in a circle around the delicious-looking spread.

'You join us at last.' Dina gestured for James, Will and Arthur to sit down.

The food disappeared quickly, shared between eight hungry mouths. As soon as they had finished eating, Brother Menid appeared in the doorway. His prompt arrival made James wonder if he'd been lingering out in the hallway the whole time.

'Good morning,' Brother Menid greeted. 'I trust you all slept well. The dawn hours have passed and your rest period is over. I am here to take you to the garden where you will begin your daily tasks.'

Will shot James a look and mouthed, *'tasks?'*

Brother Menid caught the look and did not smile. 'You are not simply guests here,' he reprimanded. 'Here you must live as we do. You must earn your meals and your rest. Come now, please follow me.'

The garden looked different in the early morning light, the grass bright and the plants full of life. Here, there was no sign of drought and everything flourished. Low bushes, flowers and clusters of herbs all grew together in harmony. Pausing on the pavilion path, Brother Menid turned to his guests once more.

'You will be working in the vegetable garden today,' he said, gesturing to James, Will, Arthur, Aralia and Tala. 'Just follow the path to your left. One of my Brothers will meet you there. Now,' he continued, turning his attention to Dina, Kaedon and Oede, 'you three are to follow me.'

While Brother Menid went one way, with Dina, Kaedon and Oede close behind him, the remaining five made for the vegetable garden. Their path led them directly past the cluster of trees James had spotted from the terrace. He looked between the branches, half-expecting to see the unidentified Brother lurking there, but the shade beneath the branches was undisturbed. When they reached the vegetable garden, no one was there to meet them. Unsure of what to do, they waited at the head of the first bed and were surprised when a voice suddenly hailed them.

'What are you waiting over there for? Come and join me.'

A hairless head popped up between some carrot tops. It was followed by a thick torso and some legs until a whole person stood before them. Unlike the Brothers they had met so far, this man was short and squat. He lacked the mysterious quality that Brother Menid, Brother Hagal and Father Eldon all possessed. Though he was bald, his skin was adorned with plaited tattoos to give the illusion of hair.

'My helpers have arrived!' he exclaimed. 'You are just in time. I need some keen weeders! They have minds of their own, always fighting back. Here.' He whisked a leafy stem from the earth and brandished it before him. The roots were stringy and the plant itself small and sickly. 'You are looking for weeds with light green leaves with dark tips, just like this one,' he explained. 'Pachu weeds. They take over everything.' He laughed as if he'd made a joke. 'Ready to tackle them?'

James, Will, Arthur, Aralia and Tala nodded mutely, taken aback by his garrulous manner. He began handing out trowels and gloves, his chatter unceasing.

'This is all the equipment you will need. They tend to come out easily. You must be sure not to use any magic on them, however. Trowels always work best.' He gestured vaguely towards the beds. 'Start anywhere you like.' He turned to go but stopped himself. 'My name is Brother Joseph, by the way.' Smiling briefly, he then turned away and hurried back to his carrots.

'Are we seriously meant to spend all day weeding?' Will complained as soon as Brother Joseph was out of earshot. He thrust his trowel into the nearest vegetable bed, uprooting several weeds at once. 'Albert must be having a joke. While the real world falls into chaos, we're stuck in a temple garden *weeding.*'

'We have to do this if we want to eat and sleep,' Arthur responded practically.

'Will's right though,' James remarked. 'According to Albert, things are worse than anyone imagined.'

'How so?' Aralia asked.

'The Belladonna is preparing for war.'

'War!' Will exclaimed loudly. '*War,*' he repeated in a quieter voice and glanced over to where Brother Joseph's head was just visible above the carrot tops.

'I overheard Albert, in the clearing by the Keeper's huts,'

James admitted. 'He was speaking to someone, though I don't know who. He said the Belladonna is preparing for war.' He chose not to mention the fact that he and Albert had been conversing just moments before.

'War!' Aralia echoed Will's exclamation. 'What sort of war?'

'I don't know exactly. A war between worlds. A war between dark and light.'

'A silent war,' Arthur stated.

'A what?' Will asked.

'A war that spreads gradually, without any specific outright conflict. The Belladonna will weaken her opponents little by little until the final battle. At that point, no one will have any energy left to fight against her.'

'Finding the remaining crystals is *our* chance to weaken *her*,' James emphasised. 'To weaken her and all those who follow her.' He noticed that throughout this conversation, Tala hadn't said a word, and wondered how much she already knew.

'She'll have doubled her army by the time we even start looking!' Will muttered darkly.

'Albert is trying to protect us,' Aralia chided. 'If this place is safe, surely it's good that we're here rather than fighting for our lives.'

'Nowhere is safe at the moment,' Will countered. 'Not here and not Arissel. Although I'm not sure how safe Arissel ever was, even before…' He glanced at James and his words trailed away.

'Even before I came,' James finished for him.

Aralia plucked at a weed and sighed. 'If you hadn't come, the Belladonna would still exist, would still be looking for a way to find the crystals and break into your world. Your presence only makes her act with more urgency. Now come on, let's get some of these weeds up before Brother Joseph checks up on us.'

Taking up his trowel, James set to work. While his hands busied themselves digging up weeds, he let his eyes wander. The garden was no longer empty. The Brothers had emerged from the temple and were busy tending to the flowers and grass. There was no sign of Oede, Kaedon or Dina. His gaze came to rest on a tree leaning against the balustrade at the nearest edge of the garden. The bark was white, similar to a birch, but the trunk was gnarled, making it look more like an old olive. Staring at it, James had a curious sensation that he'd seen this exact tree before. When or where that might have been, he didn't know, for his mind felt suddenly hazy.

All at once, he was overwhelmed by an intense dizziness. It felt like he was standing on the prow of a heaving, storm-battered ship. He closed his eyes to steady himself but instead found himself falling. The temple garden disappeared and darkness descended. A light flickered into being. It illuminated a large room furnished from floor to ceiling with bookshelves. At the far end, an old man stood facing him. His wrinkled face was adorned with tattoos, the fleshy grooves filled with black ink.

'Welcome,' he said and his voice cracked from the strain of speaking.

James felt his feet tingling as if they were resting before a fire. Looking down at them, he noticed that his clothes had changed. The blue trousers and shirt had been replaced by a long green cloak. Holding out his hands, he saw that they too were not his own. Something glinted against his chest as he moved. It was a pendant, suspended on a thick gold chain. Inside the polished casement rested a yellow-brown gem.

Hardly knowing what he was doing, James reached up to touch it. As he moved his hand, his sleeve fell back and he gasped. His own symbol had vanished and a seven pointed star marked its place.

# Chapter 7

'JAMES, are you alright? You look like you've seen a ghost.'

James heard Aralia's voice as if from far away. The book filled room before him flickered like a TV screen before going dark. Someone started shaking his arm and with great effort, he opened his eyes.

'I'm fine,' he said, though he still felt unsteady. 'Really, I'm fine.'

'You don't look it.' Will studied him intently. 'What is it?'

'I… I saw something,' James stammered. He fixed his eyes on a half-crushed Pachu weed sticking out from under his shoe. 'I was looking at that tree over there, the one with the twisted trunk, and then the garden vanished.'

'Vanished? How?' Will pressed.

'I was in a room full of bookshelves. A library maybe. I was wearing someone else's clothes only it wasn't really me. It was like I was *inside* their skin. Even the symbol on my wrist was different. A seven pointed star.'

Arthur sucked a stream of air through his teeth. 'Arvad's symbol? How is that possible?'

James raised his eyes. 'It was like I wasn't myself anymore. I wasn't just in his clothes and his body; I *was* him. I know I imagined it but it felt real.'

'Where was this library you were in?' Aralia asked. 'Was there anyone else with you… with *him*?'

'There was an old man.' James tried to recall the vision but his memory of it was already fading. 'He had tattoos on his face.'

'Like the Brothers here.' Tala pulled out a weed and dropped it between her feet. 'Maybe the library you saw is inside the temple.'

'What if Arvad had some connection to this place?' Aralia breathed. 'What if Albert knew and that's why he brought us here?'

'If that was the case, why didn't he just tell us?' Will pondered.

Before James could comment, he clocked movement in the carrot bed. Brother Joseph was emerging from the feathery fronds like some garden spirit. He was clutching a bunch of carrots which were, like his hands, caked in dark soil. Looking down at his own, mostly clean hands, James felt suddenly ashamed. They had been asked to help and so far they had only five weeds between them.

'Brother Joseph is coming over and we've hardly done anything,' he warned.

They began pulling up weeds with frenzied determination but Brother Joseph was already closing in on them.

'We could use magic,' Will suggested.

Before anyone could object, a stream of light shot from his fingertips and struck a cluster of Pachu weeds. The leaves wilted instantly and Will offered a mock bow.

'Don't gloat too soon,' Aralia reproved. 'Look!'

Where the old weeds had died, new stems were already sprouting, complete with waxy leaves and razor petalled flowers that snapped open and shut like the marginal spikes of a Venus Flytrap.

'I warned you.' Brother Joseph stood looking at the

multiplying weeds with faint amusement. 'They will fight back with all they have if you are not careful. Trowels are the best tools, as I said before.'

'I'm sorry,' Will apologised. 'It was my idea.'

Brother Joseph nodded kindly. 'Less talking and more weeding perhaps.'

He turned to go but James reached out an arm to stop him. Brother Joseph shrank back, evidently not used to anyone touching him.

James withdrew his hand. 'Sorry, I was just wondering if there's a library inside the temple. There is a book I'd like to read: *Rare Plants of Jantra*. Perhaps you've heard of it?'

This did the trick. Brother Joseph's features lit up instantly. 'I do know it, though unfortunately the archives here do not store books.'

'Archives?' Will asked.

'Yes, where we keep our records, just as our Brothers did before us and theirs before that.'

'What sort of records?' James tried not to sound too curious.

'Things that have happened here: the progress of crops year on year, landfalls, the initiation of a new Brother, guests.' He eyed the companions suspiciously. 'The archives are out of bounds to all but Father Eldon, the archivist and his assistant.' He sighed, as if he'd often dreamt of seeing inside.

James nodded. 'I understand. Thank you. I'll read the book one day I'm sure.'

Brother Joseph smiled vaguely, clearly pleased to have helped, and wandered away between the vegetable beds. James waited until he was out of earshot before speaking again.

'The archive must be the room I saw in my vision. We

have to find it.'

'That shouldn't be too difficult,' Will said. 'The temple seems pretty small.'

Aralia cleared her throat. 'It won't be easy to get inside. If entry to the archive is that exclusive, they will have taken extra precautions.'

'We'll just have to go and find out,' James replied. 'Tonight.'

The hours between morning and evening passed slowly. James, Will, Arthur, Aralia and Tala continued their weeding in silence, waiting for darkness to fall. At midday, Brother Joseph allowed them a short rest but no food or drink. It was tough working through the heat of the afternoon without refreshment but at last the day came to an end. Brother Hagal arrived to escort them to their evening meal, back through the garden to the temple. Dina, Kaedon and Oede were waiting for them in the same room they'd had breakfast in. Trays of bread and soup had been laid out on the floor in readiness. Brother Hagal left his guests to eat and did not return.

After the meal, they made their way to the bedrooms without a guide. The evening was still warm and the sky above the terrace was clear. Dina, Kaedon and Oede stepped outside to enjoy the remaining light, leaving James, Will, Arthur, Aralia and Tala inside. James sat down on his bed and closed his fingers over the clock tucked in his shirt pocket.

'What are you doing with that?' Aralia asked sharply.

'I'm not doing anything,' he replied defensively.

Aralia wasn't convinced. 'There's something you're not telling us, isn't there?' she insisted. 'I can see it in your face.'

'Alright,' he conceded. 'There's something I've been waiting to tell you since we left Arissel but we haven't had a moment to ourselves until now.' He took the clock from his pocket and held it up. 'On the evening of the festival, I noticed a row of letters on the base of the clock. They're too small to read but I'm certain they weren't there before.'

'Could they indicate the name of its maker?' Arthur asked.

James shrugged. 'I don't know but it's the same conclusion I came to.'

'The old man from your world?' Will sat down on the bed beside James and took the clock from him. 'He didn't make this clock, did he?'

'No,' James confirmed. 'Someone gave it to him for safekeeping years ago and then he passed it on to me.'

'The letters could indicate a hallmark,' Tala suggested.

'You think there is more to it than that.' Aralia looked searchingly at James. 'You think it's connected to the quest.'

James looked at the clock in Will's hands. 'Albert said there is quartz inside the clock. The same crystal is used in my phone but in a different form: silica. What if the clock, like my phone, is connected to the darkness? What if it can trace my movements? If I could find its maker, they could answer my questions. They might even be able to tell me what will happen to the clock when the barrier between worlds disappears.'

'What are you talking about, James?' Aralia laid a hand on his arm but he shrugged her off.

'The barrier between the worlds is thinning. Soon it won't be possible for me to pass between. I can already feel it happening.'

'You have already tried and failed to pass between,' Tala said quietly. 'Is that not so?'

James couldn't help wondering if she had seen him try or if she had simply guessed.

'What does she mean, you've already tried?' Aralia turned

on him, her eyes blazing.

James avoided her gaze. 'Last night I tried to go back but the clock didn't work.'

'You *what*?'

'I have to go back to my world. I have to find the clockmaker.'

'I don't understand,' Arthur cut in. 'Isn't the Belladonna trying to weaken the barrier so that she can pass between worlds?'

'That's what she believes. In truth, the weaker the barrier becomes, the harder it will be for her to enter my world.'

'Does that mean…'

Aralia started speaking but James cut her off.

'Yes, it means the way will be closed for me as well.' He took the clock back from Will and cupped it in his hands. 'There's another reason why I want to go back. D'you remember what Eir told us about Arvad?'

'He left this world entirely,' Will recalled. 'We don't know for certain if he went to your world. Eir said as much at the time.'

'But if he did,' James continued, 'then maybe he left a clue there. What if the clock is somehow a part of it all?'

His words hung in the air like a challenge, daring someone to dismiss them. No one said anything. The silence was short-lived however as Oede and Kaedon entered a moment later.

'It's getting late,' Oede said gently, 'we should all rest before a new day begins.'

Aralia and Tala bid everyone goodnight and vanished through the glass doors. In the boys' room, everyone was tucked up in bed in a matter of minutes. Oede and Kaedon fell asleep immediately but James, Will and Arthur lay staring at the darkening ceiling. As soon as they were sure it was safe, all three climbed out of bed and crept across the room to the stairs. They descended in single file and clustered conspiratorially in the hallway, waiting for Aralia and Tala. They did not have to wait long. The girls appeared a moment later and hurried downstairs to join them.

'There's another doorway at the back of the room we've been eating in,' Will whispered. 'It's hidden behind a curtain but I noticed it earlier today. We could try that way first.'

The hallway was pitch black so Arthur created a small light. It was barely more than a spark but was enough for them to see their way without tripping. The quiet that came with the night was different to that which existed during the day. It hung ominously around them, daring them to break it.

Passing through Will's recently discovered doorway, they found themselves at the top of a staircase. With Arthur in the lead, they began to descend in single file. At the base was a short passageway set with four curtained doorways. The first curtain concealed a kitchen and the second an overfilled pantry: strings of onions, mushrooms and herbs on one side and jars of seeds, grains and medicinal produce on the other.

'The temple is bigger than I thought,' James whispered, looking around the vast pantry in awe.

'It really is!'

Tala's voice drifted down the hallway, a little louder than a whisper. Turning, James saw she had wandered back towards the stairs and was gazing into a shadowy corner. She had created a small light and it revealed another staircase, a few paces beyond the first, winding a tight spiral through the ceiling.

'Come on,' Tala urged. She began to climb and everyone else hurried to follow her.

The stairway seemed to go on forever. Every time they

thought they were near the top, another spiral looped around to meet them. At long last, a small, square landing brought the stairs to an end. There was only one door at the back of the landing and it was locked. A plaque nailed just above the handle read: *An Ngur*.

'No entry,' Aralia translated. 'I think we may have found the archives.'

The door had a keyhole but no key. James ran his fingers along the top edge of the frame, hoping to find one, but to no avail.

'Father Eldon must have a key,' Arthur remarked. 'In fact, he had a set hanging around his neck when we met him.'

'You're right!' James exclaimed. 'I noticed them too. One of them must fit this door.'

'At least we know where the archives are now,' Will said in a low voice. 'The next step is to find out where Father Eldon keeps his keys when they're not around his neck. He must take them off to wash and sleep.'

'Do people like him sleep?' Aralia pondered.

'That's for us to find out,' James replied. He strode back across the landing to the top of the staircase.

'Wait, stop!'

Tala's voice halted him and he turned to look at her. She was pointing at a sliver of light that had appeared along one edge of the door. It was not bright enough to spill out onto the landing but was enough to suggest that the door was now open.

# Chapter 8

JAMES had expected the room beyond the door to be just like the one in his vision. It was however unlike any place he'd ever been to. The walls were lined solidly with shelves, all built on an angle so that the room became a conical shape. Right in the centre, a great column of curved shelves rose to the ceiling.

'Is this the place you saw in your vision?' Will asked in awe as he entered the room behind James.

James gazed up at the highest shelves and shook his head. 'There were no scrolls in the room I saw. Only books.'

Here, the shelves were stacked with hundreds of scrolls. Some had elaborate cases while others lay exposed. Thick layers of dust had gathered between the curled documents, turning the paper grey.

'This isn't what I expected for a temple archive,' Aralia remarked. 'It looks like it belongs in a fairy tale palace.'

There were no windows here and the space was lit by orbs which floated lazily between the shelves. Their soft, golden light made the room feel enchanted.

'It's no wonder only Father Eldon and the archivists are allowed in here,' Will murmured. 'The scrolls must be subject to certain conditions: humidity, light, temperature. Too many people breathing in here could change the conditions instantly.'

James nodded and pulled a fat file of cream coloured paper from the nearest shelf. The lettering was thick and black, suggesting it had been penned more recently. He couldn't read it however as it was written in another language.

'Some of these scrolls are ancient.' Arthur's voice drifted across the room. He had settled on the floor beside a particularly crowded shelf, a stack of flaking scrolls piled on his lap.

'How old is ancient?' Aralia crossed the room and sat down beside him.

'This one dates all the way back to The Awakening. This temple must have been built centuries ago.'

'What's The Awakening?' James asked curiously.

Arthur opened his mouth to reply but Tala beat him to it.

'It was an age of new thought; a time when people began to study magic as a science, not just as an unmeasurable power.'

James returned the scroll he was holding back to its shelf. 'How long ago was this age of new thought?'

The Awakening sounded much like the Age of Enlightenment in his own world, a time when humans had begun to use scientific thought and reason to understand the universe. He wondered what the people of Europe would have thought if they'd known about this world. Would they still have condemned magic and witchcraft with such severity or would they have accepted its existence as a legitimate force within the universe?

'It began around three hundred years ago,' Arthur explained, 'and lasted for more than a century.'

James nodded absent-mindedly. He wasn't sure when the Enlightenment had occurred in his world exactly, but knew it had lasted for a similar length of time.

'Arvad would have been dead by the time of The Awakening,' Will asserted. 'If he really came here, we'll have to find older records to prove it. We'll have to trace the records back three or four more hundred years.'

'I haven't found anything older yet,' Arthur remarked.

'Maybe he didn't come here,' James mused. 'Maybe the temple is connected to him in some other way. We're only assuming that he came here because of what I saw, but the room in my vision didn't look like this one.'

'Not as it is now, anyway,' Tala said. 'Maybe you saw the room as it was many centuries ago. A lot can change in seven hundred years.'

'You're right,' James agreed. 'I hadn't thought about that.'

Standing in this archive was like stepping back in time and he could only imagine the centuries of history that had been recorded here. Crossing to the centre of the room, he pulled a small scroll from the columnar shelf. As it came free, it dislodged two leather-bound scrolls standing on either side of it. Before he had time to react, both fell to the floor with ominous thuds.

'Who's there?'

A voice as hollow and cracked as the wooden floorboards boomed across the room. James froze. The voice had come from somewhere near the door, only he couldn't see anyone standing there.

'Get behind the column!' Will ordered. He grabbed James' sleeve and dragged him behind the towering shelf. Its circumference was not large enough to hide them completely and they cowered in its shadow.

'Why don't you come out?' the voice encouraged. It was deep and laced with a mild Jantran accent. 'Come out, come out, come out. I don't like to play hide and seek.'

James had been surprised to learn that many in Jantra spoke Camil as their first language, despite having a language of their own. It was an easier language to speak, Will had explained. The voice was now coming closer, creeping towards them like Poison Ivy.

'Ha, I see you!' the speaker exclaimed. 'The shadows cannot hide you now.'

The footsteps ceased. Suddenly, James felt a hand on his arm. Before he could react, the hand dragged him out from behind the column and into the light. He found himself face to face with a white-haired old man. His skin was creased like the bark of a hundred year old tree and his teeth were crooked and yellow. His nails were also discoloured and were so long that they'd begun to curve at the ends. It was not these features that were startling however, but his eyes. They were deep blue at first but quickly changed to sea green.

'You are the child taking refuge here,' the old man rasped. He fumbled in his tunic pocket and pulled out some glasses. Holding the thick lenses up to his eyes, he peered intently at James before letting him go. 'You came in the company of the Twelfth Messenger,' he continued. 'He has brought us visitors before but never ones so young.'

James objected to this comment but said nothing. He had turned sixteen just days before the Festival of Light. Will, Arthur and Aralia had also turned sixteen since their return to Arissel from Muir. Although Arthur and Aralia weren't sure of their exact birthdays, Arthur was almost certainly older than his sister. As for Tala, he didn't know, but he guessed she was a similar age. From the corner of his eye, he saw his friends moving out of the shadows to join him. The old man didn't acknowledge them.

'Albert came here himself as a boy,' he mused. 'His parents

had died tragically and he was all alone. He stayed here for a few years and often came to visit the archives. I've never met anyone quite so curious.'

'Curious?' James couldn't imagine Albert being curious. The Messenger had reprimanded him for asking too many questions on more than one occasion.

'Oh yes,' the old man said. 'He wanted to know all about the history of the temple and of Jantra. His list of questions was never ending.'

'I never knew that he stayed here,' Tala remarked.

James wondered why she would. Before he could question her however, the old man took his arm again. His eyes were a soft grey now, the colour of pigeon feathers. With his free hand, he reached upwards and drew one of the hovering orbs into his palm.

'I sense you have come to the archives for a reason,' he croaked.

James nodded. 'We were told that the archives are kept locked,' he began. 'The door just opened for us. We're not sure how or why as it was locked when we first tried it.'

The old man frowned. 'All by itself you say. How odd.' He looked away and James felt sure he wasn't telling the truth.

'Who are you, exactly?' Will then asked. 'D'you live up here?'

The old man smiled. 'I am Brother Augustus, the archivist. My duty was passed down to me by those who came before me. I live amongst the Brothers but spend much of my time up here. I am not always alone. I have an assistant who helps me. When I am gone, my role will fall to him.'

'Do you write the records?' Tala queried. 'Have you written about us?'

Brother Augustus ignored her questions and turned instead to James. His lips moved as if he was trying to say something but no words came. His forehead creased, deepening the lines that were already there.

'Why have you come here?' he eventually managed. 'What is it that you seek to know?'

James swallowed, suddenly at a loss for words himself. His wish to find the archives had been based on some vague vision of a room that had looked nothing like this one and a tattooed man who had clearly not been Brother Augustus.

'There's a tree in the garden,' he murmured at last. Before he could offer more details, Brother Augustus held up his hand for silence.

'Aah,' he began, elongating the vowel. 'I know the tree you speak of. It is an ancient yew, planted many centuries ago. In fact, there is a record of the day it was planted. It has an interesting story.' He narrowed his eyes at James and his irises turned deep purple. 'Let me find the record for you.'

He ran his fingers along several shelves, muttering to himself all the while. The orb he had been holding now bobbed above his head, following his movements. His fingers came to rest on a large stack of scrolls, bound together with gold string. Pulling a large parchment from the centre of the stack, he unrolled its many layers and began to read.

'Aha!' he exclaimed after several minutes, making everyone jump. 'Here we are.'

The page he was on was covered in scribbles, the writing so messy that it was unintelligible – to the companions at least. Brother Augustus seemed to know what it said, either from memory or a long-practiced talent for interpreting ancient lettering.

'Many centuries ago, the Minha archivist wrote of a young

man who sought refuge here,' Brother Augustus summarised. 'It is not clear why he came here, nor is his name recorded, but he stayed for many months. When his time here came to an end, he wanted to repay the Brothers for their kindness. He went into the garden and conjured a ball of light in his hands. He sent that light into the earth and even as the Brothers stood watching, it grew into a tree. A Peace Tree, or so the young man called it. If the records are to be believed, that very tree still stands in the temple garden today.'

'*Are* the records to be believed?' Arthur asked. 'Do you have any reason to doubt them?'

Brother Augustus was silent for a moment. 'The role of the temple archivist is to record the events which take place here with truth and accuracy. Yet it is difficult to believe that such a young man could possess enough power to create a tree from light.'

James frowned at the pages in the old man's hands, wishing he could read the words. 'Did anyone ever find out who he was?' He knew the answer already but didn't dare believe it, not until someone else said it out loud.

Brother Augustus sighed. 'Common legend makes no reference to this temple and we must rely on our own records to understand its history. The young man's identity was mere conjecture for centuries and only in more recent times did the Brothers here begin to guess who he really was: Arvad the Wanderer.' He stopped speaking, letting his words make their mark on those who stood listening.

James gaped at the old man's shrunken profile, his mind racing. So Arvad really had been here, inside the Minha Mound, just as his vision had revealed.

'What did Arvad look like?' he asked. 'Does this scroll make any reference to a necklace?'

Brother Augustus shook his head. 'These pages make no further reference to Arvad or the tree, but there are others. Let me fetch them.'

Raising a hand, he clicked his fingers and light sparked between them. On one of the high shelves, a scroll dislodged itself and sailed down into his open palm. He unrolled it on top of the other papers and turned it around for them all to see.

'In this last century, one of the Brothers was searching through the archives and discovered a drawing.'

He pointed to a faint pencil sketch at the bottom of the page. It depicted an oval, shaded and highlighted to represent a gleaming gem. The drawing was simple but managed to capture the exquisite nature of the piece. In the centre of the gem was another mark, so small that it might have been an error. Looking closer however, James saw that it was an upside down triangle shot through with a line.

'The alchemical symbol for earth!' he exclaimed.

'You are knowledgeable,' Brother Augustus complimented. 'The drawing dates back seven hundred years, according to the markings on the back, to a time before the Persecution. The same time Arvad was thought to have lived here. It seems that the young man gave the Brothers a second gift. A talisman which he claimed had belonged to his jeweller father.

From the drawing however, the Brothers here wondered if it was in fact made by dryads.'

'*Dryads?*' The word rushed from Aralia's mouth, conveying her surprise. 'Dryads?' She repeated in a calmer tone. 'How could the Brothers tell?'

'Because the flecks drawn inside the gem resemble those inside amphyr, otherwise known as amber. Amber is a gem strongly connected to the earth, or Aerth as it is spelt in the old language.' He wrote the word at the bottom of the paper. 'Amber is an ancient material formed from the resin exuded by conifers. The dryads were renowned for their knowledge of the earth and were, for a time, amber traders.'

'What happened to the talisman?' Tala asked.

'It was lost during the Persecution. During that time, the Brothers were condemned for their beliefs. Those who live and work here take neither the side of the light nor the dark. It has always been this way but the Persecutors deemed this unreasonable. The Minha Mound, like many other spiritual places, was sieged and the Brothers were killed. The talisman was never seen again. It became a legend here. The Brothers claimed that it was one of Arvad's gifts, but no one ever knew for sure.'

Brother Augustus rolled up the scrolls before looking up at the companions again with his now yellow eyes. 'Dawn is coming. You should not be here.' He ushered his uninvited guests towards the door. They did not protest, despite the unanswered questions resting on each of their lips. As they filed onto the landing, Brother Augustus spoke again. 'Take care,' he warned. 'There are those who would look unfavourably upon your unauthorised wanderings.'

With that he closed the door and the landing went dark. Time against them now, the companions hurried down the spiral steps and back up to the 'dining' room. Several orbs now floated against the ceiling, suggesting it was not long until the morning meal was served. When they reached the boys' room, the sky was just beginning to lighten beyond the gauze curtains. Kaedon and Oede stirred in their sleep but did not wake. Aralia and Tala left quietly and James, Arthur and Will climbed back into bed.

James lay on his back staring at the ceiling. He wondered

if the talisman in the drawing really was one of Arvad's gifts. Had he given it to the Brothers for safekeeping or had he not yet known what purpose it would later fulfil? Either way, its presence lingered within the temple walls, carrying with it the ghostly form of Arvad.

# Chapter 9

DAWN came at last. James, Will and Arthur rose with Kaedon and Oede, acting as if they'd slept well. They joined Aralia, Tala and Dina for breakfast and afterwards made their way to the garden. Brother Menid arrived to hand out their tasks for the day. James was sent to the pavilion with Aralia and Tala where a mess of seed filled baskets were waiting to be sorted. The sun was even warmer than on the previous day. Even out of direct sunlight, sweat poured down their faces. On several occasions, James found himself glancing across the garden to the old yew tree and wondering if it really had been created by Arvad out of thin air.

'James, can you hear me?'

He was startled to hear a voice in his mind. It was not Sylvia's or Tala's or even Albert's but it was nevertheless one he recognised.

'Rai?'

She hadn't spoken to him like this since the first time she'd discovered her ability on board the Arvorian ship. Nor had she told anyone else about it, as far as he knew anyway. Having had no practice, her voice sounded faint in his mind.

'I was worried... you wouldn't be able... to hear me,' she said haltingly. 'There's something I want to discuss with you... but I don't want her overhearing.'

By *her*, he presumed she meant Tala. 'What is it?' he

asked. 'We should wait until we're all together to discuss last night.'

'Just listen to me for a moment,' Aralia pleaded. 'Brother Augustus spoke of the rumoured connection between Arvad's talisman and the dryads. If this temple lies on the border to Jantra… then we're not far from Rivel.'

James glanced up at her. She refused to meet his eyes and carried on sorting seeds as if nothing else was going on.

'What's in Rivel?' he asked.

'Close to the coast is a village named Mercy.'

James remembered that name. It belonged to a dryad village, the place where Arthur and Aralia had been born.

'The dryads have great knowledge of the earth, as Brother Augustus said,' Aralia continued, her voice steadier now. 'Though I don't believe those in Mercy ever traded in amber, they may know of its properties and of the talisman.'

'Of course!' James emphasised. 'Albert *must* have known.'

'Did you say something?'

Tala looked at him and he reddened, not realising he'd spoken aloud. The way she was staring at him made him wonder if she knew that he and Aralia had been talking. He wasn't sure how she could know but her eyes gave away her suspicions.

'Nothing,' he said under his breath. 'It was nothing.' He glanced at Aralia but she was concentrating on the seed basket in her hands.

Silence fell. The three of them worked without stopping until midday when the Brothers retired indoors to rest. Standing up amongst the seed baskets, James stretched his stiff limbs. His clothes clung to his skin; the thin fabric damp with sweat. He felt desperately thirsty but there was nothing to drink. It was the custom here to refrain from all food and drink between dawn and twilight. He hadn't minded yesterday but today the heat was unbearable.

'We should go inside too,' Aralia suggested. 'If we're cooler we might be able to bear this thirst for a while longer.'

They were halfway down the pavilion path when Will and Arthur caught up with them. Both were breathless from running.

'Wait. Stop,' Will panted. 'We've got something to show you.'

James, Aralia and Tala followed them without question. Past the vegetable beds and into a part of the garden they hadn't yet seen. Here, between two low banks, ran a stream. A small bridge curved over the water, allowing easy access to the other side where crowded flowerbeds lay bathed in sunlight.

'Water,' James croaked. 'Can we drink it?'

Will nodded. 'I don't see why not. No one has told us we can't.'

Needing no further encouragement, James knelt on the bank and thrust his cupped hands into the water. Though warm from the sun it was still refreshing and he felt himself coming back to life with each sip. Will, Arthur, Aralia and Tala drank too and when they had all finished, they removed their shoes and socks and dangled their feet in the water.

'We should talk about the talisman,' Will said, breaking the silence that had fallen between them. He moved his feet back and forth in the water, stirring up small waves.

'Albert must have known,' James began. 'He must have brought us here on purpose.'

'You really think so?' Tala sounded dubious. 'He would have told us.'

Will uttered a short laugh. 'Ha! Albert never tells us

anything. He likes to keep us guessing.'

'What if the talisman really is one of Arvad's gifts?' Arthur asked, refocusing the conversation. 'It's been lost for centuries and no one has recovered it.'

'No one that the Brothers know of at least,' Will expressed.

'Arvad's first gift was kept in the vaults of the Hidden City for years without anyone retrieving it,' James reminded. 'It was the same with the sapphire ring. No one had seen it for centuries. We knew we needed to start looking for the remaining gifts, we just didn't know where to start. Now at least we know the gift is a talisman and that the earthstone is formed from amber.'

Will pulled his feet from the water. 'Where d'we start looking?'

'I think I might know.' Aralia glanced at James and he nodded encouragingly. 'You see, we're not far from Rivel and the dryad village of Mercy.'

Arthur went suddenly rigid. 'Rai, we can't.'

She turned to him with eyes full of fire. 'Why not? They could help us. You know they could.'

'You know why not.'

'Wait a second,' Will interrupted. 'Mercy is the village you were both born in, right?'

Aralia nodded. 'As halfblooded dryads and the only remaining descendants of the cursed Silene family, we're not welcome there but they wouldn't have to know us. Pachu weed flowers, for example, have illusion inducing properties that we could use to help us. If the talisman was dryad made as the records suggest, then speaking to the dryads seems like a logical starting point.'

'Why is the Silene family cursed?' Tala asked with

unashamed curiosity.

Aralia was silent for a moment. 'Our father was imprisoned for conspiring against the dryads. His innocence was only proven after his death. By then it was too late. The Silene name had already been cursed by the dryads.'

No one spoke for a moment. Arthur put an arm around his sister but didn't look at her.

'It's a good idea,' Will said at last, returning abruptly to Aralia's plan. 'The question is, how d'we get out of here? Whether Albert knew about the talisman or not, he still brought us here for safekeeping.'

'There must be a way.' Aralia stood up and began drying her feet on the grass. 'There can't just be one door out of this place.'

'What about the others?' Will asked. 'Should we tell them what we know?'

James shook his head. 'We should work out a plan first.'

A warning hiss from Arthur brought the conversation to an end. He nodded towards the bridge where an unfamiliar man had appeared. His clothes and hair suggested he was one of the Brothers but there were no tattoos above his eyes. The man's gaze was intense but his stance was awkward, as if he was uncertain of himself. James smiled at him and taking this as an invitation, the stranger approached.

'F-forgive me,' he stammered as he stopped before them. 'I m-must speak with you.'

'Who are you?' Tala demanded with unashamed interest.

'M-my name is Brother Felix. I am Father Eldon's brother. His blood brother, that is. I have lived in this place all my life and have m-met many strangers who seek refuge here. I m-must speak with you urgently.'

'Never seen the light of day, has he?' Will muttered so that only James could hear.

'F-forgive me,' Brother Felix repeated. He took a deep breath, as if what he was about to say carried great value. 'I come to tell you that you are no longer safe here.'

'Not safe?' Tala pulled her feet from the stream and stood up. 'Why not?'

Brother Felix smiled but the expression didn't quite meet his eyes. 'There is one amongst us who wishes you ill. One who seeks to expose you to those who look for you.'

'Who wishes us ill?' Will enquired.

'How d'you know that someone is looking for us?' James added. 'I thought the Brothers didn't seek to know the business of those who stay here.'

'I understand that my m-message is sudden and strange,' Brother Felix stammered again, 'but I urge you to believe me. What I say is true. I hear my Brothers whispering. Identities cannot easily remain hidden, especially in a place as small as this.' He smiled apologetically and lowered his voice to a whisper. 'I can help you but not here and not now. M-meet me at twilight by the cluster of trees by the wall. I will reveal more then.'

Clasping his hands over his chest, he bowed deeply. He then turned away and hurried back towards the temple. The companions frowned at one another but there was no time to talk as the Brothers were already returning to the garden, suggesting that the rest period was over. The afternoon passed slowly. James kept glancing up at the sky, waiting for twilight. He wondered if Brother Felix's warning was true and if it was, which Brother sought to betray them. They hadn't met many of the Brothers here but the ones they had, like Menid, Hagal and Augustus, didn't seem capable of treachery. The only way to find out was to wait.

At last the sun began to sink, leaving the sky a pale mountain blue. A few stars pricked through the atmosphere, tiny specks of faraway light. The temple garden lay silent, abandoned to the dusk. Following their long-awaited evening meal, James, Will, Arthur, Aralia and Tala hovered on the terrace outside their rooms, waiting for Brother Felix to appear. They wanted to make sure he really was coming before joining him in the garden. Dina, Kaedon and Oede had gone to speak with Father Eldon, so there was no risk of interruption. The minutes slipped by and the twilight deepened but still he did not come.

'Perhaps he's forgotten,' Tala suggested at last.

'Or he was lying,' Will growled.

Twilight passed. Brother Felix did not appear. Forced to face the reality of the situation, the companions tore their eyes away from the shadowy garden. Fighting down curiosity and disappointment, they parted ways for the night and headed back to their rooms. Slipping into bed, James once again lay awake. He wanted to believe that Brother Felix was lying but the fear of betrayal had already taken hold of him. He tried to close his eyes but could not sleep, his mind darting between Brother Felix, Arvad and the rumoured talisman. At some point, he heard Dina, Kaedon and Oede come in but after that his thoughts became a blur, caught somewhere between sleep and waking.

When morning came he felt tired and irritable. Will, Aralia, Arthur and Tala were also gloomy, prompting a sharp comment from Dina. They set about their daily tasks with ill-will, all the time scanning the garden for any sign of Brother Felix. Will asked one of the Brothers if they knew where to find him but the young man didn't know. Morning turned to afternoon and the maturing sun hurried towards its rest.

# THE EARTHSTONE

When twilight came, the companions hurried inside to wash, eat and sleep as they'd done each evening before.

This day marked a turning point. From here on, the pattern of eating, working and sleeping became familiar, bearable, but always the same. One day rolled into the next and still Albert did not come. James, Arthur, Tala, Will and Aralia searched for a way to escape but found none. There was only one door out of the temple and this was always locked, protected by some unbreakable magic. As for Brother Felix, he had simply vanished.

One evening however, as James stood alone on the terrace, he saw movement in the garden below. The flash of a long robe and the silhouette of someone lurking between the trees, in the same place Brother Felix had picked out as a meeting spot all those days ago. Heart racing, he hurried inside to fetch Will and Arthur. Only Will was there.

'You alright?' he asked as James dragged him out onto the terrace. 'What's wrong?'

'It's him,' James hissed. 'Brother Felix is in the garden.'

Will peered over the balustrade. His hair, wet from recent bathing, dripped onto the smooth stone. When he looked up again, his eyes were gleaming with frustration.

'Why is he here after all this time? I don't trust him.'

'Neither do I,' James returned, 'but aren't you curious to see what he has to say? What if he was right and we are in danger here?'

Will wiped a droplet from his forehead. 'It's been days and no one has come for us. I really think if we were in danger we'd know about it by now.'

'Fine, but even so, I think we should talk to him.' James passed back through the glass doors and Will silently followed.

Arthur had just returned from washing and had only to look at their faces to understand what was happening. He dressed hurriedly and joined them at the top of the stairs. In the hallway, they met Tala and Aralia also returning from the Spring rooms. James filled them in but would not stop to listen to their protests. The outside door was not yet locked and he slipped out into the twilight.

'James, are you sure about this?' Tala overtook him and stood firmly in his path.

'I'm sure,' he answered. Stepping off the pavilion path, he walked through the deepening shadows towards the trees where Brother Felix was waiting. The air beneath the branches was cool, mellowed by a small pool that rested between the roots. A dragonfly hovered above the water, silently meditating.

'You came.'

Brother Felix was suddenly there, standing between two birch trunks. Though his voice was the same, his appearance had altered. His tunic was torn in places and crusted with mud. The cloak around his shoulders was shredded in so many places that it hardly resembled its original form. The slashed pieces were black, as if they'd been singed. His hair too, or what was left of it, was similarly scorched. It was not these details that made James stare however, but his face. It too was dirty but not just with mud. His forehead, cheeks and lips were crusted with blood.

## Chapter 10

'YOU came,' Brother Felix repeated. He smiled nervously and brushed a clump of mud from his shoulder.

'Yes, we came.' Will appeared at James' side. 'We waited for you the first night, just as you asked. What happened to you?'

Brother Felix bowed his head. 'I am sorry. I have been travelling. The outcome of my journey was not quite as I expected.' His appearance suggested that this at least was true.

'Did something attack you?' Aralia advanced towards him. 'You should have someone look at your wounds.'

'All in good time,' Brother Felix returned. 'F-first I m-must speak with you all. I am sorry that I did not come to m-meet you before. My journey was sudden and secretive. Only Father Eldon knew. It was he who asked me to go.'

'Go where?' Will pressed. 'Did it have something to do with us? You said it wasn't safe for us here. Is that still true?'

Brother Felix's smile vanished. 'The Brothers here follow neither the light nor the dark but even we can be led astray. There is one here who would betray your whereabouts to those who would m-most like to know.'

'Who wishes us ill?' James asked anxiously. 'How d'you know?' These were the same questions he and Will had asked many days ago. Questions Brother Felix had promised to answer.

'I need not tell you who is looking for you,' Brother Felix said. 'F-for all I know, they could already be aware of your location. Few leave this temple without Father Eldon's permission and even fewer are allowed to enter it. This is not to say however that someone cannot leave or that those outside the walls will not force their way in.'

'You think one of your Brothers has already betrayed us,' Arthur stated.

'I do not think, I *know*.'

'Where did he go, this wayward Brother?' Aralia enquired. 'Why hasn't Father Eldon come to warn us himself?'

'He did not wish to worry you. I however believe that it is best for you to know. It is no longer safe for you here. You m-must leave this place. Now. Tonight.' He swallowed, as if his own words made him nervous.

'Tonight?' Will was incredulous. 'Why so soon?'

'As I said, those who wish to harm you may already know of your whereabouts. If you leave tonight, you can go where they will not find you. If you trust me, I can show you a way out of the temple.'

No one moved. James looked from Brother Felix to his friends and back again. He wanted to leave this place, they all did, but they couldn't go without first ensuring the safety of Oede, Kaedon and Dina.

'We can't go immediately,' he said firmly. 'There are things we need to discuss first.'

Brother Felix shook his head. 'You must go now! There is no time to lose. I have arranged everything for you. Your bags are waiting for you and your friends have already been informed. In fact, they have already been sent on ahead where they will m-meet you.'

'Ahead where?' Arthur asked.

Brother Felix did not answer. Instead, he vanished between the tree trunks and after some hesitation, the companions followed. Stopping by the rocks which formed a wall around this part of the garden, he pulled aside a clump of ivy to reveal a gate. The handle was padlocked shut but Brother Felix produced a key and unbolted it. A trail of light wound its way around the handle and the gate eventually clicked open.

'The gate is protected by charms that prevent people from entering and guests from leaving,' Brother Felix explained. 'Fortunately, I am able to override such charms.' He gave the gate a prod and it swung slowly open. 'Your freedom awaits.'

No one moved. James was torn between his own wish to leave this place and Albert's apparent desire to keep them here. He then thought of Oede, Kaedon and Dina waiting for them beyond the walls and made his choice. Passing through the gate, he found himself on a grassy slope halfway between the top of the Minha Mound and the bubble wrap landscape below. Everything was bathed in evening light, a soft, unobtrusive haze. Looking just ahead, he saw that their bags had indeed been brought out for them.

'Which direction are we facing?' He turned back to the garden, trying to remember where the sun usually rose and set here.

'South-west, as a rough guide,' Brother Felix said as he waved Will, Tala, Aralia and Arthur through the gate as well. 'Your friends rode north-east from here. Simply follow the stream until you come to an empty hut. Your friends will m-meet you there.' He smiled; an expression more genuine than his last. 'May your journey be a peaceful one.'

'Thank you,' Aralia uttered, though she still sounded unconvinced. 'Please tell Brother Eldon we're grateful to him for offering us his protection.'

Brother Felix nodded. He looked as if he might say something else but changed his mind. Without so much as a farewell, he closed the gate with a snap. Almost immediately, the wooden panels faded into the rock and disappeared. It was as if the temple and its garden had never existed at all.

'Well I suppose that's that,' Aralia concluded.

They slipped and slithered down the side of the mound. At the bottom, they brushed themselves off and looked around for the stream. There was no sign of it. The mounded earth was hard and dry and stretched out for miles in all directions.

'We should put our old cloaks over our clothes,' Arthur suggested. 'We don't want to risk anyone recognising our temple garments.'

'We'll be walking through the night, it seems.' Will extracted his cloak from his bag and shook it out vigorously.

'That's only partly true.' Arthur pointed ahead to where several shadowy shapes stood between the grassy mounds. 'We won't be walking.'

'What are you pointing at?' Tala squinted at the ghostly shapes.

'Brother Felix said Dina, Oede and Kaedon *rode* north,' Arthur emphasised.

'Ferastia!' Will exclaimed. 'Wild ones.'

Arthur nodded. 'There used to be small populations of them in Rivel. I've never ridden one but I know people who have. They are much shyer than domestic ferastia, so we'll have to approach them carefully.'

He led the way across the hillocky landscape to where the ferastia stood grazing. The beasts wittered anxiously as the companions approached but did not run. There were seven adults and one young one standing close together and nibbling the same patch of grass. They looked much the same as domestic ferastia, only a little larger and with longer manes. The animals watched the strangers closely but did not stop eating.

'Only one of us should approach,' Arthur whispered. 'The rest of you should stay still. No sudden movements.'

He walked up to the nearest animal, his hand outstretched. The ferastia backed away from him but when he stopped, it also became still. Without shifting its eyes, it bent its long neck towards him and nuzzled his hand. This gentle interaction seemed to calm it and the other animals relaxed too. Arthur reached forward to stroke the animal's nose. It huffed at him, as if responding to some unasked question. In one graceful movement, it sank to its knees on the grass and held still.

'It's offering its services to us,' Arthur said.

Even as the ferastia lay down, two more followed suit. They lowered themselves to the ground and bowed their heads in willing service. The others, less sure, huddled in the background watching.

'We can just take three between us,' Aralia suggested. 'We don't need one each.'

Arthur nodded. 'Tala and James, you take one. Rai, you go with Will. I'll ride alone.'

'How far is it from here to Rivel, d'you think?' Will asked as he swung himself up behind Aralia. 'If Dina, Kaedon and Oede are riding north-east, then they're also heading in that direction.'

'It would seem so,' Arthur replied. 'We should follow the stream, just as Brother Felix said.' He patted his ferastia and it rose unsteadily to its feet.

'I can hear the stream,' Aralia said. 'Listen.'

A faint gurgling sound was coming from somewhere close by. With Arthur in the lead, they rode towards the sound until they came in sight of the stream. It was barely wide enough to be called a stream and burbled a melancholy tune as it flowed through the uneven landscape.

Night soon settled over them and the world was gradually blotted out. Though the air was warm, it carried the chill of anticipation with it. James shivered and was glad for the ferastia's clear eyesight and sense of direction. He thought again of Brother Felix and his warning. If he had been telling the truth, there was a chance they were still in danger, even out here in the open. Now there were no others to protect them and no walls to hide behind. The only benefit was that if the temple was besieged, the attack would prove fruitless. He only hoped the Brothers would be safe against any intruders.

A memory niggled in his mind. On that first morning in the temple, he'd seen someone in the garden in the forbidden hours before dawn. He hadn't been able to see who it was but now he wondered if it might have been Brother Felix. His warning had been sudden and unfounded. He hadn't even been able to tell them the name of the wayward Brother. His long absence was also suspicious and it only now occurred to James that he might be the informant. His insistence that they leave the temple immediately was odd. Perhaps he had arranged for the attack to take place beyond the walls, on the route he had impressed on them to take.

'Wait, stop!' James called aloud. He tugged his ferastia's mane and it came to a halt.

'What's wrong?' Will's voice sounded close by.

'You were right to doubt Brother Felix,' James blurted. 'I

think he might be our betrayer. Think about it. He told us we weren't safe but had no real evidence. Then he disappeared for days and as soon as he came back, made sure to send us on our way. He knew it wouldn't take much to persuade us. The fact that we went straight to meet him upon his return confirmed his hope that we were still afraid for our safety. An easy fear to work with if he wanted us to leave the temple.'

'I knew we shouldn't have trusted him,' Will groaned.

'You were right,' James repeated. 'At least we're not inside the temple anymore. We wanted to escape and this was a way out.'

'What good will it be if we're killed?' Tala asked from her seat behind him. 'What about Dina, Kaedon and Oede? Brother Felix might have lied about them too. For all we know, they could still be inside the temple. We should go back.'

'We'll be putting ourselves in even more danger if we simply head back the way we've come,' Arthur countered.

Whether he said anything else or not, James didn't know. In the deep silence of the night, he heard a rushing sound. At first he thought it was the stream but the sound kept coming in waves, more like the beating of wings. Paralysed by fear, he waited for the inevitable. A flash of light split the sky, like lightning before a roll of thunder. It burst above his head and he felt Tala duck against him. One of the ferastia screamed in fright but he did not know which. Light flashed again. For a split second, the landscape was illuminated. James caught a glimpse of their attackers: four black ferastia, each carrying a cloaked rider.

'Riders!' James shouted. 'Up ahead.'

It was no use trying to remain hidden now. The riders had seen them and their only hope was to outrun them. A third bolt of light sailed through the air. James ducked but his ferastia screamed as its hooves were scorched. The beast suddenly reared and he was flung backwards. He grabbed onto its mane and felt Tala hook her fingers into his cloak. Just as abruptly, the ferastia landed on all fours again and they were thrown against its neck. Tala murmured 'whoa' as the distressed beast stumbled in the darkness. Sent into a frenzy, it began to run, travelling at such high speed that James had to close his eyes, even though it was dark.

Light zigzagged between the animal's hooves. Glancing over his shoulder through the beams, James saw Will, Arthur and Aralia close behind in a dizzying vision. Running on either side of them were two of the black ferastia. He watched as Will raised a defensive hand and cast his own light into the air. It struck several oncoming beams and a mighty crack split the atmosphere. The ground shook and for just a moment, the night was black once more. Then came the sound of stumbling hooves followed by someone screaming.

# Chapter 11

THE screaming ceased. The night was once more disturbed by a streak of blinding light. It shot through the air at high speed before exploding in a shower of sparks. Looking up through the glittering rain, James thought he saw the silhouette of a dragon. A dark shape held aloft by jagged wings. As he focused on it however, it reeled away from the light as if it had been burnt.

'Light, we need more light,' Tala shouted. 'They're gaining on us.'

At her command, James raised his hand to the sky. A stream of light shot from his fingertips and merged with those sent up by his friends. The landscape was illuminated once again, sharpened like a photograph. The cloaked riders reigned in their steeds, taken aback by this unforeseen retaliation. There was electricity in the air and the companions struck again and again, calling on all the training Kaedon, Oede and Dina had taught them.

'Look, there's a copse up ahead!' Arthur's voice rang through the night.

A dark line of trees rose from the landscape a short way ahead of them. James dug his heels into the ferastia's side and it began to run again. Though he could not see the trees, he felt branches scratching his face as the ferastia forged a path between them. Faced with fresh obstacles, the beast slowed its pace down to a steady walk.

'Rai, Art, are you here?' James called as loudly as he dared. 'Will?'

'Will and I are here,' Aralia's voice came back to him. 'Art? Are you there?'

There was no reply. James reigned in the ferastia he and Tala were riding and dismounted. He stood for a moment listening but everything lay silent. Creating a small light, he started walking back through the trees. At the edge of the copse, he stopped. Everything was dark and still. He held up his light, letting it spill out in wider and wider circles. The riders had vanished. A few steps in front of him however, a dark mass lay on the ground. He began walking towards it and as he drew closer, he realised it was one of the wild ferastia. The one Arthur had been riding. It lay on its side, eyes wide open to the night.

'Arthur are you there?' he hissed.

A faint groan came back to him. Shifting his eyes, James saw another shape caught beneath the dead animal's rear. Its body had fallen on top of Arthur's legs, pinning him to the ground. Letting his light hover above him, James knelt on the grass and tried to move the animal. It was too heavy. Suddenly, three pairs of hands joined his own. Working together, he, Will, Arthur and Aralia managed to push the ferastia's body aside and set Arthur free.

'Art, are you alright?' Aralia knelt beside him.

'I'm fine,' he grunted and rose unsteadily to his feet. 'Just bruised.'

'I'm surprised it didn't break your legs,' Will remarked but a look from Aralia silenced him.

'Where did the riders go?' Tala asked. 'Did you see?'

Arthur shook his head. 'They just vanished. Maybe they're

regrouping or adding to their forces. We should get going while we still can.'

They began walking back towards the copse with Arthur limping but otherwise unharmed. Concealed amongst the trees again, they found their way back to the ferastia. Arthur squeezed on behind James and Tala and they began to ride once more. Before long, the trees came to an end and they broke out into the open. Even though it was night-time, a soft light rested on the horizon, signifying the not so distant arrival of dawn. The summer nights were particularly short in this part of the world for which James was glad. In the daylight, the Shadows at least could not touch them. As for the riders however, he did not know. Though the early air was still, the weight of anticipation pressed down on all of them. Even the ferastia remained alert, walking with ears pricked to the sky.

'We should keep riding towards Rivel,' Arthur suggested. 'We could reach the border before sunrise.'

'What about Dina, Kaedon and Oede?' Aralia asked. 'We can't just abandon them.'

'We can't go back either,' James said firmly. He also feared for Dina, Kaedon and Oede's safety but knew the risk was too great. 'There will be riders everywhere looking for us. If we go to Rivel, we can give everything time to settle down before returning.'

As he spoke, he became aware of another sound. This time it was not the rushing of wings but the unmistakable beating of hooves. There was no time to react. A stream of light shot through the air towards them. It landed between the two ferastia and both animals leapt sideways in fright.

'We have nowhere to hide,' Arthur observed in a matter of

fact voice. 'Our best hope now is to try and outrun them.'

A new light glimmered somewhere off to their left. It was moving straight towards them; certain of its target in this open landscape. Tala ducked and James and Arthur held themselves over her as the light raced towards them. At the last minute however, it changed course and sped instead towards their attackers. Whether it hit its target or not was impossible to tell but a deep silence descended.

'Where did that come from?' Aralia breathlessly asked. 'Whoever sent it just saved us.'

'There's still a light over there,' Tala announced. 'Look.'

Glancing over to where the stream of light had come from, they saw another, much smaller light, suspended in the darkness.

'It's coming towards us,' James said.

The light was indeed moving towards them, gliding through the night like a firefly or wayward spark. It drew closer and closer before stopping right in front of them.

'Ne fil; do not be afraid.'

A deep voice startled them. The light shone brighter and the bearded face of a young man appeared behind it. His eyes were serious but a warm smile played about his lips.

'*Who* are you?' Tala immediately demanded. 'What are you doing out here in the middle of the night?'

'Saving strangers from unwanted attacks, it seems,' the young man replied calmly. His voice was lightly accented but he spoke perfect Camil. 'I could ask you the same,' he continued. 'What are five...' he paused to check his calculation, 'yes, five young people doing in the dead of night under attack from Raptuls?'

'Raptuls?' James repeated questioningly. 'Is that the name of those riders?'

'It is the name given to the beasts they ride. Like ferastia but winged. They cannot fly but their wings give them speed.' He paused to stroke both ferastia. 'Which direction are you heading in?' he then asked. 'You must be in a hurry if you dare to ride through the night.'

'We might not have made it without your help,' Aralia thanked him.

'We're heading east,' Arthur added. 'To the village of Mercy in Rivel.'

The young man nodded. 'You are not far from the border. I am going that way myself.'

'Do you have a name,' Tala enquired 'or are you simply an anonymous stranger?'

'Aldis,' the young man replied willingly. 'From the Aldia family. I have been travelling for some days and I am now on my way home to Rivel.' The light in his hand wavered, distorting his features. 'I can show you the way, if you will let me.' He did not ask their names and none of them offered to tell him.

Will glanced at Aralia. 'We have room on our ferastia if you'll join us?'

Needing no further encouragement, Aldis leapt up onto the ferastia's back behind them. He let out a soft whoop as the animal began to walk again. It responded to his voice, increasing its pace but not quite trotting.

'Can I ask you a question?' Will cast Aldis a sidelong glance and the young man nodded obligingly. 'How is it that you were able to fight off the Raptuls? There were *five* of us and we couldn't do it.'

Aldis didn't answer immediately. 'I have encountered them before. I have been trained to know what to do. It can take years to learn the right skills to fight off groups like that.'

'Groups like that?' James queried. 'You mean the darkness?'

Aldis shot him a curious look. 'Some would have you killed for believing in such things.'

'And you?' Aralia said with surprising force. 'What do *you* think?'

'I believe in the evidence I see before me. The same evidence that compelled me to save you. I would warn, however, that in Rivel beliefs like ours are not welcomed. People are afraid.'

'If they're afraid, surely it's because they can see what's happening all around them,' Arthur remarked.

Aldis shook his head. 'They are too afraid of the truth to believe in it. Their fear of what might happen makes them pretend that they are not afraid at all.'

Albert had said something similar, James recalled. The closer people were to the darkness, the less likely they were to see it. It was the same with the truth, it seemed. Silence fell between all of them. Dawn was just beginning to break on the horizon and the sky blushed pink. As the light expanded, it cast a pinkish sheen over the landscape, as though everything had been dipped in watery paint. The effect was beautiful but haunting. Closing his eyes, James searched in his mind for the village of Mercy. Pieces of landscape wove through his thoughts and he tried to hold them together. The stream was visible in every piece but the other parts would not stay long enough for him to create one solid image. He hadn't tried this kind of magic for many months and had only once or twice succeeded in creating a full picture.

The sun climbed higher as they rode and dawn became morning. Desperate to reach the Rivel border without delay, they did not stop for hours. There was no need to eat or drink as they had been used to fasting with the Brothers at the temple. Soon after midday, they crossed the border into Rivel. There was no milestone to confirm this fact but Aldis told them the official border was several miles northwards. Beyond this invisible border, the landscape stretched on as it had before, dry and featureless apart from the stream. Only the colours changed with the passing hours, rosy dawn giving way to golden day and eventually the cool blue of evening.

As the light faded, the ferastia grew skittish. The companions too became nervous of the lengthening shadows and what they might hide. The fact that Aldis still rode with them was comforting however, especially as he did not seem to fear the night. He had the vision of a hawk, his eyes piercing straight through the darkness. The ferastia could also see the way and needed little direction. Aldis whispered to them now and then and eventually guided them across the stream. They splashed through the shallows, bearing their riders safely to the other side.

'Thua, thua!' Aldis murmured to the animals in his own tongue.

They halted at the sound of his voice and stooped to drink from the stream. The day had been hot and though the ferastia did not easily thirst, they had not drunk for hours.

'We must be close to Mercy by now,' Will said. 'It's getting late.'

'We are not far,' Aldis confirmed.

'Where is it that you're going?' Aralia asked him. 'You never told us.'

There was a long pause and when Aldis spoke again his tone was distant. 'I go to the same place as you.'

'To Mercy?' Aralia queried disbelievingly.

'Are you a dryad then?' Will added before Aldis could

reply.

'No.'

His response was simple but felt somehow unfinished. No one dared press him however for his tone had sounded definite. The ferastia began to move again, refreshed after their long drink. The night was still and stars pricked through the blanket of darkness. Looking up, James was reminded of the fact that he was just a small part of something far greater. This quest was more than just a search for a crystal. It signified the preservation of an ancient magic, a force that Arvad himself had wielded. Staring at the starry void above, it wasn't hard to imagine that such power existed.

It wasn't until the early hours of the morning that Mercy came into sight. The village was built close to a great forest which stretched out for miles. The trees were tall and rich with foliage, the leaves green and lush despite the drought. Compared to the forest, the village was tiny. The peaked roofs of the houses stood out like miniature mountains against the sky. In the gloomy morning light, the buildings were part-silhouette, ghost houses in a village of shadows.

# Chapter 12

'THERE it is,' Aralia breathed. 'Mercy.'

Arthur placed a reassuring hand on her shoulder. No one else spoke, not wishing to disturb this moment of return. The ferastia came to a standstill, sensing that no one was ready to approach the village just yet.

'Should we wait until it's light?' James asked. 'No one will be up yet.'

'Much like the Brothers in the temple, the dryads thrive on dawn and twilight,' Aralia returned. 'There's no need for us to wait.'

Arthur squeezed her shoulder. 'Are you sure you're ready to do this?'

She nodded; her eyes dark grey in the pre-dawn light. 'I'm ready but there's one thing we should do first.' Reaching into her bag, she drew out a glass bottle. It was packed with dried petals and uncorking the lid, she shook a pile onto her palm. The petals were brown and curled, making them look like old berries. 'Here.' She held her hand out to James. 'Take one.'

'What are they?' James took one of the petals and sniffed it. It smelt like wet fish left in the sun on a steaming hot day and he recoiled.

'Pachu weed petals,' Aldis said with surprise. 'Where did you get them?'

'I collected a few,' Aralia replied vaguely, not wishing to

give away the name of the temple. 'The leaves are poisonous but the flowers have useful properties.'

'What kind of properties?' Will asked suspiciously.

Aralia slipped the remaining petals back in their jar and smiled. 'Illusion inducing ones. I told you that before.'

James frowned. 'Do they act like a drug?'

'They create illusions, not hallucinations! When eaten, they create a kind of aura. People who know you will no longer be able to recognise you. It changes their perception of you. You, however, will still look the same to yourself. The effects wear off quickly though and you can't eat more than one per day. Any more than that would make you sick.'

'Surely we don't all need to eat one.' Tala glanced at the shrivelled petal in her hand with distaste. 'The dryads don't know me.'

'It's better that none of us are recognised,' Arthur replied curtly. 'Apart from Aldis.'

He turned to the young man who had dismounted and was watching them all curiously. Aldis said nothing but offered a faint smile of reassurance. Pressing the petal between his teeth, James began to chew. It quickly disintegrated into a foul tasting pulp and he forced himself to swallow. Looking down at his hands, he felt an immediate sense of dysphoria. It was like his hands weren't really his own, even though his brain understood that they were. He still knew who he was even though his external body felt unfamiliar. Glancing at his friends, he saw that they too were both familiar and strange. They wore the same clothes and had the same mannerisms but their overall appearances were distorted.

'We should go,' Arthur urged. 'We don't have time to waste.'

The village houses were squat and built in higgledy-piggledy fashion. Each property was unique, with front doors of varying colours and uneven gardens in which scraggly chickens pecked at the grass. It was an unassuming place and apart from the chickens, lay still under the pale morning sky. Dismounting the ferastia, the companions headed for the main gate: five upright wooden slats held together with rusty nails.

'I wonder if our house is still here,' Aralia whispered to Arthur.

Arthur wrapped an arm around her shoulders. Together, the siblings stepped through the gate, leaving everyone else to follow. At this early hour, no one else was about and they walked uninterrupted through the village.

'I thought the dryads thrived on the dawn?' Will said. 'Where are they?'

'The dryads do not live here.' Aldis stopped walking and the companions turned to stare at him.

'What d'you mean?' Arthur asked. 'Mercy has always been a dryad village.'

Aldis shook his head. 'Not any more. This is a village of men.' His tone softened a little. 'Around ten years ago, the dryads fled to the forest. They abandoned this village and soon humans began to settle here, my family included. You should come and meet them. They will soon be awake.'

No one knew what to say. Aldis began walking again and not knowing what else to do, Arthur, Aralia, James, Will and Tala followed. After just a few steps however, Aralia came to a halt, forcing Arthur to stop with her. She pointed to a house just ahead, a tiny building with a yellow front door.

'That's it,' she whispered. 'The house with the yellow door.'

Arthur nodded. 'Amma wanted it yellow even though the

neighbours protested. She said it reminded her of sunshine even in the depths of winter.'

As they stood looking at the house, the front door was suddenly flung open. A woman

appeared behind it, dressed in a short red cloak and baggy trousers pinched in at the ankles.

'Mia jous?' Her tone was harsh and her eyes cold. 'Mia jous?' she repeated.

'Shem,' Arthur quickly greeted her. 'We're sorry to disturb you at this hour.'

The woman's eyes narrowed. 'What is it that you want, lurking by my gate?' she snapped, switching her language to Camil. 'If you are hungry, I have no food. If you are tired, I have no bed. If you are poor, I have no money.'

'We don't come asking for food, money or a bed,' Aralia reassured.

'You are thieves then,' the woman accused. 'I have nothing for you. I have nothing to hide.'

Her accent had a gentle lilt to it, almost like French James thought as he stood listening a short distance behind Arthur and Aralia. Will and Tala hovered on either side of him and Aldis, realising they had stopped, hurried back to join them. He saw the woman in the doorway and his face broke into a smile.

'Shem, Rosa,' he greeted.

She glanced at him and her expression immediately softened, though she didn't quite smile. 'Shem, Aldis. Mia jous amidi?'

'Yes, they are my friends,' Aldis replied in Camil. 'Forgive them for lingering. They merely stopped to admire your flowers.'

There were few flowers in the garden and those that did

exist had wilted in the heat. Rosa seemed satisfied with this explanation however and nodding to Aldis, closed her front door with a snap.

'The people here are wary of strangers,' Aldis warned the companions. 'You should be careful.'

'We are not strangers,' Aralia objected.

Arthur nudged her sharply in the ribs.

'Do you think I did not know that you are dryads?' Aldis asked sharply. 'You bear a resemblance to your kin.'

Aralia let out a small sigh of relief. 'What happened to our people? Did they leave Mercy freely or were they driven out?'

'People say they ran away like cowards. They grew so afraid of the rising darkness that they chose to hide in the forest. Once, they protected this land and now they cower in the shadows. They have turned their backs on any who are not their own kind.'

'Most people *still* don't believe in the rising darkness,' James said. 'How is it that the dryads knew of its influence so many years ago?'

'Not everyone is blind to the truth,' Aldis replied simply.

'Amma used to say the dryad race would one day turn in on itself,' Arthur reflected. 'It seems that she was right.'

'Come,' Aldis said, 'let me take you to my home. You will be safe there.'

'We're grateful for your help,' Will acknowledged but his eyes darted towards the forest.

Aldis caught this wandering glance and his smile vanished. 'Your desire to enter the forest is written across your features. I will not stop you from going but I cannot come with you. Perhaps when you have finished with your business there, you will come to my house. It is the one at the end of this path with the blue door.'

'Thank you,' Aralia responded gratefully. 'You've already done so much for us.'

'Sha plume,' Aldis uttered, 'until next time.'

The companions approached the forest with trepidation. Despite the heavy foliage, the branches were not so densely packed as to make entry impossible. The sound of the breeze rushing through the leaves was enchanting, an irresistible whisper drawing them into the forest. Light filtered between the branches and danced amongst the trunks like moonbeams on water. It was beautiful, bewitching even, as if this place had been taken straight from the pages of a children's fairy book. There was darkness here too, however. Moss and brambles stifled the ground with a dense coverage. There was no path through the thick undergrowth which served as a defence against unwanted intruders.

'Which way do we go?' Tala asked. 'There's no path.'

Arthur turned to her with a faint smile. 'There is a path. Look up.'

Suspended between the trees were a series of rope bridges. These were supported by strands of ivy, knitted together to form chains. The ivy was so thick that the bridges became part of the forest itself, barely distinguishable from the branches and leaves. There were other structures too, James realised, hidden amongst the foliage. Treehouses built from rough strips of wood so that they too blended into their surroundings. Ivy rope ladders hung from sloped balconies and drifted down to the forest floor.

'Dryad dwellings are often built to look like their surroundings,' Arthur explained. 'Mercy used to be like that too, centuries ago anyway. Apparently you couldn't see it from far away because the buildings were enchanted to look like the landscape.'

'It's so quiet here,' Will observed. 'Where are the dryads?'

'They won't show themselves unless they wish to,' Arthur replied, 'but they will be watching.'

'Do we stay down here or do we climb?' Tala glanced around nervously.

Arthur didn't respond. He was looking away between the trees, his eyes fixed on something no one else could see. There was a rustling sound and after a few moments, a woman appeared. She was dressed in a cropped green cloak and trousers and carried a basket full of mushrooms. Her hair was the colour of autumn leaves, the short strands twisting together like roots. She stopped between two trees and her silver eyes came to rest on the companions.

'Shem,' Arthur greeted her. 'We hope we do not trespass on your land.'

The stranger inclined her head but did not speak.

Aralia moved to stand beside her brother. 'Does the healer Amna Leigh still live amongst the dryads? We have come to see her.'

'Amna Leigh does not see people anymore.' The dryad's voice was hard and her expression did not change as she spoke. She stepped towards the companions, her feet crushing a path in the undergrowth.

'She is still here then,' Aralia presumed.

'She does not see people anymore,' the dryad repeated. 'Much has changed amongst our people.' She looked Aralia up and down, as if sensing one of her own kind stood before her.

'Please,' Aralia begged, 'we've come a long way.'

'Shem, legast si mur nei kkar.'

Arthur spoke haltingly, his tongue slowly remembering the dryad language. The words were imperfect but the female dryad's expression softened to hear them. She looked at Arthur curiously and uttered a reply in the same tongue.

'What're they saying?' James whispered to Aralia.

'She asks who we are and says she will take us to the healer. Arthur has told her we are distant cousins of hers. Come on, we must follow her.'

The dryad turned away and began to forge a new path through the undergrowth. She led the companions deeper and deeper into the forest where the trees grew taller and the leaves were thicker. After some time, they came to a great oak tree which stood across their path. The ancient branches spread out in all directions, searching for sunlight. Only the lower limbs curved towards the ground, too heavy to hold up their own weight. They created an airy cave around the vast trunk which was partly hollowed out with a cave of its own.

Ducking beneath the branches, the silver-eyed dryad beckoned for the companions to follow. Beneath the oak's ancient limbs, the atmosphere changed. It did not carry the tingling hush of the forest but a mysterious calmness. There was no time to linger here for their guide passed quickly through this enchanted cave and ducked out on the other side. Following her, the companions found themselves at the edge of a clearing. Right in the centre was an ivy covered hut, built on low stilts and accessible via a rope ladder which hung from the balcony outside the front door.

'This is the home of Amna Leigh,' their guide announced. 'Be wary, she does not welcome strangers, even distant cousins.'

The dryad stepped aside, suggesting she would not take them any further. Thanking her, the companions crossed the clearing to the hut.

'Who is this healer you want to see?' James asked Aralia.

He glanced over his shoulder to see if the dryad was still there but she had vanished.

'Amna Leigh was the elder of the dryad village when we lived here,' Aralia explained. 'Technically, she's not a healer but an Earth Reader.'

'What's that?' Will questioned.

'Someone who reads and translates the messages of the earth. I used to sit with her and watch her while she worked. She knows more about the dryad people than anyone I've met and could really help us.'

'She was ancient when we were young,' Arthur said with a smile, 'I'm surprised she's still alive.'

They had reached the rope ladder and grabbing onto a middle rung, Aralia began hauling herself upwards with surprising speed. Scrambling onto the balcony, she brushed herself off before stepping up to the door and delivering a sharp knock. It opened instantly. A woman stood before her, dressed in an old grey tunic and matching cloak. Despite her plain clothing, she bore an uncanny resemblance to the silver-eyed dryad who had brought them here.

'Shem,' the woman began. 'Mia jous?'

'Shem.' Aralia returned her greeting. 'We are looking for Amna Leigh. We are told she lives here.'

The woman looked past Aralia to where James, Arthur, Will and Tala had gathered at the top of the rope ladder. She then looked back at Aralia and her expression soured. She muttered something in her own tongue and Aralia nodded in understanding.

'I know her,' she said firmly in Camil. 'She will know me. I am a cousin.'

The woman's eyes narrowed. She stared at Aralia for a long time before turning on her heel and vanishing into the house.

The companions waited for her to return but she did not. The open doorway simply gaped at them.

'Maybe she wants us to follow her,' Arthur suggested.

Assuming that permission had been granted, they entered the house. There was no hallway; just a large, shadowy room joined to another by an arched doorway. A single orb floated between the two spaces, the dull glow only reaching a little way into each. The first room was cluttered with overflowing shelves. Half burned candlesticks and jars of herbs rested between piles of dusty books. In the middle of the room, standing between stacks of ancient paper, was a chair. The back was facing the front door but it was evidently occupied for a pair of small feet dangled between the uneven legs.

The companions hovered in the doorway, waiting for their host to invite them in. The chair began to turn, twisting slowly around until at last the occupant was revealed. To their surprise, it was not an old woman who sat there but a child. She might have been eight or nine years old and was dressed in an old grey tunic and cloak. Her silvery hair was pulled tightly away from her face by a headband, making her features look stretched. Although she was young, she sat commandingly upon the chair, her head held regally above her small frame. She did not speak and simply stared at her guests with her hard, cold eyes.

# Chapter 13

THE child did not speak for a long time. She looked at the companions one by one, her face as expressionless as her eyes. James shuddered as her gaze fell on him. He had never seen anyone quite like her. She was like a ghost, pale and cold from her silvery hair down to her bare feet.

'Elrin sa?'

When she spoke at last, her voice was hard and demanding. In an instant, her ghostly demeanour vanished and she became nothing more than a petulant child.

'Shem,' Aralia greeted her. 'We are looking for Amna Leigh. Is she here?'

The girl cocked her head, considering her answer. 'What do you want to see her for?'

Like Rosa in the village and the female dryad who had led them here, she switched easily between her own tongue and Camil.

'We wish to speak with her,' Aralia replied, still giving nothing away.

'She does not see people anymore. Did no one tell you?'

The girl slid forward on the chair but her feet still dangled a few inches above the floor. She folded her arms and glared at Aralia.

Arthur advanced towards the chair. 'Is she here? In a house this small, she can't be hard to find.'

The girl's eyes twinkled mischievously. 'She sits right here before you.'

'You are not her,' Arthur stated. 'Amna Leigh is old. Older than you can even imagine, no doubt.'

'I am she,' the child insisted. 'Did no one tell you that Amna died? I have taken her place. I am the one you seek.'

'Maybe we should talk to the dryad who let us in,' Will suggested. 'She might speak more sense.'

'I am small but not deaf,' the girl snapped. 'Amma will not talk to you. Speak to me only and tell me what you want.'

James was about to reply when he noticed someone standing in the archway between the two rooms. It was an old woman. Her back was so bent that her face wasn't visible. She leaned heavily on her walking stick as she shuffled towards the child in the chair.

'Ama,' she wheezed. 'No more games. I suppose I must see them.'

The little girl immediately abandoned her seat. She ran to the corner of the room where she hid amongst the shadows. The old woman settled herself in the chair and raised her frosty white head. Her skin was so deeply lined that her features were lost amongst the folds. Hair grew on her chin, white like the patchy strands on her scalp. She looked so frail that James feared she might snap at the slightest movement.

'Ama like to play,' the old woman croaked. 'She scare stranger away.'

'We came to see you, Amna Leigh,' Aralia said gently. 'We hope you'll forgive this intrusion.'

Their host nodded slowly. 'I know you come. My daughter tell me.'

'The lady who opened the door to us?' Tala asked.

The old woman didn't seem to hear her. 'What reason do

you come here? Amna Leigh see no one anymore. Not even distant cousin.'

Aralia knelt on the dusty floor before the ancient dryad's chair. 'You are an Earth Reader, Amna. We have come to ask for your knowledge of the gemstone amber.'

Amna Leigh raised her head a fraction further but did not meet Aralia's eyes. 'I know little of burning stone.'

'Burning stone?' Arthur said questioningly. 'Why do you call it that?'

'Because of its colour,' the old woman croaked. 'What else?'

Realising the need for a more specific question, James now spoke. 'How is amber formed?' he asked. 'Does it come from a particular region?'

'Amber is tree blood,' Amna Leigh replied shortly.

'I think she means resin,' Tala whispered.

Aralia shook her head. 'No. She means the sap drawn from dryad trees. Every dryad is connected to a particular tree. It is theirs to protect for life. An extension of themselves.'

'If dryad tree is cut down, it bleed,' Amna Leigh explained. 'Blood is white when cut but soon turn golden.'

James remembered his mum telling him once that amber was formed from tree sap. She had been showing him a necklace and earrings she'd inherited from his estranged grandmother.

'What connection does amber have to the earth?' he asked. 'Surely that's a question an Earth Reader can answer.'

'Like all gemstone, amber is product of earth. Greatest power comes from earth. All other power is weak. Century ago, alchemists found a way to turn all tree blood gold. Only the sap of the Silver Tree could not be forced to change, so ancient tales say. Amber drawn from such a tree was purest.

Its power came from earth itself. The amber formed on such a tree can only become golden if placed in fire.' She glanced at Arthur. 'That is why I call it burning stone. Alchemists did not discover this secret until it was too late. They secured great wealth, created the greatest amber trade in world, but none of it could last.'

'Who were these alchemists?' Aralia queried. 'Where did they come from?'

'Dryads from the eastern quarter of this world. They migrated over from north. Once they were our brother and sister but their search for wealth placed a great rift between our peoples.'

'I didn't know there were dryads in the east.' Aralia sat back on her heels and glanced at her brother.

'No one hear of them anymore,' the old woman rasped. 'They lived in Gulna Mountains but fled after war between Lleur and Outici. The great amber forests burned and with them the entire amber empire. The day the Golden Road fell was known throughout the world.'

'What's the Golden Road?' Arthur asked.

'Amber trading road. It passes through Gulna Mountains. Only goat herder use it now.'

James watched the old woman closely as she spoke. Her eyes wandered this way and that over the floorboards, unable to focus clearly on anything.

'These dryads,' he began carefully, 'did they ever make jewellery or talismanic pieces from the amber they harvested?'

To his surprise, Amna Leigh laughed. 'I know nothing of jewellery. We have no use for such knowledge here. We know of herbs and medicine, that is all.' She shifted in her seat, clearly tired of the conversation.

'Please,' James knelt beside Aralia on the floor, 'do you

know anything about dryad talismans that you might be able to share with us?'

Amna Leigh's features softened a little. 'Talismans were historically used to cleanse disease from dryad tree. An amber talisman possessed the power to bring tree back to life. In the same way, liquified amber could heal wounds. Dryad call this liquid Phoenix Tears. Tears of this mythical bird could heal all wound.' She dropped her head and a long breath escaped her lips.

'Thank you, Amna,' Aralia uttered. 'We have tired you out and will take our leave.'

The old woman's head snapped up. 'I sense among you two of my own,' she murmured. Her voice had changed, no longer tired and old but firm and curious. 'Will you not tell me what you are doing here before you leave.'

Her eyes travelled to the back of the room. Following her gaze, James saw that the little girl had vanished from the corner. He wondered how she had slipped away without any of them noticing.

'We are simply travellers, Amna,' Arthur said. 'We have family in Mercy.'

Leigh's eyes narrowed. She did not answer immediately. 'Few stranger enter Mercy and fewer dare enter the forest.'

She was interrupted by the appearance of her daughter. The grey-cloaked woman stopped in the archway between the two rooms and fixed her eyes upon her mother. Some silent conversation passed between them before Amna Leigh spoke again.

'My daughter gives you refreshment now. I bid you farewell.' She dropped her head to her chest as if fast asleep and said no more.

Her daughter beckoned for the companions to follow her

into the second room where she handed around a jug of water and a plate of oat biscuits. Once they had replenished themselves, the companions thanked her and she led them back through the front room to the door. Before they had time to thank her again, she had closed it behind them. One by one, they climbed down the rope ladder to the clearing. From here, they passed beneath the oak tree and walked back through the forest the way they had come. Soon the trees began to thin and sunlight seeped through the branches once more. Keen to return to Mercy, they quickened their pace and soon found themselves at the edge of the forest.

Sunlight flooded their eyes and they blinked. In this bright light, it was evident that the effects of the Pachu petals were beginning to wear off. Looking towards the village, James spotted the wild ferastia still standing by the gate. Their skin gleamed in the sunlight but they seemed unconcerned by the scorching heat. Moving his gaze just beyond them, he saw that the animals were no longer alone. Two figures stood close by, evidently deep in conversation. One was tall and the other short, and squinting at them, James realised that he knew both. The smaller figure was Amna Leigh's silver-haired granddaughter and her companion was Aldis.

'Is that…?'

His words trailed away as he noticed something else. Four black steeds had appeared in the near distance and on their backs, four cloaked riders.

'Raptuls,' Will gasped.

As soon as they were close enough to the village, the riders dismounted. Aldis and the child came forward to greet them. One of the cloaked strangers stood away from the rest and drew back its hood with a flourish. This time, the companions gasped in unison. The stranger beneath the hood was also known to them: Brother Felix.

'We've been such idiots!' Will exclaimed. 'We've been betrayed by all of them.'

'We don't have time to condemn ourselves now,' Tala said. 'They're looking this way.'

All those who stood gathered by the village gate were now looking towards the forest. The companions ducked, letting the undergrowth hide them.

'We have to leave,' James whispered.

'Leave and go where?' Aralia hissed back. 'We don't have a plan. We don't even have the ferastia. Without them, we're doomed.'

'Perhaps the ferastia aren't our only way out of here,' Arthur suggested.

Aralia turned on him. 'What do you mean?'

He smiled faintly at her. 'Draedýr.'

Kneeling in the undergrowth, he put his fingers to his lips and uttered a low whistle. It fell mute against the tree trunks and he tried again, a little louder this time. The sound rolled out and came back again in a dull echo. Straightening up, he held up a hand for silence and waited. At first, nothing happened. Then a rustling sound came from somewhere in the undergrowth.

'Stand aside,' Arthur commanded. 'Quickly!'

They cleared the area just in time. A large, sleek creature leapt from the grass and collided with the nearest tree. It uttered a sharp yelp and spun around three times before turning to face the companions. The creature looked like a dragon, small and thin with wings folded across its back. Its eyes were small and black and its head was adorned with three horns. It was not an attractive animal but its face wore a cheeky expression, with the eyes far apart and the corners of its mouth curved upwards as if it was smiling.

'Forest dragons,' Will breathed in awe. 'I've read about these little creatures.'

His admiration was short lived as the brambles parted again and two more creatures emerged. They too charged forward with steady intent and collided with the same tree as their companion. Apart from the first one being a little larger, all three animals were alike.

'Clumsy things, aren't they?' Arthur commented. 'No sense of their own speed.'

'How far can they fly?' Will reached out a hand to one of the smaller beasts. It nuzzled his palm with its flat snout, a clear invitation of friendship.

'I don't know,' Arthur replied honestly. 'To the coast perhaps. We'll be safer there than we are here at least.'

Glancing towards the village again, James saw that Aldis, Brother Felix and the riders were advancing towards the forest. There was no sign of the child.

'We don't have much time,' he warned.

The Draedýr seemed used to human interaction. They did not try to escape as the companions climbed onto their backs. James and Will took the larger Draedýr while Aralia joined Tala on one of the smaller beasts. Arthur again rode alone.

'Is everyone ready?' Arthur asked as soon as they were all settled. 'I haven't ridden a Draedýr since I was small so I don't remember how well they fly.'

'Better than they walk, I hope,' Will muttered.

Arthur clicked his tongue and the animals rose awkwardly to their feet. They waddled to the edge of the forest, flexing their wings as they went. Then suddenly they were running. Their muscular legs gave them speed and as soon as they were moving fast enough, they opened their wings. One by one, the animals launched themselves into the air. Weighed down by their riders, they beat their wings desperately, trying to gain some momentum. Finding the strength at last, they began circling steadily upwards into the cloudless blue.

Higher and higher they climbed. As the landscape fell away beneath them, the companions felt relief washing over them. With nothing but blue sky around them, their troubles melted away. Daring to look down, James saw their pursuers had reached the edge of the forest. They had not yet entered, as if they were somehow afraid to do so. Stepping away from the rest of his party, Brother Felix suddenly looked up. Confusion flickered across his face as his eyes focused on the circling Draedýr. He hesitated for just a moment before raising his hand to the sky. Streams of light burst from his fingertips. They merged in mid-air to form a single beam that sped with cruel intent towards the Draedýr and their riders.

# Chapter 14

'WE have to fly higher,' Will called. 'We're still too close to the ground!'

The Draedýr soared upwards, beating their wings to gain greater height. Far below, the ground became a blurred swathe of green and brown. Up here, the air was thinner and cooler but the sun still burned hot. To fly in such clear skies was exhilarating and despite their narrow escape, the companions couldn't help laughing as they soared into the cloudless blue. As soon as they were high enough, the Draedýr slowed their pace. The ground came into focus again but its geometry had changed. The previously flat landscape had been replaced by low slopes which, from above, looked like green waves. A dark line snaked its way between two of these slopes. It was not clear what had formed it but it appeared to be moving in the direction of the sea.

'Hey, d'you see that dark line down there?' James shouted to his friends.

'It's moving,' Tala called back. 'I think it might be people. It looks like they're heading the same way as us, towards the sea.'

Far below them, the landscape rolled on and on and the coast was nowhere in sight. The hottest part of the day had arrived and the sun beat down relentlessly from the cloudless sky.

'I thought Mercy was close to the coast,' Will shouted to Arthur who was flying just ahead.

'It is. Less than an hour by air.'

It was mid-afternoon when they first saw the sea. The water was dazzlingly blue, almost the same colour as the sky. The white topped waves sparkled in the sunlight, a thousand tiny mirrors undulating with the tide. A strip of dingy sand formed a small beach along the water's edge. It was devoid of people and the smooth sand was only disturbed by a few scraggly seabirds.

'We should land,' Arthur called. 'We're lucky the tide is low as it gives us more room for error. I'd hold on tightly.'

He issued a sharp whistle and the Draedýr responded instantly. Using just the air currents, all three beasts began to circle downwards. The air became warmer and the animals trembled with the change. They fought hard to control the rate of their descent but the air currents were too strong. It was like they were being blown about by a strong wind, only the sky was stormless. At last, exhausted by their efforts, they gave in to themselves. Folding in their wings, they allowed themselves to fall. The beach rose to meet them. Clinging on for dear life, the companions waited for the inevitable. At the last possible moment, the Draedýr opened their wings again. While this action broke their fall, they still hit the sand with force enough to send their riders flying.

James landed with his head close to a large rock. Eye to eye with its jagged side, he thanked his luck that he had missed it. Bruised and exhausted, he sat up and spat sand from his mouth. Will, Arthur, Aralia and Tala lay on the sand around him, equally bruised. The Draedýr sat between them sunning their wings, clearly unaffected by the fall.

'What a landing!' Will groaned. He sat up and looked

across the deserted beach. 'I suppose we should stay here for a while. Maybe find some shade. I'm melting.'

The only shade they could see was behind a cluster of rocks close to the water. It was patchy but provided some shelter from the burning sun. James could already feel the skin on his forehead tightening, an early warning sign. The Draedýr did not join them in the shade, preferring to cool themselves down in the shallows.

'Where are we exactly?' Tala asked as she settled herself between the rocks. 'Are we still in Rivel?'

'Rivel is a coastal region,' Arthur confirmed. 'If I remember right, this beach is called Oria Sands or *El Bas*, meaning golden sands.'

The sand was brown rather than golden, the same colour as the grass which stretched all the way along the edge of the beach. Even the houses above the dunes were brown and uninviting, built from muddy bricks and coffee-coloured tiles. Only the sea seemed welcoming, the deep blue water sparkling without cease.

'Here, take a look at this.' Will was peering intently at his map which he'd spread out on the sand between the rocks. The ink had bled in places from exposure to the elements but the general shapes of the continents were still visible. 'We're somewhere around here.' He pointed at Rivel, just above Henlos on the east coast of the northern continent. 'We could easily travel along the coast from here and back into Jantra. Once we've re-joined Dina, Kaedon and Oede, we can return to Camil.'

'What would we go back to Camil for?' James asked.

Will shrugged. 'Where else can we go? It might not be safe in Arissel but at least it's somewhere familiar. We can pick up more supplies, and then, maybe, journey south like we always planned.'

This suggestion was logical but James' mind was already set on a different journey. 'There's one other place we could go,' he said quietly.

'Where?' Even as Aralia asked this question, she realised what he was hinting at. 'No!' she exclaimed. 'It's too dangerous and you know it.'

'More dangerous than going south?' He rubbed his dry eyes but the motion only made them feel worse due to the sand still stuck to his lashes.

Tala cleared her throat. 'Would either of you mind filling the rest of us in?'

'We should go east,' James stated, 'to the Gulna Mountains.'

'The Gulna Mountains?' Will's eyes grew wide. 'Amna Leigh said the dryads don't live there now. We don't even know if their race survived.'

'I know,' James acknowledged. 'I heard her too but...' He paused to find the right words. 'Let's say the talisman really is one of Arvad's gifts. Let's also say it was made by the eastern dryads from trees growing in the ancient amber forests. The dryads might not live in the mountains anymore but they must have left some trace. Clues about their history that we could use to help us. The talisman could be anywhere in this world and going east would give us somewhere to start.'

'It's true that we have more clues connecting us to the east than the south,' Arthur remarked. 'People must remember the dryads and if not people, then books and records.'

'What if we go there and find nothing?' Aralia asked. 'Time isn't on our side.'

'That will remain the case whether we go east, south or simply back to Arissel,' James pointed out.

'It makes sense to go east,' Tala said, taking James' and Arthur's side. 'If we really are looking for an amber talisman, it seems logical to go to the place where the greatest amber trade in the world once existed.'

Will glowered at her. James wondered why his friend resisted this plan. He was normally the rash one, willing to leap into adventures without thinking first.

'It seems we're divided,' Aralia observed.

Before anyone could comment, Will uttered a low hiss. He was peering between a crack in the rocks and his knuckles were white where he was pressing them into the sand.

'Riders,' he croaked, 'on the dunes.'

Crouching behind him, James also looked between the rocks. Three ferastia had appeared above the dunes and were making their way towards the beach. Each carried a rider but from here it was impossible to see much more than their general outlines.

'Stay low,' Arthur whispered. 'The rocks should give us cover.'

'Only if they don't come too close,' Will returned but ducked anyway.

There was no time to cover their tracks and nowhere to hide the Draedýr. All they could do was keep low and hope the riders didn't come too close. It wasn't long however before they heard the dull thudding of hooves. Though the ferastia weren't hurrying, their hooves still sent tiny tremors across the sand. They were coming closer to the rocks, the vibrations strengthening by the second. Suddenly, the hooves stopped. There was a thud as one of the riders jumped down onto the sand.

Holding still, James became aware of a change in the light patterns around him. Turning his head a fraction, he saw that a shadow had fallen across his previously sun drenched foot. Slowly, he raised his eyes, hardly daring to imagine who or what he might see. A man stood above him. His hard gaze pierced the shade between the rocks and made the air feel suddenly warmer. A ray of sunlight fell across his shaggy hair beneath which an earring glittered. Looking at the man, James suddenly realised that he wasn't a stranger after all.

'Kaedon!' He jumped to his feet, hardly knowing what to think or say. 'What're you doing here?' he managed to ask.

'*Kaedon*?' Will echoed in disbelief.

'Get up.' Kaedon's eyes bored through each of them in turn. 'All of you,' he demanded.

'You've led us on quite the chase.' Dina appeared behind Kaedon, her eyes burning with equal intensity. 'What were you thinking?' she snapped and her lips pursed into dangerously thin lines.

'It's a long story,' Will tried.

Dina placed her hands on her hips. 'Well you'd better start telling it.'

'It wasn't intentional,' James began. He stepped out from between the rocks, his hands held up in a gesture of peace. 'One of the Brothers told us we'd been betrayed. He told us to leave by order of Father Eldon. He promised us you'd gone on ahead and would meet us.'

'We never left the temple,' Kaedon stated, 'not until we found out you were missing anyway. One of the Brothers told us you'd escaped.'

'Was his name Felix by any chance?' Will asked dryly.

'I have a feeling,' Dina interjected, 'that we all dealt with the same Brother.'

'He was the betrayer,' James said, 'but we ignored our suspicions because we were desperate to leave the temple.'

'If we had known you were still there, we would never have left,' Tala added.

Dina turned to her in surprise, as if she'd forgotten her presence amongst their party. 'Why didn't you come back when you realised the truth?' she asked after a pause.

'It wasn't safe.' James chose not to mentioned Aldis and the Raptuls just yet. 'We decided to travel to Mercy instead.'

'The dryad village?' Oede joined their party, having thus far remained with the ferastia. 'What were you doing there?' His eyes fixed themselves on Arthur and Aralia.

'We were seeking details about Arvad's next gift,' James answered honestly. Surprise registered on the faces before him. 'Arvad was in possession of a talisman believed to have been made in the amber forests of the east.'

Oede moved to stand between Kaedon and Dina. 'How did you come by this knowledge? The amber forests are no more. The eastern war destroyed them and the dryads too.'

'The Mercan dryads told us about the amber forests,' Arthur replied quickly, 'but we learnt about the talisman from Brother Augustus, the temple archivist. According to temple records, Arvad once visited the Minha Mound and left the talisman as a gift.'

Kaedon shook his head in disbelief. 'And you believed the words of someone you barely knew? Someone who could equally have lied to you and betrayed you like Brother Felix.'

'The actions of one Brother don't condemn them all,' Tala said sharply. 'Albert trusted Father Eldon and believed the temple was safe.'

Her words were met with silence. Already the sun was beginning to sink and clouds had gathered over the dunes, turning the grass purple. The sea reached up to touch the dying light which had turned the waves into an ever changing watercolour painting. Only the air was still, holding its breath in anticipation of twilight.

'Tell me,' Dina demanded, 'what are you doing here by the sea?'

'Can you not guess?' Tala asked bluntly.

'You wish to travel east.' Kaedon did not sound surprised. 'You wish to travel to the site of the amber forests and learn about the talisman.'

'Are our plans so predictable?' James questioned with a faint smile.

'To me, yes,' Kaedon said seriously. 'I've spent months training all of you and trying to understand your wild ambitions.'

'Is it possible?' Aralia enquired.

Kaedon turned to her. 'Is what possible?'

'You've travelled to more places than any of us, no doubt. Is it possible for us to travel east from here, over the sea?'

Kaedon didn't speak for a long time. He simply stood staring out at the horizon. The evening was warm and the air tingled as the heat of the day merged with the coolness rushing in from the sea.

'We'd need a boat,' he said at last.

'What about flying?' Aralia gestured to the Draedýr still playing in the shallows.

'On those things?' Dina asked sharply. 'They don't look strong enough to carry passengers, let alone fly.'

'They are Draedýr,' Arthur explained. 'Dryad beasts.'

Before Dina could comment on this fact, James spoke again. 'The real question is whether you are for or against this journey. Will you come with us?'

Dina, Kaedon and Oede looked at one another, a silent conversation passing between their eyes. At last, Dina spoke.

'When Albert committed us to this quest, he warned us about the impulsive natures of our charges. But he also told us they were brave and intelligent and guided by strong instincts.' She smiled faintly. 'Our role is to offer training, advice and protection but at the end of the day, this quest belongs to you. You must follow your instincts just as Albert said you would.'

'I imagine that means we are with you,' Kaedon summarised.

'How long will the journey take?' James asked. He glanced at Will but his friend was looking out to sea and his expression gave nothing away.

'In a fast boat, it would take five or six days to reach the western coast,' Kaedon calculated, 'but by air it depends on the speed of those animals. We may have to plan our route around islands so they can land and rest in between flights.'

'Once we reach the eastern continent, we will need to travel through Lleur to reach the mountains,' Oede added. 'The Gulna Mountains form a border between Lleur and Outici, though Outicans call it the Napis range. The two regions are in a peaceful war with one another.'

'How can a war be peaceful?' Tala queried.

'The regions are in a long standing disagreement with one another but they don't take up arms against each other,' Oede replied.

'We should plan our route tonight,' James said, returning the conversation to the journey at hand. 'We may be able to leave at first light.'

With evening already well advanced, he and Will began to build a fire between the rocks. Kaedon, Aralia and Arthur settled the ferastia and the Draedýr while Dina and Tala handed out supplies: bread, vegetables and fruit taken from the temple and preserved in waxy paper. Each of them ate only a little, knowing they would need food for the journey ahead.

When the meal was over, Will unrolled his map again. Following some careful calculations, Kaedon plotted a flight route over the Eeron Sea which lay between the most northerly regions of the northern and eastern continents. On paper, the route looked straightforward enough but they all knew the reality would be different. The sun set over the dunes as they worked and the air gradually cooled. Soon the sky became dark and the fire went out. With their plan mostly in place, they decided to call it a night and get some much needed rest. Kaedon offered to take first watch, leaving everyone else to drift off into uneasy sleep.

Exhausted from the day, James lay down between the rocks and slipped easily into dreamland. He dreamt he was standing by the sea, his bare feet submerged in the waves. A static charge rippled the air around him, so strong he could almost see it. He stood still, wondering at the cause. He sensed a presence behind him. From the corner of his eye, he saw a hand stretching toward him, clawing at his cloak. He stepped backwards and felt himself teetering, like he was on the edge of a precipice, even though the sand was firm under his feet. He tried to regain his balance but it was too late. He fell, hurtling headfirst into an unknown darkness.

# Chapter 15

JAMES sat up, stiff and cold, just as the dawn light was creeping into the sky. The sea was a strip of beaten silver, reflecting the pearly grey morning. His head was spinning, as if some part of him was still falling through that deep abyss. In dreaming, the darkness had seemed endless and only in waking did it vanish at last. His mouth tasted stale and gritty and grains of sand crusted his lips. They were in his hair, his eyes, his clothes. He fixed his eyes on the water, still and inviting in the already warming air.

'Do not move!' Strong hands were suddenly on his shoulders, pressing him flat to the sand between the rocks.

Turning his head to one side, James saw Oede kneeling above him. The hands holding him suddenly let go.

'We are not alone,' Oede announced. 'We cannot be seen.'

'What d'you mean?' James asked. 'Who else is here?' Pushing himself onto his elbows, he looked between a crack in the rocks. The far end of the beach was teeming with people. Cloaked strangers weaving their way around one another with apparent purpose.

'Who are they?' Will also raised his head to look.

'Fighters,' Oede replied without inflection. 'They have come to set sail.'

'Fighters from where?' Arthur nudged himself a space between Will and James. 'Where are they going?'

Oede pointed out across the water to where a ship was anchored. It was long and narrow with white sails and a tall mast. A smaller vessel was making its way between the mother ship and the shore. The fighters gathered on the waterline, stacking equipment ready for transfer.

'I think the question is who are they here for,' Dina murmured. 'They are not just fighters. They are slaves.'

James found himself unsurprised by this revelation. 'We saw them from the air,' he said aloud. 'They were walking below us for a while.'

'Why are slaves being used as fighters?' Will asked. 'Surely the Belladonna has trained warriors to fight for her.'

'Why waste warriors on smaller battles?' Kaedon responded. 'It is better for her to let her slaves and prisoners die first. Only when the real battle begins will she call upon her strongest fighters.'

'Only when there is war,' James said.

The Belladonna was using the slaves and prisoners like chess pieces, pawns that would enter first into battle. Their lives were disposable. They would break the ranks and die first; unrewarded and unremembered.

'Where are they going from here?' Aralia continued the current line of questioning. 'What battle are they being sent to fight that requires them to travel by boat?'

'There are rumours of a place in the east,' Oede replied, 'a place like Arvora. It is my belief that they are being sent there. Their battle is not for the battlefield.'

'They fight unseen forces,' James stated. 'They die trying to enter my world.' In his mind's eye, he saw the frightened face of the slave woman in Arvora who had been forced to pass between the worlds and had died trying. He could still see the lightning in her veins and could smell her flesh burning.

'If they're going east, we should follow them,' Tala suggested.

Will shook his head vehemently. 'No way are we boarding a slave ship.'

'I didn't mean we should join them! No one in their right mind would board a slave ship. I meant we should follow them. From the air, just as we planned.'

Listening to her, James realised that she must not know about their journey on the Arvorian slave ship. Albert clearly hadn't filled her in on every aspect of the last adventure and for that he was grateful.

'Following the ship could help us achieve safe passage,' Kaedon agreed. 'If we fly high enough, we can trace its route without being seen. If it's not going the same way as us, then we simply follow our original route.'

'If that is our plan, then we must wait for them to make a move,' Oede concluded.

By the time the sun appeared just above the waterline, the beach had been cleared. Slaves and equipment had been transferred to the main ship, the rowing vessel raised and the sails made ready in hardly any time at all. Now, as the sun turned the waves pink, the ship began to move. As it slid away from the shore, an invisible wind filled the sails, bearing the vessel forward over the waves. Taking this as a cue, Kaedon stood up and brushed the sand from his clothes.

'We don't have long,' he stated. 'The slave ship sails on magic and will therefore travel faster than any normal vessel.'

It didn't take them long to gather up their bags and smooth over the disturbed sand. Arthur called to the Draedýr and they rose from their resting place behind the rocks. The ferastia Dina, Kaedon and Oede had arrived on had disappeared during the night, guided by their wild instincts. The Draedýr, though only half tame, had stayed. They knelt when Arthur bid them to do so and held still as the companions mounted. Pulling several coils of rope from his bag, Kaedon passed one to each set of riders.

'Tie yourselves to your beast and to each other,' he instructed. 'We don't want anyone falling into the sea.'

He knotted a section of rope around Dina's waist before tying the end to his belt. James, Tala and Will also bound themselves together and Arthur, Aralia and Oede took up the final coil. The Draedýr did not seem to mind the makeshift reigns looped about their necks and stood patiently awaiting their next instruction.

'We're ready for take-off,' Kaedon said as soon as everyone was secure. 'Arthur, the task is yours.'

James felt suddenly nervous. He had always known that the journey would be dangerous, whichever route they chose. To fly however was to be exposed to the elements and to the Shadows. Tension hung over the beach, a cloud in an otherwise clear sky. As if sensing this change in atmosphere, the Draedýr began to move. They waddled along the beach, picking up speed as they went. Their legs moved faster and faster until they built up enough momentum to launch themselves into the air. Wings beating steadily, they began circling upwards, away from the quiet surf and the deserted shore.

The air was still, waiting for the full glory of the morning. Alone on the dunes, the little houses slept, their chimneys smokeless at this early hour. Out on the water, two small boats rode the waves. Gulls flocked around each vessel, suggesting they belonged to anglers. Further out to sea, climbing the higher waves, was the slave ship. The white sails turned pink as the sun rose above the water. The waves and the sky also blushed and James was reminded of the old sailors warning about red skies at dawn.

'It will be a long flight,' Kaedon cautioned as the Draedýr began to level themselves.

'There may be a storm.'

'Shouldn't we wait until it has passed before we fly?' Aralia asked.

Kaedon shook his head. 'It may not come at all and if it does, we will just have to ride it out. We don't have the hours to waste.'

As the sun rose, the silver sheen vanished from the horizon. The sea glimmered invitingly, the white tipped waves catching the now golden sunlight. From above, it looked like someone had spilt a tube of glitter on a crumpled blue table cloth. This cloth stretched on in never-ending folds, filling the vast space between the shoreline and the horizon. It was not long however before the beach and the dunes were lost from sight. Further out at sea, the waves no longer lay still. Only the slave ship dared tackle them, intent on its voyage to an unknown harbour. For the companions, the excitement of first take-off soon wore off. Time passed by and the minutes turned steadily into hours. James' eyes began to ache from staring too long at the dazzling water and he rubbed the bruised colours in his vision.

'There's nothing but sea for miles!' Tala's voice broke the stillness of the air.

'We won't see land for several hours,' Kaedon answered. 'At sea, one must look up to navigate, not down. The waves are untrustworthy but the sky is a constant. For now, we simply fly towards the sun while it still lies in the east.'

'We won't have long with the sun,' Dina warned. 'The

storm is already brewing.'

A thick bank of cloud had gathered on the horizon. It lay below the arc of the sun, hanging alone in the otherwise bright sky.

'It will be with us by afternoon,' Kaedon predicted. 'If we're lucky, it might pass us by but sea storms aren't usually that kind. We may just have to ride it out and fly above the clouds if we can.'

In the distance, the dark cloud split in two, framing the sun to an unsettling effect. James looked down at the still bright waves. Right now they lay calm but a storm would change that.

'We've survived a sea storm before, in Eir's boat from Arvora to Muir, remember?' Will said.

Dina, Kaedon and Oede had not been present then, nor had Tala. James remembered the heaving waves beneath Eir's boat and the wood splintering as the Shadow had attacked it.

'We barely survived that,' he replied with a shudder. 'If we hadn't reached land when we did we would have drowned.'

Will fell silent. On the horizon, the clouds continued to multiply, despite the sun's best efforts to hold them back. Still the storm did not strike. It lingered on the horizon, dark and brooding.

'Perhaps it will miss us after all,' Dina said.

Her hopes were swiftly dashed. Soon the sun disappeared altogether, imprisoned by the clouds. A light wind picked up, courting the waves in an energetic dance.

'We should fly higher before it's too late,' Arthur called. He shouted to the Draedýr and they responded by circling higher.

The rain struck with sudden and violent force. A deluge of water burst from the sky, soaking them all instantly. The droplets were freezing and the relief offered from the heat of the last few hours was only temporary. A strong wind whipped up out of nowhere and turned their skin to ice. The Draedýr became so slippery that it was difficult not to slide off their backs, even with the ropes holding them all in place. The air whirled with rain and the horizon vanished behind a thick grey curtain. It was as if evening had come early, though it was only just past midday. The heavy rainfall was brief but as soon as it lessened, the thunder came. It cracked across the sky like a giant whip and the air shook with its force.

'We're losing height, not gaining it,' Kaedon shouted.

'The wind is too strong,' Arthur called back. 'The Draedýr are struggling.'

A bolt of white light branched across the clouds. Startled by the brightness, the Draedýr dropped closer to the heaving swell. Daring to look down again, James suddenly caught sight of a light glinting on the waves.

'Did anyone else see that?' he shouted above the noise of the storm. 'There's a light on the water. I think it might belong to a ship.'

No one answered him. He kept his eyes fixed on the waves where the light was now flashing on and off in regular motion. He wondered if it might be a signal; the last hope of a distressed ship.

'What if it's a signal?' he shouted. 'There might be a boat in trouble.'

'There's nothing we can do,' Kaedon's voice drifted back to him. 'We can't fly low enough to help. Those who go to sea know the dangers.'

'There will be people on board,' James insisted. 'They'll never survive against those waves.'

Thunder crashed in his ears, drowning out any response.

'The waves are unnaturally high,' he heard Oede shout at last. 'I've never seen anything like this.'

The lightning ceased and the sky became pitch dark. It felt like they were passing through the heart of a hurricane, spinning through a deadly void.

'Something isn't right.' Kaedon's voice sounded again. 'This is no ordinary storm. The darkness is artificial, a cover for something else.'

Even as these words left his lips, James became aware of a rushing sound. It came from somewhere above but it was too dark to see anything. He did not need the power of sight however to identify the sound as the rushing of wings. He held his breath, waiting for something to happen. Lightning filled the sky again and in that momentary brightness, he saw a dark shape plunging towards the sea. It struck the water, sending up a great wave all around it. The distress signal began to blink again. James watched in horror as a second shape dived towards it and the light was again snuffed out.

As another roll of thunder faded in the sky, James realised he could no longer hear the rushing of wings. He was sure the sky had begun to lighten as he could now see the faint outline of the swollen clouds. Though the storm was still raging, the artificial night was gradually lifting.

'They're not here for us,' Dina said in a cracked voice. 'They're here to escort the slave ship. Anything that gets in their way will be destroyed. Small boats, for example, lost in a storm.'

'We should see if there are any survivors,' Oede joined but made no further comment.

The Draedýr dropped again towards the sea. Cold air rushed upwards and the waves rose to meet them. James felt the air sucked from his lungs and the skin on his face flapped as if it was made from cloth.

'I can't see anything on the water,' Arthur called as they continued to fall. 'No light, no bodies, no torn up boat. I...'

'Wait!' Tala cut across him. 'I see something. I see the light.'

There it was, the same light glimmering between the waves. It was faint but lasting and seemed to float alone on the wild water. As the Draedýr swooped lower however, it began to blink again, on and off over and over and over.

'There's someone in the water!' Tala exclaimed. 'They're holding the light.'

Behind the blinking beam, someone was struggling against the waves. Holding onto his Draedýr with one hand, James reached out towards the victim. His fingers brushed the water but he wasn't quite close enough to grab hold of them.

'Take my hand,' he called. 'We're here to help you.'

The waves parted and he found himself staring into the frightened face of a little girl. Her eyes glinted in the light she so desperately held, making her look almost demonic. Before he could speak to her again, a wave broke over her head. She re-emerged moments later gasping for air.

'Take my hand,' James tried again. 'Please.'

She watched him closely but did not respond. It was then that he saw why. Her right hand was clamped around something in the water, a bulky shape that was keeping her afloat. It was too large to be a plank but was light enough to remain buoyant. As he leaned forward to take a closer look, he realised with sudden horror that it was a body.

# Chapter 16

JAMES stared at the body with revulsion. It was lying face down in the water, rising and falling with the motion of the waves. Fighting against his feeling of nausea, he reached out to the little girl again. She continued to stare at him and did not try to take his hand. Every inch of her had gone into survival mode as she fought to keep her head and the lamp above the waves.

'She'll freeze to death if we don't pull her out quickly,' Kaedon shouted.

'She won't let go,' James called back. 'She's holding onto a body.'

The Draedýr carrying Kaedon and Dina swept past him and he felt the rush of its wings.

'Grab her hand,' Kaedon commanded. 'Just take it. We'll hold the body. As soon as she lets go of it, pull her up between you. We move, now.'

Time seemed to stand still. Then everything began to move in slow motion. Held fast by Dina, Kaedon leaned down to secure the body. Following this cue, James grabbed hold of the little girl's hand. Surprised by his touch, she let go of the body but as soon as she realised what she had done, she began to scream. James tried to pull her from the water but she sank her teeth into his hand. He did not let go. She began to thrash about in the water and the lantern fell from her grasp.

'Can one of you help me?' James called over his shoulder to Will and Tala.

Tala shifted forward so that she was as close to him and the child as possible. Leaning down, she took the child's other hand firmly in her own and tugged. Unable to fight anymore, the girl went limp. James and Tala hauled her onto the Draedýr's back where she crumpled between them. As soon as the child was secure, James turned to observe Dina and Kaedon's efforts. They were struggling to pull the body from the waves. Even with help from Oede, Arthur and Aralia, the sodden corpse was too awkward to lift onto the Draedýr's back.

'It's too heavy,' Dina declared. 'We'll have to let him go.'

'Him?' Tala asked.

'Yes. The child's father perhaps.'

'Is he definitely dead?' Will enquired.

Dina nodded. 'He is dead.'

She let go of the dead man's arm and Kaedon followed suit. The body fell into the waves and was lost amidst the heaving swell. The little girl watched with wide eyes. Her face was wet but her tears were lost in the rain.

'We should fly on,' Oede urged. 'The wind is picking up again. The storm has shortened the daylight hours and it will soon be night.'

Will pulled out his map but a gust of wind snatched it from his fingers. He tried to catch it but it vanished into the vast atmosphere.

'We've already been blown off course,' Kaedon said dully, 'and we've lost sight of the slave ship. The longer we keep flying, the further off course we could be heading. Keep your eyes peeled for somewhere to land.'

James looked down at the surging water stretching on for miles in all directions. There were no boats and no islands in sight and his heart sank. There was nothing out here but the sky and the waves. The real world felt far away and this journey like some bad dream.

'The Draedýr are tired from flying through the storm,' Arthur warned. 'They won't be able to go on much longer.'

At his command, the beasts began to circle upwards again. Their wings worked slowly; the muscles weak from fighting against the storm. They hung just below the clouds, unable to muster enough strength to fly higher. The hours rolled into one as they travelled onwards. The sky brightened temporarily before growing dark again as evening descended. Between the shifting clouds, glimpses of a clear twilight sky brought some sense of hope. Still, the sea surged like an inky beast below and there was no sign of land.

'We're flying north-east,' Kaedon suddenly called. He pointed through a gap in the cloud to where a few bright stars pricked the atmosphere. 'We haven't drifted as far off as I feared but we should change our direction.'

'Our direction isn't our greatest worry at the moment,' Arthur said. 'The Dreadýr are losing height again.'

'Then our search for land continues until we can look no more,' Kaedon replied shortly.

Even so, the Dreadýr changed direction, angling themselves towards the east. The clouds had covered the stars again but Kaedon seemed satisfied with this change of course. Though the storm had ceased, the air was cold and the companions shivered in their wet clothes. James and Tala tried to keep the little girl warm between them but she was shivering violently. Whether from shock, the cold, or both it was difficult to tell. As the Dreadýr sank towards the sea again, the surging waves sent showers of water over them.

'We're running out of time,' Will called. 'We'll be in the water soon.'

No one answered him. Still the Dreadýr sank lower until their claws brushed against the water. Though the waves had calmed a little in the aftermath of the storm, they were still powerful enough to overturn a small boat.

'Can the Dreadýr swim?' Dina's voice betrayed her fear. 'If they can't, then we'll have to.'

'Where would we swim to?' Kaedon placed a hand on her shoulder. 'We're out in the middle of the Eeron Sea. There is nowhere for us to go.'

'Not nowhere.' Tala spoke so quietly that only James heard her.

'What did you say?' he asked.

'Just look,' she urged. 'Look ahead of you.'

Where the waves rose and fell, a dark mass had appeared on the water. It was not the smooth side of a ship or sea creature but a cluster of jagged rocks. As they flew closer, it became evident that the rocks formed a tiny island. It rested alone in the middle of the ocean, no more than fifteen metres in diameter. The Draedýr needed no encouragement to land on the island. They collapsed on the rocks with their wings outstretched, too exhausted to fold them in. Using the last of their own strength, the companions dismounted onto the island.

There was no shelter here from the biting sea wind. Pulling a damp blanket from his bag, Kaedon hung it between two rocks. He tied it down with ropes to create a makeshift tent. Taking the rescued child from Tala's arms, he set her down beneath it. With no kindling to light a fire, Oede created a false flame. It burned brightly between the rocks but offered little heat. The companions huddled around it in their wet clothes, trying to find some warmth.

'We have to eat,' Dina said. She began pulling rations from her bag; fruit and oat biscuits which were soggy from the rain. 'Pass the food around,' she instructed, 'but spare a little for the Draedýr.'

The little girl took the food handed to her by Aralia without question. She ate a small piece of oat biscuit before squashing the rest between her fingers and dropping it into her lap. Still soaked to the bone, she shivered where she sat but would not allow Aralia to wrap an arm around her. Her eyes began to droop and she slipped into an uneasy slumber. Around her, the companions fought their own fatigue but it won in the end. They slept, dreaming of storms and crashing waves.

James woke up to the sound of screaming. Sitting bolt upright, he looked for the little girl. She had left the shelter and was sitting beside the fire, screaming from the top of her lungs. In an instant, Aralia was by her side, holding her.

'What's wrong with her?' Will sat up too and put his hands over his ears.

'She's cold,' Aralia said desperately. 'She'll die from hypothermia if we don't get her warm.'

James unzipped his bag and pulled a blanket from it. It was still damp but it was better than nothing. He tossed it to Aralia who wrapped it around the child's shoulders.

'We should huddle around her,' he suggested. 'Our heat will keep her warm.'

He put an arm around Aralia and another around the child. Will, Tala, Dina, Arthur, Oede and Kaedon packed in around them. The little girl stopped screaming and went limp in Aralia's arms. Her breath became shallow and her eyes flickered open and shut.

'Our heat is not enough,' Aralia whispered.

As if sensing the urgency of the situation, one of the young Draedýr roused itself and stumbled over to join the huddle. Nosing its way to the middle of the group, it sat down beside the child. Holding its body against her, it opened its wings to form a wind break around her.

'Wise creature,' Oede murmured. 'Its body is warmer than all of ours combined.'

'Even with its warmth, we'll be lucky if she survives,' Dina said darkly.

Aralia poured a drop of water between the child's lips but she would not swallow. The droplet leaked out from the corner of her mouth and landed on the rocks. There was nothing anyone could do but sit and wait while the girl continued to sleep like a child princess laid out to rest. Somehow, the hours passed. The wind lulled and the night darkened. There was nothing out here but the continuous sound of the waves slapping against the rocks. Though the tide rose, it did not cover the island completely and the companions huddled in the centre, waiting for dawn.

It came at last and they watched through salt crusted eyes as the sun rose. The waves became less menacing, splashing playfully around the rocks. No one had slept again save for the child who lay as she had done all night. Beside her, the Draedýr also slept, its wings folded protectively around her. The other animals had not moved from their original places.

'We won't be able to fly with the child in this condition.' Oede glanced over his shoulder at the girl from where he stood at the edge of the rocks.

Kaedon rubbed his stubbled chin thoughtfully. 'We can't stay on this island either. Our supplies will run out.'

'We have enough for two days at most,' Dina informed him. 'We don't know how far it is to the western coast. The sooner we leave, the better our chances.'

With supplies under ration, none of them ate that morning. The time passed unbearably slowly with nothing to do but stare at the sea. The sun grew hotter and with little protection from its fierce rays, they baked and burnt on the rocks. When the heat became unbearable, they splashed their faces with cool seawater but the salt formed crumbling masks over their faces. The current was too strong to take a swim, as observed by the waves tugging at the rocks.

Staring up at the sky, James thought about the clock in his pocket. Even though it had been soaked in the storm, the hands ticked on steadily against his chest. He wished it could take them all away from this place but knew this wasn't a reality. He was the only one able to use it as far as he was aware but now it wasn't even responding to him. Sighing, he fixed his eyes on a wayward cloud shaped like a bird with its wings outstretched. It was beautiful yet lonely floating across the endless sky.

'We're no longer at risk from hypothermia at least,' Will said with false cheerfulness. He sat down next to James and wiped the sweat from his reddening brow.

'Just heat stroke instead,' Tala groaned. 'I don't know which is worse. To freeze from cold or suffocate from heat.'

'I'd rather freeze,' Dina said thoughtfully. 'It seems less traumatic.'

'How about neither?' Aralia suggested.

'What would you rather?' her brother asked with a faint smile.

'A natural death or at least a bolt of light to end things quickly.'

These weak attempts at light hearted conversation somehow kept them going. Stuck in such close proximity to one another, there was little room to breathe or think. Nor was there much privacy, with only a small cluster of rocks to hide behind when nature had a calling. All through the long day the child did not wake. As the sun began to sink, all hope of leaving the island before nightfall vanished.

'We should try to sleep,' Oede suggested at last. 'How can we survive another day if we do not rest? We can take it in turns to watch the child.'

Aralia offered to stay awake first. Everyone else lay down on the warm rocks and closed their eyes. James lay awake for a long time, aware of his tingling sunburn. At some point he must have fallen asleep however for he was woken up by the sound of someone shouting. He sat up, forgetting for a moment where he was. The sun had only recently set over the sea and the waves were stained red. Twilight had begun to descend and the sky was filled with a dusky light. It felt like he'd been asleep much longer but hardly any time had passed. He turned towards the voice. Aralia was sitting on the highest rock on the island and a stream of light rose from her outstretched palm into the evening sky.

'Hey, what're you doing?' He jumped to his feet and hurried towards her.

She didn't answer. He was about to speak again when he saw something moving on the water. It was a boat, not a large one like the slave ship but a fishing vessel. A shadowy figure sat in the bow while another frantically worked the oars. The boat tacked towards the island. As it drew nearer, the first figure stood up and shouted something to Aralia. It was a man, dressed in rain gear and thick sea boots.

'What's he saying?' James joined Aralia on her rock. 'Can

you understand him?'

'They can't row right up to the island. It's too dangerous.' Kaedon stood up stiffly and waved to the men in the boat. 'If we want them to help us, we'll have to swim out to them.'

Dina, Will, Tala and Arthur had also woken up. Only the child slept on. The companions gathered up their things and took them over to the other side of the island. Oede carried the girl in his arms but she did not stir.

'We go one by one,' Kaedon instructed. 'Will, you first. Tie this rope around your waist. I'll hold the other end.'

Will knotted the rope around himself and stepped down into the water. The half-submerged rocks gave way almost immediately and he was forced to swim. He reached the fishing boat in a few short strokes and the men hauled him aboard. Aralia and Tala went next, followed by Dina and James. Kaedon and Oede came last, supporting the child between them. On reaching the boat, the fishermen lifted the girl gently aboard while Oede and Kaedon dragged themselves over the side.

The vessel was only just large enough to hold all of them, even with the crates of fish pushed aside. The companions sat on the benches that stretched from one side of the hull to the other, shivering despite the warm air. The fisherman who had first shouted to them pulled a flask from his belt and handed it to Dina with a smile. Trusting him completely, she took a sip before passing it round. The liquid inside tasted alcoholic but proved pleasantly warming.

'Arba.' The man at the oars spoke for the first time. He was taller than his companion and somewhat more imposing. He sported a scraggly beard, the result of many days at sea, and his dark eyes took everything in without blinking. 'Threntsa,' he continued. 'Arba thrensta.'

'Arba,' Oede said calmly.

'Cha reo mana. Perech?' The fisherman smiled, revealing missing front teeth. 'Cha reo.'

Oede processed his words slowly before answering. 'Lleur. Jai sa?' The fisherman nodded and held up a finger. 'They say just a day more to reach the coast of Lleur,' Oede translated. 'They are going that way anyway and can drop us off.'

'Ka noda,' the first fisherman added. 'Hasa?'

'No birds.' Oede looked back at the Draedýr still resting on the rocks. 'We'll have to leave them behind.'

'They'll be lighter without us anyway,' Arthur stated. 'When they are ready, they will find their way home.'

As if knowing a decision had been made, all three animals looked up. Arthur bowed his head to them and they mirrored this gesture of thanks. They did not try to follow the fishing vessel as it drifted away from the shore into the deepening twilight.

# Chapter 17

THE night was long and passed like a delirious dream. Waking in the early hours, James was surprised to see land already in sight. A dark band lay across the horizon, not yet touched by the dawn. This sighting should have brought him hope but he had no energy left to celebrate. He watched through bleary eyes as the distance between the vessel and the shore grew gradually smaller. The land began to take on more substance. A grey coastline faced the water, flat and unimposing. There were no coves or cliffs, just rocks descending gradually into the sea. Straight ahead of the boat and beyond the rocks lay a beach. The sand here was not golden but pure black.

'The famed black beaches of Lleur,' Oede announced.

Beyond the beach were more rocks and a dense wilderness of trees and undergrowth. There was no sign of habitation anywhere; no boats tied to the rocks or footprints on the sand. Everything lay still, disturbed only by the occasional splash of a wave against the shore. The fishermen guided their boat alongside the rocks. The taller man, Kashvi, set down his oars while his companion, Kai, dropped anchor.

Both men had travelled from an island off the coast of Merai, a region at the tip of the northern continent, and were heading south to Uban which rested on the west coast of the eastern continent. This was their homeland, they had told

Oede, but whether they spoke the truth or not was hard to tell. Neither had revealed what they were doing travelling such a great distance in a small fishing vessel. The pair were friendly enough however and the companions were grateful for the safe passage across the Eeron Sea.

With their boat safely anchored, Kai and Kashvi climbed out onto the rocks and began helping their passengers ashore. The companions thanked them profusely and Oede translated these sentiments into the fishermen's own tongue. With thanks exchanged, the men returned to their boat and raised the anchor. The companions watched as the vessel drifted away from the shore, carried by the rolling swell. Turning away from the sea, they then began clambering over the rocks to the beach. Kaedon carried the child who only now began to stir. As he laid her gently on the sand, she opened her eyes and looked up at him in bewilderment.

'It's alright,' he reassured her. 'You're alright.'

She pushed his arm away from her and sat up. Her cheeks were faintly flushed and her eyes sparkled with the remnant of her fever. She jumped to her feet but her illness had weakened her and she fell onto the sand again. Unwilling to give up, she tried again and this time steadied herself. No one tried to stop her as she walked down the beach and over the rocks to the water's edge.

'What d'we do with her?' Will asked as the girl settled herself on a large rock. 'We can't take her with us.'

'I think there are more pressing issues,' Dina said sharply, 'like whether we have enough food to last us another day and which way we should head next.'

'We should pay our respects to the dead before we plan the next journey,' Oede advised. 'The child needs a farewell.'

Dina nodded. 'You're right, I'm sorry. We will first allow

her a goodbye.'

Oede made his way down the beach towards the child. She watched him warily but did not try to run away. Oede tore a strip of cloth from his cloak and tied it into a knot before handing it to her. She took it in both hands, evidently understanding its significance. She dropped the knotted cloth into the sea and it sank beneath the waves.

James turned to Dina. 'What are they doing? What's the cloth for?'

'In many parts of the world, a knotted cloth symbolises grief and farewells. It represents the ties between the spirit realm and the real world and the letting go of the physical form that houses the spirit during its time on this earth.'

'In some cultures, a talisman woven from reeds is used,' Tala added. 'I've seen this done once before.' She did not elaborate.

Down on the rocks, Oede took the child's hand and led her away from the shore. The waves chased after them; horses with billowing white manes. Soaked to her knees, the child sat down in the sand and took off her shoes. Kneeling beside her, Oede began to build a fire from scraps of dried seaweed. Though he used magic to set them alight, the flames were real and warm. Squatting next to him, Dina handed him the bunch of fish Kai and Kashvi had given them as a parting gift. They were still fresh, their silvery skins plump and gleaming. Taking a knife from his belt, Oede deftly gutted and filleted them before skewering them on seaweed stalks and holding them above the flames. The flesh began to roast, sizzling with natural oils and turning golden.

When the meal was ready, he divided the cooked flesh between them all. It tasted like salt and the sea and to their starving stomachs was like a banquet. The little girl ate a little, picking at small flakes. Her eyes never left the circle of strangers sitting around her. Her expression was always the same, watchful and serious, giving nothing away. The companions looked back at her. There was nothing to the child. Her bones stuck through her skin making her look malnourished and her face was thin and gaunt.

'What is your name?' Dina asked the child as soon as she had finished eating.

The girl stared at her and said nothing.

'We are just trying to help you,' Aralia added gently. She tried to adjust the cloak which had slipped from the girl's shoulders but the child pushed her away.

'Here, let me try something,' Will said. He printed his name in the sand and pointed to himself. 'My name is Will.'

Some kind of recognition registered in the girl's eyes. Her lips parted and a sound came out. 'Dara.'

'Dara?' Aralia repeated. 'Is that your name?'

The girl nodded. 'Dara.' She wrote the word out in the sand, the letters large and uneven.

Aralia smiled and pointed to herself. 'My name is Aralia.' She went around the circle, naming each of them in turn. Dara nodded in acknowledgement and her expression lightened a little.

With introductions complete, everyone sat back to consider their surroundings. The beach was short and the only route away from it was through the tangled undergrowth.

'The black beaches of Lleur.' James repeated Oede's earlier announcement. 'How far do you think we are from the mountains?'

Kaedon pulled a crumpled map from his pocket and spread it out on the sand. The ink was faint and the cartographer far less skilled than the one who had penned Will's map. There was little detail and the lines between regions were inaccurately drawn.

'It may take weeks to reach the mountains, depending on which part of the coast we're on,' Oede said. 'Regardless of our precise location, we'll have to pass along the border of the nameless region. It is safest that way.'

'Nameless?' James asked.

'The territory was disputed for years between Elika and Lleur. Eventually they split it between them and left it unnamed. Centuries ago it was called Metria but not anymore. It is deemed an offence to call it that. It's safest for us to cross into the nameless region and then into Outici rather than travelling the length of Lleur.'

'We have our route, then,' Kaedon concluded. 'To leave this beach, we must first head east but as soon as we can, we will turn south.'

'We should get going.' Dina stood up and stamped out the remains of the fire. 'The day is still young and the weather is in our favour.'

Gathering their belongings, the companions then began walking up the beach, erasing their footprints as they went. The rocks between the sand and the undergrowth were low and smooth, making them easy to clamber across. Dara took the lead, no longer ill and frail. Her steps were light and she jumped from rock to rock without a care. Everyone else hurried to keep up, trying not to fall between the cracks. Before long, the terrain began to change as the undergrowth took over. They were forced to forge a path between bowed branches and knotted stems, unable to see where they were going. The sea and the beach disappeared behind them, hidden from view by the dense vegetation. The air felt different here, humid and close.

'Watch out for snakes,' Oede cautioned as they ploughed onwards. 'There are many species in this part of the world.'

'Bat serpents too,' Will added with a grin.

James made a face as his friend turned to look at him. 'What're they?'

Will's grin widened. 'Winged snakes with vicious teeth that suck your blood.' He pinched Tala on the back of her arm. Rather than squeal as he'd evidently hoped, she spun around and slapped his hand away.

'Maybe it's best that we don't know about all the bloodsucking creatures out here,' Dina said disapprovingly but the corners of her lips twitched.

James ducked beneath a wiry branch to hide his smile. An unseen thorn pricked his thumb and blood pearled on the tip. He raised the wound to his lips but Oede grabbed his wrist to prevent him.

'It's not just snakes that are poisonous,' he warned.

The undergrowth stretched on for miles. The humidity was almost worse than the scorching heat they'd previously endured. Here the air stuck to their clothes and their skin. The salt on their faces melted and trickled into their eyes, making them burn. It was hard not to think about water and as the morning wore on they became more and more irritable. Though the sun was trapped behind hazy clouds, it warmed the atmosphere to an unbearable degree. Moisture gleamed on the leaves of the surrounding plants as they too suffered. By midday – an estimated time based on the position of the sun – it felt like they'd made little progress. It was impossible to tell how many miles they'd travelled without knowing exactly where they had come from in the first place.

Tensions were rising high when Kaedon suddenly called

for them all to stop. He held up his hand for silence and pointed through the trees to where the outline of a building had appeared. It stood alone amidst the dense undergrowth, its ramshackle roof choked with leaves. Reserving comment for the moment, the companions crept towards it. The undergrowth suddenly parted and they found themselves standing at the edge of a clearing. The leaf encrusted building stood to their right but it was not the only one. Clay walled huts encircled the clearing, all facing inwards. All bore signs of fire damage, smoke stains marking the baked walls. Several of the roofs had also been damaged, sagging where the same fire had burned irreparable holes.

'I wonder what happened here,' Dina said in a low voice. 'It looks abandoned.'

At the centre of the clearing was a stone well. James peered inside. The bucket was still attached to its chain and thirsty after the long walk, he lowered it down. There was a dull splash as it hit the bottom, followed by a clunk. The handle creaked as he reeled it up again, relieved to feel the weight of the bucket had changed.

'Anyone thirsty?' he asked with false cheeriness.

The bucket reached the top and he peered inside. Rather than carrying water however, it was filled with reddish muck. Half buried in this sludge was a dead fish, its skeleton smashed into tiny fragments. Disappointed, James let go of the bucket and it plunged back to the bottom of the well where it landed with a thud.

'The fire marks aren't particularly old,' Kaedon remarked, running his fingers along the blackened wall of one hut. 'The village can't have been abandoned long, although the dry well might suggest otherwise.'

James opened the door of the smallest hut. A cloud of ash

swirled around him, carrying the stench of smoke. The room before him had been destroyed by the fire. There was nothing left apart from a fireplace piled with the remains of another fire and footprints marked permanently onto the earthy floor. It was then that he saw a body, lying face down by the back wall. The corpse was so badly burnt that there was almost nothing left of it. He stepped closer, hardly daring to breathe. Beneath the papery skin gleamed parts of a skull. The smell was sickening and staggering backwards, he was sick against the wall. Behind him, the door creaked and he spun around. It was Kaedon.

'Come out of here,' he encouraged, 'it's not safe.'

'There's a body,' James gasped, 'or what's left of it anyway.'

'It's not the only one,' Kaedon grimly replied. 'Come on, let's get out of here.'

Stumbling over the debris, James went back out into the hazy sunlight. The air in the clearing tasted fresh compared to the stench inside the hut. He saw Will, Tala, Arthur and Aralia coming out of another hut, all looking as grey as he felt. Oede and Dina stood by the well with Dara between them.

'There has been a massacre here,' Oede said quietly. His face looked pained; an expression James had never seen on him.

'It's no ordinary massacre,' Kaedon added, 'nor an ordinary fire. The huts have been burned from the inside out.'

'Dark magic,' Dina murmured.

'It was *her*,' James accused, 'the Belladonna.'

'She's not the only one possessed by darkness,' Oede reminded. 'There are others: looters, madmen, coldblooded murderers who also know dark magic.'

James looked at the huts, so ordinary on the outside but tainted by darkness within. The clearing began to spin around him. The sky, the huts and his friends became a blur. When everything settled again, the scene before him had changed. Though he still stood in the clearing, it was now night time and he was surrounded by people who were not his friends. As he watched, these cloaked strangers raised their hands and cast streams of light into the sky. Rather than strike the huts however, the beams fizzled out in mid-air and sparks rained down on the matted roofs. The smell of smoke reached his nostrils. Acrid fumes began pouring from cracks in the roofs and walls. The huts were burning from within and those trapped inside began to scream.

# Chapter 18

'JAMES, what's wrong?'

The vision vanished and James opened his eyes. He was leaning against the well, shaking from head to foot. Though he could no longer see or smell the smoke, he could still hear screaming and beyond this, the sound of someone laughing. It was her, he knew it was, though he couldn't tell if her voice was real or imagined.

'*She* wanted this,' he said. 'She might not have commanded this particular massacre but it happened because of her.'

Before he could say any more, there was a rustling sound in the bushes. Everyone froze, half expecting some wild animal to leap forth into the clearing. Instead, when the leaves parted, a child appeared. Whether a boy or a girl, it was hard to say, for they were dressed in a loose smock and their face was hidden behind a mop of sandy hair.

'Just a child,' Dina said with relief.

Will rolled his eyes. 'Another one!'

On seeing them, the child stopped short. Behind the hair, a pair of dark eyes glittered, giving the child a lizard-like appearance.

'What are you doing here?' Dina demanded. 'Are you alone?'

The child stared at them a moment longer before turning away and vanishing between the bushes once more.

'Hey, wait!' Dina called but her only reply came from the swishing leaves.

'We should follow them,' Tala suggested. 'Come on.'

Pushing their way between the bushes in the child's wake, they soon broke out onto the edge of a marshland. Long grass stretched on for miles in front of them, veiled by a light marsh mist. In the near distance, a cluster of stilted houses stood out on the landscape. It was towards these that the child was running, bobbing up and down between the grasses like a field hare. The companions hurried to follow. The ground was spongy but did not give way beneath them. They were not alone on this strange, flat landscape. There were people scattered across the marshes, hard at work. Some looked up unsmilingly as the companions passed by but others took no notice at all.

'They must be Cutters,' Oede remarked. 'I would imagine they cut the grass for trade.'

'What for?' Tala wrinkled her nose against the acrid smell emitted by the grass each time it was touched. 'It smells awful.'

'The smell is to ward off predators.' Oede ran his fingers along a tall blade and a cloud of yellow dust rose from it. 'It's called seismonastic movement.'

'Is the dust poisonous?' James asked.

'To animals but not to humans.' Oede cleaned his fingers on his robe. 'At least, I think that is the case but I don't know for sure.'

Even the air felt poisoned here. Not by scent or sound but by something out of reach. A presence lingering at the edges of the landscape; a shadow James could not shake off.

The first house they came to stood slightly apart from the others. It was small and squat, a single storey building with a thin balcony running around the perimeter. The androgynous child had disappeared but an old man was just emerging from the front door. He held a pipe between his lips and as he limped across the balcony, it began to smoke. Leaning on the railing, he blew out a stream of smoke before noticing that he wasn't alone. Shrinking back from the edge of the balcony, he shouted something over his shoulder into the house. Two younger men appeared in the doorway, both nursing daggers at their belts.

'They are distrustful of magic,' Oede warned as the companions came to a standstill beneath the balcony. 'We should be careful.'

He hailed the three men standing above them. They looked surprised to hear him speaking their language but did not turn away. One of the younger men said something back and Oede frowned, trying to process his words.

'They ask who we are,' he translated slowly. 'They want to know why we are here.'

The second young man also said something, his tone harsh and guttural.

'We are not the first to come by here today,' Oede continued. 'There were others, many. At night.'

'Others?' Will asked.

Oede's face changed as he listened to the men speaking. 'The locals here call them Throl or Night Creepers. For one month, they pass through every seventh night.'

Something about these words stirred a memory in James' mind. In Eriphas, one of the seven trading villages in Henlos, the Arvorian slave ships had been rumoured to pass through every seven nights.

'Slaves,' he said aloud.

Oede nodded. 'They say the last group came by just hours

ago.'

'Perhaps they were responsible for the village massacre,' Arthur suggested. 'Perhaps they came from the ship we tried to follow.'

Oede nodded again. 'It's possible. The men here say that the last group were led by a man named Or. They have seen him here before. This name means one who bears a scar on his face.'

A chill ran down James' spine. There was only one man he knew with a scar on his face. One who led the slaves from town to town in service of the Belladonna. All at once, he understood why the air felt contaminated here. The Belladonna's willing servant had been here just hours ago and his evil presence still lingered.

'Kedran,' Aralia whispered.

James looked at Oede, waiting for any further information. If Kedran had passed through this way it meant that the Belladonna's poison had spread quicker than anticipated. He knew her influence was growing, gathering between the cracks and crevices, but hadn't realised quite how much.

'How is it that we always end up in the same places as Kedran?' Will asked. 'Is he following us or are we following him?'

The three men moved away from the balcony railing and came down the wooden steps which extended from the wall to the ground. All three had leathery skin and their hands were scratched in many places, presumably from cutting the wiry grass. Some wounds were still fresh while others had hardened into scars.

'Teodor, Ottho, Wilf.' The old man gestured first to himself and then to the young men behind him.

Oede nodded in acknowledgement and returned the introduction, though none of the names he offered were their own. Teodor bared his teeth in the semblance of a smile and beckoned for everyone to follow him out into the marshes. He led them to where three women were hard at work, sweat streaming down their bare arms and faces. One of the women straightened up as the group approached. She was middle-aged, judging by the streaks of grey in her hair, but her shoulders were broad and her arms muscular. She spoke a few words to the old man, her tone harsh and colloquial, each word delivered as if it were followed by a full stop.

Reaching into her basket, Teodor pulled out a bunch of ivory handled knives. He passed one to each of them without explanation. James took the implement between his fingers. It was light and the blade was razor sharp. Kneeling on the soft ground, Teodor took his own knife from his belt. Grabbing a bunch of grass, he sliced the blades off at the base. From the bunch in his hand, he selected a lighter stem and deftly peeled back the outer skin. A creamy liquid oozed forth and whipping a glass bottle from his pocket, he caught the juice inside it. Now he spoke again, directing his words at Oede.

'He asks us to work for him in return for food and a bed,' Oede translated. 'The liquid is used in medicine.' He listened to Teodor again before continuing. 'The grass grows daily in this season but new shoots are torn. Must be picked,' he corrected himself. 'If cut the wrong way, they turn poisonous.'

'How d'we know if the grass is new?' Will asked.

'The blades are a lighter green.'

'Alright then,' Will replied with a hint of sarcasm and looked doubtfully around at the swathes of identical grasses.

'The marshes are boggy because long ago there were

trenches here,' Oede went on, ignoring Will's comment.

'War trenches?' James queried. He could think of no other purpose.

Oede shook his head. 'Trenches built by slaves long ago. Teodor does not know what for. Cutters are superstitious people, forced from their original homes to settle here. Terrible things once happened here.'

James knew only one story, from the history of this world at least, which told of trenches being dug.

'The Dark Master Jasper,' he said. He spoke too loudly for Teodor's head snapped up. The old man's eyes burnt with fear.

'Fnja ek marm, Jasper,' he rasped.

'A curse on Jasper,' Oede translated.

Teodor stood up and, flanked by Ottho and Wilf, left them to their work without another word.

'What has Jasper got to do with the trenches here?' Tala asked as soon as the men were out of earshot.

She hadn't been with them in Arvora, nor in the Garian slave town. A town the slave boy – named Lirim by Aralia – had called Arima, meaning City of Souls. James had assumed she'd know about such things but now realised no one had informed her.

'He forced his slaves to dig trenches, to search for a way into my world,' James began. 'The slaves had, and evidently still have, a history here.'

'Some say the Golden Road became a slave route, used for humans rather than amber or gems,' Oede added quietly.

'How is it that you know the Cutter's language?' Aralia asked him. 'Have you spent time in the east before?'

Oede did not look at her as he spoke. 'I spent several months travelling the regions along the western coast and I learnt several of the local dialects.' He reached up to touch the necklace at his throat. The leather strap was visible but the green stone pendant was hidden beneath his cloak.

'We should get to work.' Dina cut off any further questioning. 'It's almost evening.'

The companions spread themselves out and began to work. Only Dara did not help as she was still too young. She sat on a nearby tuft of grass, watching them. The late afternoon sun was hot but the companions worked without pause. It was difficult to spot the young shoots amongst the old and by the time evening came, they had only a handful of new blades between them. The sun cooled quickly as twilight approached, like a slice of heated metal dipped into freezing water. The Cutters finally stopped working and began making their way back towards the houses.

Teodor came out onto his balcony as the companions approached. He leaned over the railing and gestured to a partially covered area beneath the hut. It concealed a bucket on a rope which acted as a makeshift shower. They took turns to use it, rinsing away the grease and salt of far too many days. Those waiting their turn went up to the house. Teodor was not the only one at home. Several people were gathered around a long table in the front room. It was heaped with food: bowls of vegetables, meat, bread and crumbling cheese. In celebration of the quarterly Harvest Feast, Oede explained.

There was no more work that night. Just food and plenty of vinegary wine. When one bottle was dry, out came another and another until they lined the low windowsills like miniature ice sculptures. The glass glinted in the lamplight: blue, green, white. There were no orbs here. In fact, there were no signs of magic at all. As the twilight deepened outside, Teodor and his guests began to sing rowdy songs.

Oede, Dina and Kaedon drank as much as they dared but James, Will, Arthur, Tala and Aralia sat back and watched, spectators of some strange show in which they played no part. It was warm inside the hut. Not the muggy kind of warmth that induced headaches but the relaxing kind that contributed to easy sleep. Dara dozed off in her chair and Oede carried her into a corner and wrapped her in a blanket that Teodor handed him.

'Their heads will ache tomorrow,' Will whispered to James. He nodded at Dina and Kaedon who were still sipping wine and trying unsuccessfully to join in with the singing.

It was almost midnight when a knock sounded at the door. Everyone around the table froze as if struck by some spell. The singing ceased and in the ensuing silence, Teodor crept over to the door and opened it. A child stood on the balcony, wrapped in a dark cloak. She was obviously frightened for she trembled as she spoke. She delivered a short message to Teodor before vanishing into the night. The old man shut the door. He stood staring at the wood for a long time before turning around and uttering a few brief words.

'What did he say?' James whispered to Oede as the room filled with voices again.

'He says there were beasts spotted above the valley.'

'What valley?' Tala asked. 'What beasts?'

'That is all I know.'

Teodor's guests began filing out of the house. Only Ottho and Wilf remained. When everyone had gone, the old man shut and bolted his door before turning to Oede. His eyes, once again, were full of fear. He spoke quickly and Oede frowned as he tried to keep up.

'He says there has been a massacre at a nearby village and that more slaves are coming this way. They will pass by in just a few hours. There are two groups... there are never two groups in seven days. Beasts of the air, Shadows, haven't been sighted for many months. Something is changing.' He paused while Teodor took a breath and then continued. 'The people here fear darkness. There is a valley beyond the marshes where they dare not enter. It is the way the slaves go and never return. They say it is cursed. The locals call it Dau Lur, or Grey Valley, though its real name is long forgotten.'

James shivered. 'Could you ask him if the valley goes in the direction of the Gulna Mountains?'

Oede passed his question on in broken phrases. 'The valley rests on the border of the unnamed region,' he translated as Teodor spoke. 'If we follow it, we will reach the Gulna Mountains.'

'Which part of the mountains?' Kaedon enquired. 'Where does the Golden Road begin?'

Oede shook his head as Teodor responded to these questions. 'He says he does not know.'

The hut was quiet now. Teodor sat down on a chair beside the front door, rigid and alert. His sons joined him, leaving the companions to rest. Blankets had been laid out for them and they tried to make themselves as comfortable as possible on the wooden floor. James endeavoured to stay awake, suspicious of Teodor and his sons, but fatigue soon overwhelmed him and he fell fast asleep.

The sound of knocking startled him awake. Glancing over to the front door, he saw Teodor rising to open it. The bolts clicked and the door creaked as it swung inwards. James craned his neck to see who stood on the other side but the visitor was concealed by darkness. Teodor spoke quickly to this late night visitor and his voice sounded almost pleading. As James watched, one of the young men stepped out from the shadows. It was Wilf. He carried blanket in his arms beneath which something moved. Teodor stood aside and Wilf handed his burden over to the mysterious stranger. James held his breath, grateful for the thick shadows on this side of the room.

'Stay still.' Oede's voice was loud in his ear.

Glancing over his shoulder, James saw that Oede was also watching the door, his golden eyes blinking like an owl's. Teodor's voice was becoming more and more agitated. The stranger tried to enter the house but Wilf blocked his path. Suddenly, there was a flash of light. It burst through the door and struck Wilf in the chest. The young man fell to the floor with a thud and lay still. Teodor let out a great howl and crumpled to the floor beside his son. Out on the balcony, the stranger simply melted away into the night.

Ottho tried to comfort his father but the old man pushed him away. Not wanting to intrude but unable to simply sit back and watch, James shook off his blanket and stood up. His movement caught Ottho's eye. The young man turned on him, eyes blazing and James felt the full fury of his gaze. He noticed that Ottho was holding something. Yellowing papers covered with running ink. Papers that were both ancient and familiar. Glancing over to where he'd left his bag, he saw the zip gaping open like the razored mouth of some carnivorous fish. It was his turn to look at Ottho with mounting fury.

The young man grinned at him and raised his hand. There was a spark of light and the dry pages burst into flame. James tried to grab them but found he couldn't move. Frozen to the spot, he watched in speechless horror as the rare pages of Arvad's tale burned.

# Chapter 19

THE room was silent. James watched the fiery flakes of paper falling to the floor like snow. Where they settled on the floorboards, they became no more than powdery clumps of ash.

Ottho continued to smile as the papers burned. 'Andra,' he whispered. 'Capta kut, Sku.'

'Don't listen to him, James,' Oede said. 'It is time for us to leave.'

Still kneeling on the floor over his son's body, Teodor began murmuring to himself. His words were taken up by Ottho who stood looking at James with a mixture of fear and hatred.

'We must leave,' Oede urged again. 'Take up your bag and go out onto the balcony.'

A movement in the corner of the room caught James' eye. Arthur, Will, Tala and Aralia had all woken up and, like him, were watching Ottho intently. Only Dina and Kaedon still slept, undisturbed by the rising hostilities. Fighting against his more primal instincts, James brushed passed Ottho and swiped up his bag from the floor.

'Wait on the balcony,' Oede ordered. 'All of you.'

James went out onto the balcony without another word. His friends followed him. They did not have to wait long before Dina and Kaedon joined them and last of all, Oede.

Ottho followed them to the door, still echoing his father's chant. His voice drove the companions down the balcony steps and out onto the marshes. The landscape was pale and bare in the early dawn light. It was cool too, a low marsh mist shrouding everything. The atmosphere was suitably eerie for a place where Jasper's slaves had once lived and worked. Looking up over his shoulder, James saw Teodor had joined Ottho on the balcony. The pair stood watching as the companions hurried away across the marshes.

'Let's get as far away from here as possible,' James muttered. 'These people are crazy.'

'They are wary of magic, that's all,' Oede replied.

'Why were they chanting?' Will asked curiously. 'Do they believe in evil spirits?'

Oede was silent for a moment. 'They were casting a protection spell over the house to expel evil. Not just the evil brought by the darkness but the evil present in all magic and in all those who command it. Those like the traders, like all of us, and especially you.' He looked unblinkingly at James.

'Me!' James exclaimed. 'They don't know anything about me.'

'Everywhere we go, people are just beginning to learn of a wanderer. They do not see this individual as someone who has come to save the light but as someone who brings the darkness. Most people don't know who you are when they meet you but they sense the darkness around you.' Oede reached up to touch his necklace, as if doing so would ward off some unseen evil.

'Where you go, the darkness follows,' Dina now murmured. 'The Shadows are everywhere, watching and waiting. Simple people can feel their presence like a scar on the landscape.'

James was silent for a moment. 'Ottho burned the pages of Arvad's tale,' he then said quietly. 'That's what he took from my bag. He must have known what they were.'

'Everyone knows Arvad's tale and is aware of its rarity in written form,' Kaedon joined. 'To someone like Ottho, your possession of a story like that indicates your willingness to practice magic.'

James couldn't help feeling sorry for the Cutters and everyone like them. To be fearful of magic was to disarm oneself in a world where the darkness was rising. Once upon a time, he too had been wary of magic but he now understood its integral role in protecting this world as well as his own.

'Hey, wait!' Will's voice suddenly cut through the morning air. 'Where's Dara?'

Everyone stopped and looked at one another in alarm. Dara was not amongst them, nor was she anywhere on the surrounding landscape.

'Did we leave her sleeping?' Dina rubbed her forehead. 'How could we forget her! She's just a child.' This reprimand was directed towards herself as much as anyone else.

Kaedon shook his head. 'Her bed was empty. I assumed she was with the rest of you on the balcony when we came out and I didn't think to check.'

'There's only one way to know for sure,' Arthur intervened. 'We'll have to go back inside.'

'I will go,' Oede volunteered. 'I at least can understand their language.'

A memory stirred in James' mind, a recollection that filled him with sudden dread.

'Wait!' he exclaimed and Oede halted in his tracks. 'You won't find Dara inside the hut.'

'Where then?' Dina demanded. 'Did you see her go

somewhere?'

James shifted uncomfortably. 'I can't be sure, and it's only now I realise it, but Wilf handed something to the stranger at the door before he was killed. Something wrapped in a cloak. It was moving.'

'You think it was Dara?' Dina said sharply. 'That isn't possible.'

'It *is* possible.' Oede's statement silenced Dina. He looked at her with concern in his eyes. 'I believe it was a trader at the door.'

'What would a trader want with a child?' Aralia asked.

'The slave trade grows ever greater with the Belladonna's power,' Oede replied, 'so much so that even ordinary people are targeted. Sacrifice or be sacrificed.'

James frowned. 'What does that mean?'

'Either you offer a sacrifice or you yourself will be sacrificed. Teodor and his sons may have offered the child to the trader out of fear. The sacrifice of another would guarantee their own freedom.'

'But Wilf died,' Tala said. 'How does that make sense?'

'It does not,' Oede replied, 'but people like Teodor act out of fear. Fear blinds them to the truth.'

'Why Dara?' Will questioned. 'Why not me or James or any one of us?'

Oede raised his shoulders in a slight shrug. 'A sleeping child will not fight back and can easily be carried. I believe it's as simple as that.'

'If she has been taken, then we have to follow her,' Dina stated.

'We'll lose time if we go after her.' Kaedon wrapped his arm around Dina's shoulders. 'What kind of life would she have anyway without anyone to care for her?'

Dina detached herself from his half-embrace, eyes blazing. 'We don't know whether she has anyone to care for her or not. We don't know anything about her. If she was your child, would you sit back and let her go?'

'The traders can't be too far ahead of us,' Oede interrupted. 'We can follow them. The only way out of the marshes is through the valley Teodor spoke of. The traders will be going that way too. If we hurry, we might be able to catch up with them.'

The stilted village shrank on the landscape behind them as they continued their journey across the marshes. The mist cast an eerie shroud over the landscape but this began to lift as the sun rose. The marshes stretched on for a great distance. There were other stilted villages but many houses stood alone amongst the wavering grasses. After some time, even the houses vanished from the landscape, replaced by low bushes and trees whose roots absorbed the moisture in the earth and made it less spongy. The companions stopped just once before midday to pick some wild berries from a Lala Tree. The oval fruits looked like plums but tasted more like bananas. Energised by this small meal, they walked on beneath the warming sun.

Suddenly, Arthur stopped in his tracks and uttered a short exclamation. In the soft earth between his feet was a footprint. The edges had begun to dry, preserving the print perfectly where it lay. Just beyond it was another and another, weaving a path through the grass. Whether the prints belonged to the traders or not was impossible to tell but the sight of them gave the companions hope. It was not hard to follow the trail through the marshes. The landscape became fresher and greener around them as they walked. Soft moss replaced the tough marsh grasses, spreading over everything like green velvet. The ground gradually rose into slopes on either side of their path. These became higher and higher until they blocked out the sunlight and plunged everything between them into shadow. It was like a giant axe had swung down and cleft the landscape in two.

'Dau Lur,' Dina murmured. 'We've entered the Grey Valley.'

James glanced instinctively upwards, half expecting to see Shadows roaming the skies. There were none, just one or two lonely clouds drifting across the vault of blue.

'It looks too green and fresh to be called the Grey Valley,' Tala remarked.

Along the centre of the valley ran a clear stream. Unable to resist, Will knelt on the mossy bank and thrust his hands into the water. He drank deeply from his cupped palms before sitting back on his heels with a grin.

'The water tastes sweet,' he announced. 'You should all try some.'

'This place is beautiful.' Aralia sat down beside Will and let a handful of water filter through her fingers. 'It's hard to imagine slaves passing through here.'

'Beautiful places can hide dark secrets,' Oede observed quietly.

'The footprints end on this bank.' Kaedon squatted on the ground to better observe a wide area of compressed moss. 'The flattened moss suggests the slaves may have stopped here.'

Where the footprints had been so regularly scattered before, there were now none. Nor were there any on the other side of the stream where the narrow bank was bordered by rocks. The most obvious way through the valley was down the centre, following the flow of the stream.

'We'll have to keep going through the valley and trust that the traders took the same route,' Dina said. 'The shade is deepest there so at least we'll stay cool.'

The air in the valley was close yet damp. While the ground was dry and firm, the lush moss suggested recent rainfall. Still weak with dehydration, the companions sat on the bank of the stream and drank until their thirsts were sated.

'Has water ever tasted this good?' Will splashed a handful over his hair and face.

James tried to answer him but suddenly felt lightheaded. It was like he'd just stepped off a roller coaster and was trying to find his balance. His vision was blurred and he blinked several times to try and clear it. Though he'd only just drunk from the stream, he felt thirsty again and cupped his hands beneath the water once more.

'Wait!'

Arthur's voice stopped him. He turned towards his friend but could hardly see him through his hazy vision. His tongue felt like sandpaper and unable to resist, he lifted his hands to his lips and drank.

'Don't drink the water!' Arthur's tone was commanding.

'Why not?' James croaked. He felt thirstier than he had all day and dipped his hands in the stream again.

'We're so thirsty,' Will pleaded. 'Aren't you?'

'My mouth is full of sand,' Tala added. 'If I don't drink, I'll shrivel up.'

'The water is making you feel thirsty,' Arthur said urgently. 'Stop drinking it. You'll feel better. Trust me.' He spoke slowly, as if he too was struggling.

'I feel dizzy,' Dina slurred and tried to stand up. She lost her balance but Arthur caught her.

'Resist the temptation to drink,' he commanded and bent

down to smack Will's hand away from his mouth. 'We don't know what the water will do to us if we keep drinking it.'

'It must be enchanted,' Oede said. He was the only one of their party who did not seem affected. 'We should have realised. *I* should have realised.'

'We'll die if we don't drink,' Will complained. 'We're in the middle of nowhere.'

'We won't die,' Oede reassured, 'but we should rest and let the effects wear off. There's a tree on the slope behind us. We can rest under it for a while.'

Stumbling to their feet, they edged away from the stream towards the slope. They climbed towards the tree with the last of their strength. The trunk was slim but its roots were thick and twisted into little dents and hollows. The companions flopped down between the roots and closed their eyes. James felt his limbs growing heavy with fatigue. He laid his head against the tree trunk but found he could not sleep. He looked out over the valley, watching the shadows lengthening as the sun lowered in the sky. The moss seemed to shift and change around him, making him feel like he was in the middle of a green sea. Feeling faintly sick, he closed his eyes and his head finally stopped spinning.

'Will!'

James awoke with a start. He could hear Tala calling Will's name, over and over again with increasing persistence. He sat up and opened his eyes. On the other side of the tree, Tala, Aralia and Arthur were squatting by Will's side.

'What's wrong with him?' Dina appeared at Tala's side, followed by Kaedon and Oede.

James stumbled over to join them. Will lay with his head against the tree trunk and his body tucked between the roots. His skin was pale and his chest moved up and down with shallow breaths. Tala shook him by the shoulders and a stream of water gushed from his lips.

'He must have drunk more water,' she said.

'I think this is the culprit.' Arthur nudged a discarded water gourd lying close to Will's hand.

Will made a series of gurgling noises, as if he was trying to speak. He rolled himself onto his side and tried again. 'You should try it,' he slurred. 'The best water I've ever tasted.' The effort of speaking made his eyes roll and he fell silent again.

'It's like he's drunk,' Kaedon observed. 'Delirious too.'

Will opened his eyes but was unable to focus his gaze on anything. 'Beautiful, isn't it?' He tried to gesture at the landscape but his hand fell limp by his side. 'The whole valley is shimmering.'

'He's hallucinating,' Aralia said. 'I might have something to help. We have to make him be sick.'

She delved into her bag and pulled out one of the numerous herb bottles she kept inside. Prising Will's lips apart, she sprinkled a pinch of fine, yellow powder onto his tongue. He started coughing, the powder making his saliva foam. His chest began to heave and seconds later, he was violently sick onto the moss.

'He'll be sick until his stomach is empty,' Aralia warned. 'I've mildly poisoned him and when he's finished, I'll administer the antidote.'

'Mildly poisoned!' James exclaimed. 'Are you sure you know what you're doing?'

Aralia nodded. 'I've seen it done. Now, we might need to hold him down because the effects can be unpleasant.' She pulled a face and pinned her hands around Will's arms.

James and Arthur took a leg each while Tala held his head in place, tilting it to one side so that he didn't choke.

'Won't this dehydrate him too much?' James asked.

'It's a risk we'll have to take at the moment,' Aralia replied. 'The effects of the water might be worse.'

As the poison set in, Will was sick over and over again until no more liquid came up. Aralia dropped the antidote between his lips and they waited. Before long, he began to writhe like a snake shedding its skin. Foam spilled from his lips and dribbled down his chin onto the grass. He tried to shake off the hands holding him but they pinned him down until he was too weak to fight anymore. He fell back against the tree trunk and drifted into a delirious sleep.

# Chapter 20

'WILL he be able to walk again soon?' Dina asked, looking anxiously down at Will's sleeping form. 'We can't linger here for too long. The longer we wait, the further away Dara gets.'

'We'll have to wait a while longer to find out,' Aralia replied. 'For now, our job is done. We should rest too.'

Will's breathing had become more regular and Aralia left his side. Everyone else gradually peeled away, save for Tala who sat holding Will's hand. She caught James looking at her and couldn't hide the blush rising in her cheeks. James didn't know how he hadn't seen it before and wondered if Will felt the same or if he still secretly believed that Tala was cursed. He smiled to himself and sat down between the tree roots. All he could hear was the sound of the stream trickling through the valley below. His mouth felt like sawdust but he tried to ignore the sensation. Fumbling in his pocket, he drew out the clock. His fingers brushed against the dials but did not linger there.

'What're you doing?' Arthur sat down beside him and fixed his gaze on the timepiece.

'Nothing.' James hurriedly tucked the clock back in his pocket.

Arthur didn't reply. His gaze had drifted down into the valley where the shadows lay long and deep. Something was moving close to the stream and as his eyes adjusted, James realised it was a line of people.

'Slaves,' James whispered.

Arthur nodded. 'Stay low.'

He crawled over to where everyone else was sitting and conveyed the same message. Pressed against the grass, they all watched as the line of slaves stopped beside a kink in the stream. One by one, they leapt across the water to the opposite bank where they vanished into thin air.

'We have to cross the stream,' Arthur whispered incredulously. 'There are no footprints on the other side for a reason.'

Dina stood up abruptly. She stood facing the valley, her eyes glassy and distant.

'Dina?'

She did not seem to hear Kaedon's voice and her eyelids drooped, as if she was half asleep.

'What's she doing?' Tala asked. 'Is she sleepwalking?'

'She doesn't sleepwalk.' Kaedon was by Dina's side in an instant. He took her arm and she did not try to shake him off.

'She's hallucinating then,' Tala assumed.

'I've been here before,' Dina suddenly said.

'What do you mean?' Kaedon asked with concern. 'You haven't been to the east before.'

Dina turned her face away from him. 'Before.' Her hands began to tremble and she held them up in front of her.

'Before when?' Kaedon tried to make her look at him but she refused.

'Long before. When the valley was much the same but there was no stream. They named it after me.'

'What're you talking about?' James stood up but she would not look at him either.

'The valley. The Valley of Alcyone.'

Her words struck him forcefully in the chest. He knew that name. It belonged to one of the seven sisters, the cluster of stars that brightened the night sky in this world and his own. The namesakes of the sacred women Arvad had known, two of which he, Will, Arthur and Aralia had met, though not in living form. First Celaeno in Lover's Wood, then Taygete at the bottom of Celaeno's Lake where the seastone had been found.

'Who is Alcyone?' Kaedon asked.

'One of the seven sisters,' James replied distractedly. 'This valley was her betrothal gift, presented to her by one of Arvad's brothers. He named it after her. Just like Electra's Temple, Celaeno's Lake and Taygete's Waterfall.'

'What has Dina got to do with all of that?' Kaedon's voice rose with his concern.

Sensing eyes upon him, James turned to find both Tala and Aralia watching him. They sat side by side, their animosity forgotten as they watched over Will together. Two of the reincarnated seven sisters. He looked again to Dina, wondering how he hadn't guessed it sooner.

'There are seven sisters living in this world right now,' he began, 'not sisters by blood but women bound together by a shared fate. A fate that links them to Arvad and his quest. These sisters are reincarnations of the original seven sisters. Dina, it seems, is one of them. She is Alcyone.'

Kaedon gazed at Dina with a mixture of disbelief and dismay. She turned to him and took his hand. A different kind of fire rested in her eyes, soft and green like the valley.

'Do you know what my name means?' she asked.

He nodded. 'Fair judge.'

'It has another meaning too: from the valley.' She turned to look at James and her voice sounded in his mind. 'I didn't know until now. Not with my conscious mind at least.'

He held her gaze. 'None of us did. Not even your sisters.'

'Tala and Aralia,' she said. 'I should have known.'

'How is this possible?' Kaedon asked and the internal conversation was broken.

'I'm not certain,' Dina said out loud.

James looked over the darkening valley. They had come this way by chance, choosing to travel through the unnamed region rather than through Lleur, yet here they were in a place that connected them to the quest and to Arvad. Then again, maybe it wasn't chance. If the amber talisman really had been made by the eastern dryads, perhaps Arvad had passed through this valley seven hundred years ago. He had a way of connecting all his clues together for the right people to find.

'Will's awake.'

Tala's voice broke his thoughts and he looked towards his friend. Will's eyes were open and he was trying to speak.

'Where are we?' he croaked. 'What happened to me?'

'The water poisoned you,' Tala informed him.

'Water,' Will groaned. 'I'm so thirsty.'

'Can you stand up?' James asked. 'If you can walk, we can keep moving.'

Will tried to sit up but immediately fell back. He tried again and this time managed to pull himself upright, resting his back against the tree.

Tala took his arm. 'Take it easy. Don't rush it.'

Holding onto her and pushing against the tree, Will managed to stand. He took one step forward but lost his balance and fell against Arthur.

'We'll all have to help him,' Tala said. 'He can't do it on his own.'

Kaedon took hold of Will's other arm and with Tala's

help, eased him away from the tree. Little by little, they began to edge their way down the slope towards the stream. James, Arthur, Aralia, Oede and Dina followed patiently behind. By the time they reached the stream, evening had descended. The shadows in the valley merged and deepened, making it difficult to see anything. Reluctant to create a light, the companions stumbled on through the velvety gloom.

Where the slaves had crossed the stream, several large stones protruded from the water. Using these as stepping stones, the companions crossed over one by one. Kaedon led the way, supporting Will over one arm. On the opposite bank, they all stopped and stood waiting for something to happen. The valley looked the same as before, only now they were looking at it from a different angle. Behind them, a wall of rocks cut them off from the mossy slopes which towered over the valley.

'Where now?' Tala asked. 'There's nowhere for us to go from here.'

'That's not true.'

Dina's voice drifted back along the bank from where she now stood half-hidden between two boulders. A light hovered above her, illuminating a narrow split between the rocks just wide enough for a person to squeeze through if they were so inclined.

'You're joking, right?' Will assessed the gap with evident displeasure.

Dina shook her head. 'I can't see another way. Can you?'

Without waiting for his reply, she squeezed herself between the rocks. Arms outstretched, she began pulling herself through. Kaedon followed her and held out his hand to Will who somehow found the strength to join him. Entering last, James soon broke out onto a path behind his friends. Rocky walls towered above them on either side, creating a narrow path between them. Dina continued to lead the way and before long, James became aware of a rushing sound somewhere ahead of them.

'Can anyone else hear that?' he asked.

It was not the sound of wings but of running water. He did not have to wait long to find out the source. Skirting around the edge of a protruding rock, he saw a wall of cascading water before him. Three waterfalls tumbling down the rocks like great silk curtains billowing in a wind. At the bases of all three, the water converged to form a deep pool.

'We'd best not drink it this time,' Dina said and subconsciously touched her dry lips. 'This time we carry on.'

To their left, the slopes became higher and the path rose with them. The night grew thicker and they stumbled on under the light of a single orb. Once or twice they were forced to stop to let Will rest but his strength gained as the night wore on. At long last their path came to an end. The rocks suddenly fell away to reveal a new valley far below them. They were higher up than anyone had realised, their path so gradual in its ascent that the full extent of the incline had gone unnoticed. From this height, they could see beyond the valley to where a line of mountains rose beneath the light of a new moon.

'Are they…' James let his words trail away.

'The Gulna Mountains,' Oede finished for him. 'It's been years since I last set eyes on them.'

'Are they as you remember them?' Dina asked.

Oede nodded. 'Just as treacherous. Those peaks are unscalable. The Golden Road passes between them.'

The path they were on now dipped again, descending into this second valley. The companions walked with fresh energy, watching the sky as it began to lighten with the coming dawn. This valley was far less impressive than the one they had left behind. The grass was wiry and dark and the smooth slopes were disturbed by clusters of houses. There were people here too, working in the fields they'd marked out with stones. Evidently used to the presence of travellers, they did not look up as the companions went past. From above, the valley had looked small but the path through its centre was long.

By the time they reached the centre of the valley, the sun was already climbing towards midday. Here, in the valley's heart, they came across a young man travelling the same path. He was tall and thin and carried a heavy bag on his back. As he drew closer, he shouted out a greeting in his own tongue which Oede haltingly returned. The young man smiled, his cinnamon coloured skin glowing in the full light of midday. He began speaking rapidly and only stopped when Oede held up a hand for silence.

'We do not understand your language,' he said in Camil. The young man frowned and Oede spoke again, this time in a different tongue. The young man's smile widened and he fired off a rapid reply.

'He says there are not many travellers on this road, just slaves,' Oede translated slowly. 'He wonders who we are.'

'Has he seen slaves today?' James asked. 'If so, were they going towards the mountains?'

'He has seen them,' Oede answered. 'They were going that way. The villagers refuse to say anything about them. There is a long-standing deal that the traders leave the villagers alone in return for their silence about the illegal trades that happen here.'

'Is this young man a villager?' Dina enquired.

Oede nodded. 'Yes but he comes from a different valley.

There are seven valleys here. All rest in the shadow of the mountains. The Golden Road can be accessed via the next valley. In these parts, the road goes by another name: Ryk Lenska, meaning Path of Dust.'

The young man seemed eager to go and thanking him, Oede let him continue on his way.

'How far to the next valley?' Kaedon asked.

Oede looked up at the sky. 'We should arrive with the sunset.'

They began to walk again. As the mountains drew closer, they could see the blue tips against the cloudless sky. Determined to reach the foot of the Gulna range by nightfall, they did not stop again, nor did they come across anyone else to halt their journey onwards. Above them, the sun arced past its highest point before beginning its downward journey. The transition between one valley and the next was not marked by any border. The only indicator that they had moved between was the change in the landscape. Now the ground began to rise again, merging with the surrounding slopes so that the valley formed a U-shape rather than a V.

The grass became sparse and was soon replaced by loose shale. This formed a path which ran up one of the slopes before eventually reaching the foot of the mountains. Here it began to ascend more steeply, cutting a clear route between the rocks. Between one half of the path and the other stood a hut. It was little more than a wooden shed with no windows and a door hanging off its hinges. Nevertheless, the roof was intact and it was towards this that the companions climbed.

They reached it just as the sun was beginning to set. Pulling aside the door, Kaedon peered into the space within. 'It's an old goat hut,' he announced. 'There's enough room for all of us inside.'

James paused in the doorway. The hut was comprised of a single room. It was empty inside, save for the ashy remains of a fire. Before entering, he cast one more look up at the jagged mountains. From here, he could just make out a narrow yellow ribbon between the slopes, sometimes following the ridge but at other times suspended like a drawbridge between the peaks.

'There it is,' Oede murmured behind him. 'The Path of Dust.'

# Chapter 21

AFTER just four hours sleep the companions rose from their beds on the floor of the goat hut. It was barely dawn but they knew they had already lost too much time. Gathering their things, they left the hut and began to ascend the mountain path. The loose shale made the going tough even though the route was not particularly steep.

The Golden Road came into sight just as the sun was rising. The early light turned the yellow shale golden and it was easy to see how the route had gained its name. With the sunlight beaming down upon it, the path really did seem to be made of gold. A rusty archway marked the beginning of the road. An inscription engraved on a plaque at the top read: Ryk Lenksa.

'You can imagine what the road must have looked like years ago when it was packed with amber traders,' Will remarked.

'I think I prefer it this way,' Aralia said. 'Just listen to the silence.'

Up here, the only sound was that of their shoes crunching over the shale. The silence engulfed them. Not the pressing silence of closed spaces but the vast stillness of the great outdoors. Side by side, the companions passed through the archway and onto the road. It was much the same as the mountain path, though perhaps a little steeper.

'Ready?' Kaedon asked, raking his eyes over each of them. 'From this point the route will only get harder.'

He didn't wait for an answer and began to climb the path with renewed strength. Everyone else followed, their sights firmly set on a stone that marked the top of the path. They reached this point without any trouble and stopped to gape at the scene before them. The direction of the route had now changed. It no longer climbed up the mountainside but became a flat and narrow bridge between this mountain and the next. The rock fell away beneath it, plunging into a deep valley below. The bridge was just wide enough for them to walk across. They took turns to cross it, not wishing to place too much weight on it at once.

James stopped to admire the view which from the bridge was even more breath-taking. A river ran through the centre of the mountain valley. It stretched all the way to the sea which was little more than a blue band on the distant horizon. It was awe-inspiring to stand above such a vast, unmarred landscape. Dragging his eyes away from the scene, James crossed to the other side of the bridge. Looking ahead, he was surprised to see they were no longer alone on the Golden Road. Two men were walking towards the bridge from the opposite direction. One was old and the other young and both carried huge backpacks. They did not seem surprised to see the companions and doffed their hats in greeting as they approached.

'Llueti.' The old man spoke first, a wide smile spreading across his features. 'Llueti,' he repeated.

'What is he saying?' Tala asked Oede.

Oede did not answer her. Instead, he turned and spoke to the old man. 'We speak Camil,' he said clearly. 'We come from the northern continent.'

'Ah Cima!' The old man's smile widened.

'We're looking for the home of the eastern dryads.' Aralia spoke slowly and deliberately. 'We understand they once lived in these mountains.'

Both men looked at her but it was the younger one who answered. 'Draida?' he asked. 'Sul e Draida?'

'Yes,' Oede replied hurriedly. 'We are searching for the Draida.'

The young man nodded but did not take his eyes off Aralia. 'Emra kisk. Ri nsu.' He drew his fingers across his throat and let his eyes roll.

'Emra is a word I know,' Oede said quietly. 'It means slave. These men must have passed the traders on this road.'

Kneeling on the shale, the young man picked up two stones. One flat, the other pointed. He began to draw on one with the other, sketching a series of mountain peaks and two paths passing between them. One wound through the middle of the mountains while the second branched off to the left. On the first path he placed a cross and on the second, an arrow.

'There must be two routes we can take,' Kaedon observed. 'The one with the arrow departs from the Golden Road.'

The young man pointed to the path marked with the cross. 'Emra kisk,' he repeated. 'Ri nsu.'

'The slaves pass along the Golden Road,' Oede murmured. 'The second route is a better way through the mountains.' He glanced at the stone again where the young man was busy drawing a series of lines over the main road.

'What's he drawing?' Will asked.

'A checkpoint,' Oede replied with a tone of surprise. 'I thought these would be abandoned but it seems they are not. They must now belong to the traders.'

The young man stood up and handed the stone to Aralia. Both he and the older man tipped their hats again before walking away down the road. The companions called their thanks after them but neither looked back.

'We should keep going,' Dina instructed. 'We have to find the second path.'

The sun matured and the day grew older with it. The Golden Road stretched on and on, curving around rocky outcrops and forming bridges between crevasses and peaks. It was a little like the Great Wall of China, James thought. Though he'd only ever seen pictures and videos of it, this path seemed equally magnificent.

It was just as the sun was turning golden that the path they'd been looking for came into view. Much like the young man's drawing, it branched away to the left of the Golden Road. It was not so much a path as a narrow passage hemmed in by rocks. Of the two routes, it was the more treacherous, but they hoped it would spare them an encounter with the traders. They entered the passage in single file, with Kaedon taking the lead again and Oede bringing up the rear. Though the rock walls were tall, occasional cracks in the surface revealed slivers of the reddening horizon, where white clouds sailed like ships across a bloody sea.

Pausing to admire the view, James saw that the Golden Road was still visible below them. Between two rocky outcrops, he could just make out the checkpoint the young man had drawn for them. It looked abandoned but as he craned his neck, he saw there were two people standing just beyond it. He couldn't tell whether they were guards or traders but either way, he was glad they did not have to pass through the checkpoint.

'It seems we were saved by strangers,' Oede said over his

shoulder.

Knowing that it was unwise to linger, they climbed on. The mountain passage seemed endless, surrounded by nothing but the cooling rocks and darkening sky. At the head of their group, Kaedon came to a sudden halt.

'What is it?' Dina asked.

Kaedon stood aside and pointed to a shape lying on the ground before him. It was neither a rock nor an animal carcass but carried the same bulk as both.

'Is that... Is that a body?' Aralia asked tremulously.

Kaedon did not speak. He knelt over the shape and a light glimmered in his hand. It illuminated the still face of a young girl. She was not particularly old, ten or eleven perhaps. Her skin was frozen blue and her holey brown cloak barely covered her lifeless form.

'Just a child,' Aralia said. 'It's too cruel.'

'Why is she up here all alone?' James wondered aloud. 'She's dressed like a slave.'

'The darkness doesn't stop for anyone: not men, women or children, or even the young, the old and the sick,' Tala stated.

'She must have died trying to escape the traders,' Arthur added quietly.

'I thought the slaves couldn't escape,' Will said. 'They're bound by magic.'

James couldn't help thinking of Dara. She was a similar age to the child here. Even though he hardly knew her, he did not wish her any harm.

'It feels wrong to say, but the presence of a slave must mean we're still heading in the right direction,' Kaedon said. He lifted the body onto a pile of stones to the side of the path and wrapped the holey cloak more closely around it.

Everyone gathered around. They each took up a handful of stones and placed them on the child, burying her unnamed and forgotten amongst the mountains. His throat tightening, James stepped away to look between a gap in the passage wall. His eyes came to rest on a wide basin hollowed into the side of the mountain. The far side of the basin was almost sheer and was marked with rows of rectangular holes. Looking at these holes, James suddenly realised that they were windows. Heart racing, he called for everyone else to join him.

'Hey, come and look at this!'

His friends gathered around him and he pointed between the gap in the rocks.

'Is that what I think it is?' Dina asked.

James nodded but didn't speak.

'At long last we have reached the home of the eastern dryads,' Oede filled in for him.

As they stood staring, a shadow moved across the base of the slope between two of the windows. It was a person, though their black clothing made them almost invisible in the gathering twilight. Watching them, James felt suddenly cold. He could feel the air tingling, not with a pure, ancient magic but with a much darker power. It was the same feeling he had sensed in the marshes. A deadly poison spread by the Belladonna and her forces. Even as he thought of her, he felt a presence at his shoulder. Invisible and intangible but unmistakable. Little by little, she was penetrating his mind, even though he tried to block her out.

'Who is that?' Aralia asked, pointing to the figure in the basin below.

James said nothing though he knew who it was. Or, the Cutters had called him. Kedran.

'It's him, isn't it?' Aralia then whispered. 'Kedran.'

Again James said nothing.

'It seems he too knows of the eastern dryads,' Kaedon mused. 'By the power of deduction we can also assume that he knows of the talisman.'

'If he knows, then *she* knows,' Will emphasised.

'That part was not so unexpected,' Dina said. 'The more puzzling question is why bring slaves here? Unless...' she trailed away and looked at Oede.

'Unless this is the site of the eastern Arvora,' he finished.

'Do you really think it could be?' Arthur asked.

Oede raised his hands in a gesture of uncertainty. 'There is only one way to be sure.'

Standing sideways, he pushed himself through the gap in the rocks. One by one, everyone else followed until they all stood in a row along the edge of the basin. Though steep, it was not sheer like the slope on the opposite side. Kedran had now vanished, leaving the way clear for their descent. Using their hands for support, they began to descend backwards down the slope. Loose stones scattered away from their feet and clattered down the mountainside. By the time they made it to the bottom of the slope, the last remnants of twilight had vanished. A slender moon slipped out from behind some clouds to light their way across the mountain bowl. They crept around the edge where the shadows were darkest, hoping they wouldn't be seen.

Even the lowest row of windows was a grown man's height from the ground. Kaedon was only just able to hook his hands around the sill. With great effort, and with a helping hand from below, he managed to heave himself upwards and through the hollow opening. The sill was just wide enough for him to kneel on and balancing himself, he reached down to help the next person. Aralia took his hand and he pulled her up to join him. Once safely on the sill, he lowered her down on the other side. He passed James through next, followed by Will and then Tala.

It was dark and cold inside the mountain. Standing still, James listened for any sounds but all he could hear was his own breathing.

'Rai?' he whispered. 'You there?'

'I'm here.'

There was a soft thud followed by a grunt. Holding out his hand, James conjured a light. Its faint beam illuminated Will and Tala standing beneath the window. Curious to see more of their surroundings, James spun around. They were standing in a long stone passageway. The walls were built from sandy yellow stone which gleamed like marble in the soft light. The passage was striking in its height and scale but displayed no carvings or adornments.

'It's so different to Mercy,' Aralia murmured. 'So grand.'

It wasn't long before their party was whole again and they began to move down the passageway. The stone floor echoed with their footsteps despite their best efforts to be quiet. At the end of the passage, a stone arch led them through into another. This one was much the same only here the walls were stained with paint. Though the colours were fading, they had been deliberately brushed onto the polished walls to depict scenes; people dressed in flowing robes, fruit laden trees, and baskets piled high with golden treasure. There were animals too, ferastia, dragons and mountain birds.'

'They're murals,' Will whispered.

'These are not just any murals,' Oede said. 'They tell the story of the dryads and their lives as amber harvesters and traders. The Golden Road runs all the way down this passageway.'

At times the paintings were broken up by archways leading into different rooms. Entering one such room, the companions stopped to stare in awe at the space before them. Even in here there were murals, moments in time frozen on the walls. These scenes were more complete, untouched by the natural elements for centuries. The colours were still bright in places; red, yellow and green with occasional touches of white and gold. There were no people in these murals, just trees. Hundreds upon thousands of trees. The leaves whispered to one another, preserving the voices of the dryad ghosts who still dwelt here in the dark.

# Chapter 22

WALKING the perimeter of the room, James' gaze fell on a statue standing against the back wall. Holding up his light, he saw that it was the figure of a woman. She stood on a pedestal, dressed in a long robe with her hands clutched to her chest. There was something familiar about her, almost as if he'd seen her likeness before.

'Electra.' Dina came up behind him. 'Where I come from, people worship her.'

'We saw her statue in the temple just outside the Hidden City,' Will recalled. 'Electra's Temple.'

'I've never been inside it,' Dina confessed. She reached out to touch Electra's stony hand. 'Others have told me that it's a special place.'

'Why would there be a statue of Electra here in the east?' Aralia also came to stand in front of the statue. 'The Mercan dryads certainly don't worship her. They believe in earth spirits rather than gods and goddesses.'

Dina now ran her fingers along a ridge on the stone robe. 'Electra is not a goddess confined to one belief system. She is named after a star and therefore is more universal than most deities. Her name, in some translations, means amber.'

'Even so, why is she here?' Arthur asked.

'The presence of this statue is simple,' Oede said. 'If Arvad's talisman really was created by the dryads here, it should come as no surprise that there is a link to the seven sisters also.'

'That's true,' James murmured. 'The gift for the firestone, the coin, was connected to Electra and the sapphire ring once belonged to Celaeno. It would be strange, though, for Electra to be tied to more than one gift.'

'Maybe she was never really linked to the coin,' Will suggested. 'There may not have been any connection between the temple's name and the sisters' duty to protect the firestone.'

'Our best chance of finding out the truth is to keep exploring.' Kaedon's voice cut across the room and the conversation was brought to an abrupt end.

The sharpness of his tone made James wonder if he was still struggling with the knowledge that Dina was one of the sisters. He hadn't spoken about it since they'd left the Valley of Alcyone but he kept looking at Dina as if he wasn't quite sure who she was anymore. Either she didn't notice these looks or she chose to ignore them. Perhaps she too was coming to terms with her new identity.

Leaving the room behind them, the companions continued down the passageway. At the end, a wide arch led them into what appeared to be an entrance hall. A wooden door stood at one end, the surface carved with elaborate designs. It must have looked different from the outside for none of them had noticed it on their approach. In this space too, the walls were covered with murals. The Golden Road flowed through every scene, a continuous yellow line. It stood out against the other colours which all faded into the same shade of brown. Like the other rooms they'd entered, the hall was cool and silent with no sign of Kedran or the slaves.

'Kedran must be here somewhere,' James said in a low

voice. 'He can't have vanished that quickly. Wherever he is, the slaves must be too.'

At the back of the hall, a grand staircase led up to another floor. In the hollow space beneath it, a second stairway descended into an unknown darkness.

'Up or down?' Will asked.

'Down,' James answered though he wasn't sure why.

He began to descend, keeping his hands pressed against the walls on either side of him. The air grew colder and a draught blew upwards from below. His light went out and he reignited it only to find that the stairs had already come to an end. Holding up his light, he gaped at the space now illuminated around him. He was standing in a great cavern through which a black river flowed. The water was completely still and his light reflected off the glassy surface. Down here, the walls had not been polished smooth and maintained their natural formations. Undeterred by the rougher surfaces, the mural painters had carried on the story they had begun in the rooms and passageways above. Many of the scenes had faded but traces of their former glory remained.

'Incredible,' Arthur murmured. 'I've never seen anywhere like this.'

A wooden boat was moored against the earthy bank. The paint had peeled along the waterline but the frame looked solid enough. Kaedon knelt to inspect the oars laid ready in the rowlocks. Evidently satisfied, he swung himself into the boat's shallow base.

'What are you doing?' Tala placed a foot on the rocking gunwale to steady it. 'There can't be much down here.'

'We can't know that for certain unless we explore,' Kaedon replied. He held the boat steady for her and she reluctantly clambered aboard.

There was just enough room for all of them on board the vessel. As soon as they were all settled, Kaedon took up the oars. The boat slid through the black water, taking them deeper into the heart of the mountains. Down here, the atmosphere carried a sense of sadness. This place had clearly been abandoned for many years and James wondered at its history. He looked up at the cavern roof and shivered. The air had cooled significantly. There were now icicles hanging above the boat like stalactites. Though small at first, these freezing spikes grew thicker and longer until they were all forced to duck to avoid being skewered. Even the walls became slippery with ice, encasing the river in a freezing tunnel.

'Should we turn back?' Will asked through chattering teeth. 'We'll freeze to death if we carry on.'

Even after the heat they'd endured on their journey so far, this cold was unbearable. The icy tunnel was beautiful but frightening too. The only sound between the freezing walls was the gentle swish of the bow cutting through the water.

'Maybe you're right,' Dina said, glancing at Will. 'There can't be much down here.' She laid a hand on Kaedon's arm. 'Let's go back.'

Kaedon frowned. 'I would if I could but there's a strong undercurrent pushing us this way. I can't row against it.'

James reached out to touch the tunnel wall. The ice was so cold that his fingers stuck to it and he couldn't pull them away. Even as he fought against it, he thought he saw something beneath the glassy surface. A pale shape caught within the frozen layers. He didn't have to look twice to realise that it was a face, the eyes closed and the mouth open in a scream.

'Stop rowing!' he gasped. 'My fingers are stuck to the ice.'

Kaedon immediately pulled in the oars but the boat kept moving forward. 'The current is too strong!' he exclaimed.

Already stretched to his limit, James tugged at his hand again. This time it came free and he fell back inside the boat. Wordlessly, he pointed towards the face in the ice but everyone else had already seen it.

'There's more than one!' Will exclaimed in horror. 'Look!'

There were now a dozen or more faces staring back at them from the icy depths. Though the sight was gruesome and somewhat frightening, no one could tear their eyes away.

'A massacre,' Tala said under her breath. 'The end of the dryad story.'

James shuddered. In this world, the dead lingered longer than they were welcome. He'd never believed in ghosts but in this world, it was impossible to deny their presence.

'Why would anyone wish to murder the dryads?' Aralia questioned. 'It seems so unnatural.'

'War, perhaps,' Oede answered.

James frowned. 'A war between whom?'

'Many regions in the east. Everyone wanted a share of the amber trade and when the dryads refused, war broke out. The amber forests were reportedly destroyed. Most people assumed the dryads fled their home and vanished but it seems that many did not escape.' Oede gestured to the icy walls. 'A terrible fate.'

'I wonder why no one took a claim on this place,' Arthur wondered aloud. 'Most of the murals have been preserved and there is so much space here.'

'Most people don't like lingering at the sight of a massacre,' Kaedon replied bluntly.

'Look,' Dina interrupted before anyone else could speak, 'we've reached the end of the tunnel.'

Just ahead of them, an earthy bank rose from the water, bringing their short journey to an end. The bank divided the river from a circular pool at the centre of the small cave they now found themselves in. All around this pool, triangular stones had been pressed into the ground in a seemingly random formation.

'What d'you think those stones are?' James asked as the boat knocked against the bank.

'Burial stones,' Arthur responded. 'The Mercan dryads use them too. These caves must be burial chambers. Proper burial chambers for planned ceremonies rather than the chance graveyards of a brutal massacre.'

Kaedon stood up and the boat wobbled beneath him. Stepping onto the bank, he held the vessel still while everyone else disembarked. Aralia went to stand by the edge of the pool but no one followed her.

'Be careful,' Dina warned, 'we don't know what the pool is for.'

'It's a Ryth Pool,' Aralia said calmly.

'A what?' Will asked.

'A Ryth Pool. According to legend, the water inside such pools has the power to reveal truths about the past and the future. Our mother used to tell us a story about a woman who became so obsessed with her own future that she jumped inside a Ryth Pool trying to realise it. Naturally, she drowned.'

James went to stand beside Aralia. The surface of the pool was smooth and dark like polished jet. He gazed into the water, half hoping to see a vision of his own past or future. Aralia took his arm and drew him away.

'I don't know if my mother's story was true but let's ere on the side of caution and stay away from the pool.'

James turned his attention to the cave instead. It was much smaller than the first and there was only one mural, painted onto the curved wall surrounding the Ryth Pool. It depicted a white tree with a fountain of water gushing from its trunk. At the point where the water and wood met there was an area of light painted in the shape of a woman.

'Electra,' he whispered.

Behind the tree, sweeps of watery paint had been brushed across the wall like mist. The wall's uneven surface made it look like the mist was moving. On the top branches of the tree was a circle of reflected light. It came from the Ryth Pool where the orb James held was mirrored on the water. Though the surface lay still, the reflection on the wall began to waver. The haloed circle transformed into dancing flames. These fiery tongues licked at the painted branches but could not burn them. Beyond the white tree, the cracks in the cave wall took on the appearance of many trees.

'The amber forests,' Will breathed.

The scene changed. The cracks reshaped themselves into dark caves through which the flames raced. Billowing smoke turned the rocks black and when the flames faded, ice began to form where they had been. The bodies of the dryads who had been suffocated by the smoke now became imprisoned in an icy tomb.

'Water has a memory,' Oede murmured as the vision began to fade. 'The particles absorb human emotions and can change shape accordingly. Shout angry words at water and it will become ugly, sing its praises and it will become beautiful. The water inside this pool remembers how the eastern dryads met their end.'

'So the vision we just saw was a memory, then,' James said.

'The tree in the mural must have some significance,' Will

cut in before Oede could reply. 'I've never seen a white tree before.'

Aralia ran her fingers over the base of the tree trunk. Though the paint was faded, it still carried a luminance to it, as if it really was burning. 'It isn't white. It's silver.' She let her words sink in before continuing. 'Amna Leigh spoke of such a tree. One whose sap was so pure it could not be tampered with, even by the great dryad alchemists. The only tree of its kind. She was trying to tell us that the amber used in Arvad's talisman came from this tree.' She paused again and looked at James. 'What if she wasn't just referencing the talisman however but the earthstone itself?'

James stared at her. The *earthstone*. He had been so concentrated on finding the talisman that he hadn't stopped to think about the crystal.

'If the legend is to be entirely believed then the crystals were formed by the elements themselves, not by magic or man,' Arthur commented. 'Therefore it's entirely possible that the earthstone came from this tree.'

James gazed up at the mural, trying to imagine the tree standing amongst others in the great amber forests. 'It's also possible that this tree still exists,' he said quietly. 'What if it not only created the earthstone but serves to protects it as well? The gifts Arvad gave the elements in return for the crystals carried the curse of eternity. Just like the Chinjoka dragon was bound to protect the firestone and Celaeno's Lake to protect the seastone, perhaps this tree was granted eternal life.'

'If that's true, we have to return the gift to the tree in order to set the earthstone free and break the eternal curse,' Will concluded.

Before anyone could speak again, the air was disturbed by

a humming sound. It shook the ground and cast vibrations across the surface of the Ryth Pool. Looking around the cave, James noticed for the first time a tunnel leading outwards from it. The entrance was small and hidden in shadow, but it was through here that the sound came. The tone was deep and captivating and stepping towards it, James realised it was the sound of chanting.

# Chapter 23

STANDING by the tunnel entrance, James felt the sound vibrating through him. He could almost separate one voice from the next, a mix of tones but all equally tuneless. The chanting was spoken in another language but the words were indiscernible, all belonging to the same droning hum.

'Come on,' he said over his shoulder, 'let's follow it.'

The tunnel was shorter than anticipated. At the end of it, a stone stairway rose through the roof and into an unknown space above. James paused, unsure, but Dina nudged him in the ribs and he began to climb. The stairs were long and steep. A cool draught blew in from somewhere, suggesting they were no longer underground. Soon enough a glimmer of light appeared and they broke out into the open air.

It was dark outside but the moon still glowed above the mountains. To their surprise, the companions found themselves standing on the edge of a precipice protruding from the dryad mountain. The side closest to the mountain was just wide enough to hold all of them but the far edge only had room for one. James wasn't afraid of heights but the view below the precipice made his toes curl. There was nothing between this narrow ledge and a ravine many miles below. It was from this ravine that the chanting came. The sound swelled upwards, bouncing off the mountains in ghostly echoes.

Though the sky was dark, the ravine was filled with light. Burning torches formed a line down the centre, held aloft by all who stood there chanting. People dressed in brown robes, their heads uncovered and shaven. As James watched, a new line of people began filtering through the ravine. They were not dressed like the chanters, but nor did they appear to be slaves or traders. Their faces were covered with silver masks and they walked with a lightness that suggested they were not human. Behind these masked figures, there came a third line. Dressed in thin white shifts, the latest arrivals walked without dignity or strength, stumbling over the uneven ground. They were all young women, James noticed, just a little older than himself. He looked for Dara amongst them, though he knew she was too young to be there.

The chanters suddenly uttered a great shout. One by one they melted away to the edges of the ravine to allow the young women through. The white clad girls huddled at the centre of the ravine, all facing outwards. Several torchbearers closed in around them. There was a flash of light and all the torches went out. In the darkness that descended, all James could hear was the ragged breathing of his friends close behind him. A new light glowed in the centre of the ravine. It carried a bluish tinge, like winter twilight. It illuminated the young women first before expanding to fill the whole ravine.

Just beyond the waiting people, a new figure appeared. Dressed entirely in black, it moved slowly towards the central circle. James observed the newcomer with mounting dread as they passed between the lines of shadowy torchbearers. He felt his throat constricting, as if someone had their hands around his neck and was gently squeezing. With each step the figure took, the invisible hands tightened. He gasped for air but the poisoned atmosphere could not sustain him.

'James?' Dina shook his arm. 'Are you alright?'

He couldn't speak. Couldn't even turn to look at her. He was still conscious but his body would not respond to the signals in his brain.

'He's shaking,' Will observed. 'James, can you hear us?'

In the ravine below, the mysterious figure had stopped. One of the young women in the central circle dropped to her knees, unable to hold herself upright any longer. There was no mercy for her. A bolt of lightning shot from the hand of one of the masked observers. It struck the girl in the chest and her life was instantly snuffed out. In his hazy stupor, James again recalled the death of the young woman in Arvora. She too had been shot down by a bolt of light following her failure to pass between the worlds. Her body had been carried away by white coated men and women but here there was no such dignity. The girl's body disintegrated where it lay and became a pile of ash.

'We should go.' Kaedon's tone was urgent. 'We should go now.'

James tried to move but his feet wouldn't obey. A voice was whispering in his mind and he closed his eyes, wanting to hear it. The ravine disappeared and he found himself standing at the edge of a different precipice. There she was, right in front of him, half of her face covered by a silver mask.

'What do you want from me?' he asked, finally finding his voice.

Her lips did not move but he heard her speak. 'You know what I want.'

'You want the crystals,' he answered, 'and you want me.'

She laughed but her mouth remained motionless. 'The crystals are superfluous to me. I can achieve greatness without them. What I desire is the ability to pass between worlds.

Once I have that, neither you nor the crystals will be able to stop me.'

'You'll never find a way into my world,' James said defiantly.

She laughed again. 'Won't I?'

The precipice vanished. He was now standing in an office at the top of a London building. He knew he was in London because he could see the Gherkin through the window. The office was full of people, all working mercilessly as if their lives depended on it. No one spoke to each other and the only sound was the consistent hammering of computer keys. A door at the back of the office opened and a man appeared. He was dressed in a crisp grey suit that accentuated his thin frame. His hair was also thin and grey and his expression was marred by worry lines. James stared at the man in disbelief. He tried to move but again found himself paralysed.

'Dad?' he whispered.

His father did not acknowledge him. He simply strode over to the nearest desk and dropped a file of papers onto it.

'He cannot hear you.'

She was still there, lurking somewhere in his subconscious. An evil presence controlling the vision he now stood within. The atmosphere inside the office suddenly changed. The computer screens began flickering and error messages appeared on each of them. At the back of the room, a shadowy figure appeared. A light flashed from its hand and struck a woman in the chest. She fell across her desk and lay still. The veins in her hands and arms turned black as if with poisoned blood. James retched but nothing came up. He was no longer of flesh and blood but a ghost.

'I have not found a way to pass into your world in physical form but I am still able to reach inside.' Her voice was no longer inside his mind but close to his ear. 'Those in your world sealed their fate the moment they invented technology. Anyone who helps me will be rewarded but those who resist me will die. They will not be able to fight against my power. How can you fight something you don't even know exists?'

'Stop it,' James cried out. 'Just stop it.'

'One day it will be daddy, the next day mummy. But oh, you shouldn't mind that. They've forgotten all about you. But then, did they ever really care?'

James considered her words. She was right. His parents bought him presents on his birthdays and at Christmas and took him on holiday once a year but when else did they really care? His dad, Philip, started work early and finished late most days, not because he needed the money but because he didn't know how to stop. His mum, Louisa, often stayed late with him and then they would go out for dinner together. Sometimes James joined them but he often ate alone at home, under the pretence that he was at a friend's house.

'They might not spend time with me but they would never abandon me,' he said aloud. 'I won't let you hurt them.'

'Your words are meaningless,' she snapped. 'All you have to do is take my hand, step over the precipice, and you will be safe. *They* will be safe. I promise I won't harm them if you give me this. It's just one small step.'

'I don't believe you. How will you protect them when their world is consumed by war?'

'There won't need to be a war if you help me. Think of the lives you could spare by taking one simple step.'

James shook his head vehemently. 'You don't care who lives or dies, so long as you have power. I will stop you, even if it takes me the rest of my life.'

'I know where the gift is that you seek.'

Her words caught him off guard. He opened his mouth to speak but no words came out. She laughed, a horrible, clawing sound.

'I can see in your eyes that you long to know,' she crooned. 'Your blood pulses with it. Do you think the great Arvad would be so careless as to hide the talisman in plain sight, in a burnt forest where it was first made? No, he was far cleverer than that.'

'He didn't hide the gifts,' James said. 'They became lost over time.'

'That is a half-truth. Arvad hid the gifts himself. Two were found, the ring and the coin, but were later lost by those who did not understand their purpose. Those who knew of Arvad and his quest were few and far between. Some tried to solve his riddles while others sought to cover them up. As the age of peace descended, his quest became no more than a meaningless treasure hunt pursued by fanatics.'

'Arvad's name is known to most people,' James countered, 'even if they do still think of him as no more than a myth.'

'His name is now known because of you.' Her voice dropped to a whisper. 'People have begun to learn of a boy who is destined to find Arvad's crystals. An individual Arvad spoke of in his writings. He did not know the identity of this person but he was convinced it would be someone who followed the light. When he vanished from this world, those who knew about his quest soon forgot. They saw no reason to believe in the powerful magic he claimed to possess. Even now, those who know his story do not quite believe it.'

'The Lost Years,' James said under his breath.

She did not speak again immediately. When she did, her voice was even softer than before. 'Where did he go in those lost years?' she murmured in his ear. 'The question has never truly been answered. But you know, don't you?'

James nodded despite himself. 'Some people believe he went to my world.'

'Ah, yes,' she whispered.

This time he felt her presence beside him. He turned towards her but the office suddenly disappeared and he found himself once more upon the lonely precipice. Looking across the gaping chasm, he saw her standing on the opposite side as she had been before. A dark figure in a silver mask.

'It seems you are not the only one who can pass between,' she said. Although she looked further away, her voice still sounded close in his ear. 'What would Arvad wish to do in your world, I wonder, apart from see it for himself?'

James suddenly realised what she was getting at. This part of the conversation had come full circle, starting and ending with Arvad's gifts.

'You think he hid the talisman there.' He spoke without emotion, presenting a fact for her to confirm or deny.

She laughed. 'Not just the talisman but the earthstone itself. Do you not see? It is the perfect hiding place where only you can find it.'

James gaped at her. 'Arvad didn't know who would find the crystals. He didn't know it would be someone from my world.'

Before he could continue, a new voice sounded in his mind. It was familiar and he realised it was Sylvia's. Her tone was urgent and he listened to her carefully.

'James, wake up. You must wake up. Make the right choice.'

He blinked and realised his eyes were already open. It was not Sylvia's voice he now heard, nor the Belladonna's, but Aralia's. She was shaking his arm and repeatedly speaking his name. Shifting his gaze, he saw that he was still standing above the ravine. The black clad figure had vanished and the torches had been relit. As he stood entranced, a bolt of lightning split the sky above. The moon withdrew behind a cloud and the torches were once again snuffed out. In the darkness of the night, he heard the Belladonna's voice again.

'Do it,' she hissed. 'Do it now. Show me the way and I will not harm you.'

James felt her anger and involuntarily reached for the clock. Hardly knowing what he was doing, he turned the dials. He heard the voices of his friends as if from far away but could not understand what they were saying. A feeling of faintness overcame him and suddenly he was falling. His chest compressed and he forgot how to breathe as he slipped into the depths of time and space.

Almost immediately, he realised something was wrong. Other shapes moved in the darkness around him, oddly distorted forms that looked almost human. He could hear screaming and a chill passed over him. The darkness went on and on, as if it had been stretched and was never meant to end. It felt like he was drowning in a surging sea of ink and he gasped for air. His mind began to fade and closing his eyes, he let the sea take him.

# Chapter 24

JAMES regained consciousness somewhere he didn't know. He was sitting on a bench at the side of an empty street lined with buildings. The streetlamps were just beginning to fade, the orange bulbs dim against the morning sky. A few pigeons waddled around some bins, stepping over squashed cigarette butts and plastic wrappers. Otherwise, the street lay still. As he looked around, his eyes came to rest on a group of people huddled in front of a whitewashed window. They were all watching him intently. He suddenly felt like an animal trapped in a zoo; the target of unwanted observations.

'Where the hell are we?'

One person broke from the group and advanced towards the bench. Their face came into focus and James saw that it was Will. He blinked several times, wondering if he was having a bad dream.

'Will?'

The remaining three figures also came towards him. Looking at them with aching eyes, James realised that he knew them too. Their bodies were faint as if they weren't really there at all.

'Rai, Arthur, Tala?' He rubbed his temples, trying to comprehend what was happening. 'Where are the others? Where are Dina, Oede and Kaedon?'

'We don't know,' Will replied steadily. 'We don't even

know where *we* are.'

James wondered if there was a chance they were still in the other world. Maybe the clock hadn't worked or maybe he was dreaming. Looking around at the street however, he realised this couldn't possibly be true. The whitewashed windows, the overflowing bins, the scrawny pigeons; these all belonged to his own world, to dreary old England. He realised now that the street was familiar. Leaning forward on the bench, he looked down to the far end where a sign swung uneasily above the last shop on the terrace.

'We're on Silver Street,' he said.

'Please tell me that's somewhere in the Gulna Mountains,' Will groaned.

Tala glared at him. 'Does this place look like the mountains to you?'

'We're not in the mountains,' James confirmed. 'We're in my world.'

His friends stared uncomprehendingly at him. No one spoke for a long time.

'How is that even possible?' Will asked at last.

'It's not.' James rose unsteadily to his feet. 'You're not really here.'

'It doesn't look like you're here either.' Aralia touched his arm. 'Your body is as faint as ours.'

For the first time since arriving here, James looked down at himself. His body was hazy at the edges, like he was a ghost in his own world. It was a sign of in betweenness, of not belonging.

'It's like we've been split between worlds,' he murmured. 'We're a reflection of our real bodies. It's the same way Albert looked in the airport and the black coated men at Victoria Station. The same way *she* looked in my father's office.'

'It's just not possible,' Arthur said. 'Maybe for you it is, but not for the rest of us.'

'The fact that we're even here suggests it is possible,' he countered. 'It's no use standing out here on the street debating it for hours when there are things we have to do.'

'What things?' Tala asked but James had already walked away.

The pigeons scattered as he went past but he hardly noticed for his sights were firmly set on the shop at the end of the street. He felt like a stranger in his own world, a shadow lingering where it didn't belong.

'James, where are we going?' Will hurried to catch up with him. 'This street is a dead end.'

James didn't answer immediately. He kept walking, only stopping when he'd reached the end of the street. The last shop in the terrace looked closed, with blinds drawn over the windows and clear signage on the door. James however knew better than to believe in appearances. He twisted the knob and the door opened with a satisfying click.

'How do these lights work if not by magic?'

Arthur's voice made him turned around. His friend was gesticulating at the fading streetlamps. James couldn't help smiling. It was novel to be the knowledgeable one standing on home turf.

'The lights run on electricity,' he offered. 'Most things here use electricity and data.'

'Data?' Tala asked.

Again James smiled. 'My phone, for example, uses data to function. Data can be dangerous. It can be tracked by the wrong kinds of people.' He withheld any further explanation and his friends did not press him.

Above his head, the shop's sign creaked in a light breeze.

The gold lettering looked as fresh as it had the first time he'd seen it.

'Count the Hours,' Aralia read aloud. 'This is the clock shop, isn't it?'

James pushed the shop door and it swung inward, accompanied by the rusty tinkle of an old fashioned bell. The room beyond was dark but the natural light spilling through the doorway cast a faint sheen over everything. As he stepped inside, James was struck by a wave of sound. Hundreds of analogue clocks all fighting to be heard. Cupping the little gold clock in his hands, he felt its rhythm slowing to match that of its brothers and sisters.

'I wondered when you would come back.'

A familiar voice crackled from the shadows. A light flickered on and a hunched silhouette appeared in the doorway behind the desk. The figure stepped into the light and James found himself looking at the clockmaker. The old man's face had not changed, the skin deeply wrinkled and the eyes bright and engaging.

'You should not be here,' he croaked. 'It is not safe.' He adjusted his thick glasses to see James better.

'I'm not really here.' James approached the desk and placed a hand on the worm eaten wood.

The old man did not take his eyes from James' face. 'You come as a shadow.'

He looked well, James thought, despite his scrape with death at Victoria Station not so many months ago. His eyes still glittered with a fierce intelligence and he stood without aid of a walking stick.

'It will take more than that to get rid of me,' the clockmaker continued. 'My old frame is a little more dented perhaps but I'm none the worse for it.'

James reddened, embarrassed that his thoughts had been so easily read. 'I wasn't sure what had happened to you.'

The clockmaker dismissed this expression of concern with a wave of his hand. 'You shouldn't be here,' he said, repeating his earlier warning. 'You are in danger. The time is coming.'

He spoke in such a way that James was unsure if the words were directed at himself or the room in general. He waited for the old man to speak again. The crackle of a radio in the background captured his attention. As the connection stabilised, a voice began speaking and he strained his ears to listen.

'Today is a sorry day indeed. Thousands of people across the country have fallen victim to unprecedented cyber-attacks. The attacks may seem random, occurring on public and private computers, but experts have reason to believe they were targeted.'

The radio crackled again and the voice changed.

'At four o'clock this morning, a series of attacks took place in four major cities across the country. There is speculation as to whether these attacks were linked or merely random occurrences. Investigations are being carried out. The victim count stands at twenty-five with several people in critical conditions in intensive care. One survivor described the situation as 'terrifying, like an invisible shadow swept in and…'

The voice suddenly stopped and James realised the clockmaker had switched off the radio. He was watching James closely, as if in expectation of a question. Seeing the look, James chose to remain silent. The last time he'd listened to this radio, the voices had been predicting the national power cut that had occurred just moments later. He couldn't help wondering if the attacks he'd just heard about had even happened yet. Either way, he knew the Belladonna had to be behind them. Her influence was growing stronger and time was running out.

'Some events come to pass, others do not,' the clockmaker said. 'It is not safe here. You must go.'

James didn't move. 'How is it that I'm not really here?' he asked. 'I come from this world. I'm not exactly a stranger.'

The old man peered at him over the rim of his glasses and sighed. 'Darkness rises. It seeps into the towns, villages and fields. Ordinary people are falling prey to it, even here, in the so called ordinary world. The barrier between worlds is thinning.'

Sylvia had spoken the same words. She had explained their meaning to him but he found himself asking the clockmaker for further clarification.

'What is the barrier exactly? How is it thinning?' He watched the old man carefully but the wrinkled face gave nothing away.

'As time stretches, the worlds drift apart,' the clockmaker said. 'The darkness seeks to prevent this from happening by drawing them closer again. The more time stretches, the harder it will become to pass between. There will come a day when perceptive time overtakes literal time.'

'What does that mean?' James asked. 'It has something to do with the clock, doesn't it?' he added hurriedly.

'It relates to how humans perceive time versus the idea that time isn't real. It is only humans who make it so by measuring it. Everything in this world is bound to time because that is the human way.'

'But the clock,' James pressed, 'it's somehow connected to all of this, isn't it?'

The clockmaker nodded. 'Two things I know. The clock

was made in a place of great power, in another world that goes by another name. Emryth. It is a finely crafted piece with complex mechanisms that contain traces of white quartz and diamond. This is how it keeps time in both worlds.'

'Diamond?' James frowned. 'Why diamond?'

'It is unusual I admit. Diamonds can, in the right circumstances, provide timekeeping signals. In a similar way, the precise frequency of quartz makes it an excellent timekeeper. Many of the clocks in this shop contain quartz but yours is the only piece with a diamond.' A sigh escaped his lips. 'The more time is meddled with, the weaker the barrier between worlds becomes and the greater the risk of the clock stopping for good.'

James swallowed. 'Stopping?'

While he had known for some time that it would become harder for him to pass between worlds, he hadn't realised that the clock would stop. Some small part of him had hoped that the timepiece would be able to transport him between worlds, even after the barrier had vanished.

'The clock is bound to its maker,' the old man said, 'but I sense that is why you are here.'

James nodded. 'There's a name on the clock. It wasn't there before. I think it belongs to the maker.'

He placed the clock on the desk. The old man eyed it hungrily but didn't pick it up. He simply looked at it, muttering to himself all the while. Eventually, he allowed himself to touch it. His old fingers ran gently over the gleaming metal. It was as if he was greeting a much loved pet after a long separation.

'I'd forgotten how beautiful it was.' He turned the piece over in his hands and his eyes found the tiny row of letters etched onto the base. 'The name of the maker of a piece like this only appears for one reason. Time is running out.'

'What time?' James tried unsuccessfully to mask the fear in his voice. 'All time?'

'The maker's of course. When the maker dies, the clock will stop once and for all.'

James frowned. 'But the clock already stopped. It wasn't working when I found it here.'

'In rare instances, and in the presence of great power, time can be *paused*. If the maker found a way to do such a thing, the clock would temporarily stop. It was made seven hundred years ago and the hands lay still for seven centuries until you made them start again. The maker of this piece is not immortal and will one day die. When the clock stops, you will no longer be able to pass between worlds.'

The old man's words drove a knife through James' chest. He was conscious of his friends lurking in the doorway behind him but the clockmaker had not acknowledged them, making James wonder if he could even see them.

As if responding to this thought, the old man glanced at the doorway. 'It would be wise to invite your friends inside,' he said gruffly. 'I see them just as I see you.'

They came at his invitation, trailing into the shop with wide eyed wonder. They looked at the old man as if he were an alien species, someone who lived an entirely different existence to their own. The clockmaker watched them carefully but his expression gave nothing away.

'How is it that you know of our world?' Will boldly asked. 'The world you referred to as Emryth.'

The clockmaker's face lit up with a smile. 'It is rare, I'll grant you, for someone from this world to know of Emryth. I am what is called a Time Keeper, someone who resides in this world but is aware of the other. I cannot enter it but I know of its presence. I am one of one hundred keepers across this earth. We have never met but together we watch for unusual happenings on this side of No Man's Land.'

'I never knew,' James said, surprised by his own lack of knowledge.

'You never asked.'

'What is your name?' Aralia stepped into the circle of light surrounding the ancient desk. 'We only know you as the clockmaker.'

James again felt embarrassed. This was another question he had never asked. The clockmaker had known who he was before he had ever entered this shop so no formal introduction had ever been made.

'I've had many names. I was born Kai but I prefer Orion. A little flamboyant perhaps, but when you've been around for as long as I have you don't mind that.' His eyes wandered back to James and his smile faded. 'I cannot read the name.' He placed the clock back on the desk. 'It is written in symbols rather than letters. The man who brought it here, not long after it had been made, never told me the name of its maker. He simply wished for the clock to be kept safe here. I did not know its significance then.'

James had often wondered whether he was meant to find the clock or whether he had stumbled across it by chance. A sudden realisation dawned on him. If Arvad really had crossed between worlds, perhaps he had once possessed this very timepiece. He must have been the one to transport the clock between the worlds after it was made. Perhaps he had chosen to stay in *this* world to protect the clock from the darkness. Centuries after his death, someone must have found the clock and brought it here, to the shop on Silver Street. Whether this stranger had understood the true significance of the timepiece he would probably never know.

If all this had happened, it was possible to believe that the talisman and the earthstone really were hidden in this world as the Belladonna had said. He shuddered to think of her. She had persuaded him to turn the clock dials and in doing so, he had exposed his world. She had asked him to show her the way and he had obliged. His desire to know if the earthstone and the gift really were hidden in this world had overtaken all other sense. Once the darkness had passage between the worlds, the crystals would have little power to stop them.

Breaking from his thoughts, James looked across the desk at the clockmaker. The old man was watching him closely but he did not try to speak. James felt a thread of fear knotting in his stomach. A sudden, deep seated fear of the unknown.

# Chapter 25

THE clockmaker did not speak again for a long time. He simply stood gazing at the clock in James' hands as though he longed to hold it again himself. His lips occasionally moved but he spoke no words aloud. At long last, he dragged his eyes away from the clock and gave voice to his murmurings.

'The man who brought me the clock told me of a place in the southern regions of Emryth. A place where there is a tower that stretches to the stars. You must take the clock to this tower to find out its truth.'

'You were alive then,' Arthur said, 'seven hundred years ago?'

The clockmaker looked at him thoughtfully. 'You could say that. I am of this generation but others have passed before me and I am of their blood. I have their memories, as if it was I that was there all those years ago. It is the way of the Time Keepers. We only die when our task is done.'

'And yours will be done when the clock stops ticking,' Aralia murmured.

'I suppose it will. There are those who seek to end my life but they cannot do so until my task is complete. Not even Shadows.' He glanced at James, his eyes recalling the attempted assassination at Victoria Station.

A sound outside the shop startled them all. The clockmaker hurried to dim the light. He glanced nervously at the door, as if expecting someone to burst in.

'You must go,' he urged for the third time. 'There are those in both worlds who would seek to find you here. People whose hearts have turned black though they might not know it with their conscious minds.'

James stood firm. 'I have just one more question and then I promise we'll go. Did the man who brought the clock here say where he had found it?'

The old man's eyes narrowed. 'What makes you think he found it? It is my understanding that he was given it. Why do you ask?'

'Because I believe that this clock once belonged to Arvad the Wanderer.' He didn't know if the old man would know Arvad's name but he had to try it.

'To my knowledge, Arvad never came to this world,' the clockmaker replied without hesitation. 'I know his name from legend and nothing more. He never came to this world. Time Keepers across this world have never recorded such an occurrence.'

James blinked at the old man in disbelief. 'That's not possible. He must have come here. She said he did.'

'It was only a rumour, James,' Aralia reminded. 'Eir didn't know if it was true.'

'No, not Eir. The Belladonna.'

At the mention of her name, the clockmaker banged his fist upon the desk, making them all jump. James had never seen his calm demeanour break before.

'The darkness wants only one thing, James Fynch, and that is the ability to pass between worlds. Evil only imagines evil. Arvad never came here. The crystals and the gifts spoken of in the myths do not exist on this earth at least.'

A sinking feeling settled itself in James' stomach. He knew

that the Belladonna had been manipulating him but he desperately wanted to believe that Arvad had hidden the earthstone in this world, a world whose name contained the element the crystal was born from.

'Return to Emryth and finish your quest,' the clockmaker murmured. 'It is the only way to save us all.'

Stepping out from behind the desk, he began ushering them towards the door. His feet shuffled over the floorboards, clearing a trail of dust behind them. The bell tinkled again as he opened the door and waved the companions out onto the street. Last to leave, James turned back one final time.

'Thank you for helping us. Thank you for everything.'

'Be careful, James Fynch,' came the reply and the shop door swung shut.

Morning had broken over Silver Street. The streetlamps had faded altogether and the sun had risen, gilding the peaked roofs of the buildings. Though the air was warm, a light breeze pushed clusters of clouds across the sky. James turned to his friends whose ghostly eyes were fixed upon him with a mixture of expectation and awe.

'We should go,' he said.

Part of him longed to stay here, to take a train to Kent and visit his house on Greenwood Avenue. It always looked lovely in the summer, full of flowers planted by a neighbour, Mrs Grits, some years ago. He had never given the flowers any thought but thinking about the house now, the garden belonged in his mental image. At this time in the morning, his parents would be just setting off for work. For a mad second, he wondered if he could turn up at the office and surprise them, but deep down he knew this could never happen.

'James, come on,' Will's voice interrupted his thoughts.

'We should go. You said it yourself.'

James nodded. 'It's hard leaving when I don't know if I'll ever be able to come back again. My parents…'

Aralia took his arm. 'You will be back,' she reassured. 'You will. Now let's go. There's nothing for us here and it's time we returned to Dina, Kaedon and Oede.'

James turned his back to the shop. The journey here had not been entirely wasted; he knew that. If they hadn't come here, they might not have learnt about the diamond inside the clock, the star tower or the Time Keepers. He was glad to have seen the clockmaker but as he turned away from the shop, he felt sure that he'd seen the old man for the last time.

'Hold on to me,' he said aloud to his friends. 'Don't let go.'

Will, Arthur, Tala and Aralia all grabbed hold of him. He turned the clock dials full circle until they pointed to eleven fifty. Silver Street and the clock shop faded from view and everything went dark. It stayed dark for a long time. James was no longer sure whether his friends were holding onto him or not. The air was unusually cold, like there was a frost. His limbs were numb and all he could feel was his heart beating against his chest. He floated easily through the continuum of space and time, unthinking and unfeeling as his body was woven into the fabric of the universe itself.

'James!'

He thought he heard his name being called. It sounded far away and he wondered if he'd simply imagined it. Then it came again and he realised that he had stopped moving. Opening his eyes, he saw that he was sitting on a swathe of silvery grass. A white mist swirled around him, engulfing him in its hazy depths.

'James!'

Hearing his name a third time, he looked over his shoulder. Aralia was standing behind him, her body wrapped in the same ghostly shroud.

'Where are we?' Another voice spoke. From amongst the swirling cloud, a familiar figure appeared.

'Dina!' James exclaimed. He jumped to his feet and hurried towards her but she held up a hand to stop him.

'Where are we?' she repeated.

Kaedon and Oede appeared behind her. They too looked hazy; ghosts like everyone else.

'What are you doing here?' James asked. 'You weren't with us before. Where did you just come from?'

'With you *where*?' Dina asked. Her sharp eyes bored right through him.

'No Man's Land,' James said. 'That's where we are now, I mean.'

'No Man's Land!' Kaedon exclaimed.

'The place between worlds.' Will appeared at James' side. 'What are we doing here?' he asked and the certainty in his voice vanished.

James closed his eyes, trying to still his thoughts. 'Why *are* we here?' he asked the air. 'Why No Man's Land?' Opening his eyes again, he looked directly at Will. 'I haven't been here since the first time I crossed between worlds.'

'Some people can't go beyond No Man's Land,' Tala said suddenly and everyone turned to look at her in surprise. 'Albert told me that some people are unable to cross between worlds,' she continued, 'even if there was a way.'

'What does that mean exactly?' Will asked.

Tala sighed. 'It means that certain people don't have the right composition of elements in their body to make such a transition.' She glanced at Dina, Kaedon and Oede. 'This is more common in adults than in children.'

Dina looked mildly put out. 'It seems unlikely that Kaedon, Oede and I should all suffer from this biological failing.'

'None of you should be here, regardless of biological make-up,' James stated. 'I don't understand how this has happened.'

'James, we need *you* to stay calm.' Aralia put her hands together as if in prayer. 'You're the only one who has been here before.'

James wasn't sure if he was imagining it, but there were shapes moving about in the mist. He'd seen these shapes before when he'd stood here with Albert. There were no cries or screams this time but he was sure the spirit folk of No Man's Land were watching them.

'We have to find the mirror,' he announced, finally coming to his senses. 'Before *they* find us.'

'*They?*' Oede raised his eyebrows questioningly.

'I'm not exactly sure what they are. The spirits or souls of those who get trapped here. Centuries of people who have tried and failed to cross between worlds.' He glanced anxiously around him. In the mist, the passing spirits looked like cloud shadows racing across fields on a summer's day.

'You're going to have to stop for a moment and explain what in the world you're talking about!' Dina said sharply.

James looked down at his ghostly feet. 'No Man's Land is an in-between place. Those who try to cross between worlds can become trapped here.' Dina opened her mouth to ask another question but he cut her off. 'We don't have time to talk here. I'll explain the rest later, I promise.'

He turned and walked away. He had no idea where he was going but had little choice but to walk somewhere. Albert had guided him through the mist the first time but there was no way to recognise anything in this mist. He tried closing his eyes, hoping he might see the route ahead in his mind's eye but there was nothing.

'D'you actually know where you're going?' Will hurried to catch up with him. 'Where is this mirror?'

James didn't stop walking. 'Albert guided me before.'

'What if we're trapped here?' Aralia asked anxiously. 'What if we stayed too long in your world and we can't get back? I don't know if any of you have noticed, but our bodies are even fainter than before.'

'We can't be trapped here,' James stated firmly. 'We just need to find the mirror.'

'What if we are?' Will joined Aralia's line of questioning. 'Maybe we meddled with time for too long. Apart from you, none of us are meant to cross between worlds. It shouldn't even be possible.'

'You heard what the clockmaker said,' Arthur added. '"The more time is meddled with, the weaker the barrier between worlds becomes". Maybe we're weakening too.'

James shivered. He thought it was in response to Arthur's words but he then felt something move behind him. It did not feel like a living presence but nor was it a ghost. A light breeze ruffled the edges of his cloak and he held still, not daring to turn around. He saw Will's face change and his eyes fixate on something just beyond his left shoulder.

'What is it?' He tried to sound calm. 'What's there?'

An unfamiliar voice answered him. It echoed around him as if he was standing in a vaulted room rather than outside.

'You come at last,' it whispered. 'The leader, the healer, the warrior and the wise. I welcome you to No Man's Land, to the realm between the worlds.'

'Who's there?' James gulped.

'You know me but we have never met,' the voice returned. 'Look at me and you will see.'

Slowly, James turned around. There was nothing behind him but the swirling mist.

'Show yourself,' he demanded.

The hazy outline of a human figure appeared in the mist. He stared at it for several seconds before realising that it was himself. Not his usual self but a shadow, a gaunt and ghostly form with wide, horrified eyes.

'You see what you are and what you will become,' the voice whispered. 'Many others have seen the same in themselves and gone mad because of it.'

'What d'you mean?' James stepped towards his shadowy self. 'Are we trapped here?'

Aralia came to stand beside him. 'Is this our fate?' she asked quietly. 'Are we going to die here?'

There was a long pause before the voice came again. 'That is for you to decide. You bear great strength, little sister. You all do.'

'Sister?' Aralia spun around. 'Who are you? Show yourself!'

'I already am.'

The voice stopped speaking and a new shape appeared in the mist before them. At first, it looked like a woman but the edges then hardened to become the frame of a mirror. Behind the polished glass, a silver lake stretched on into the limitless distances of No Man's Land.

# Chapter 26

'MY name is Asterope.' The voice sounded stronger now but still the speaker did not reveal herself. 'I see amongst you three of my sisters. Your spirits live within me, just as mine lives within each of you.'

'Asterope's Glass,' James said with sudden clarity. 'This mirror is Asterope's Glass from the legend of the Seven Sisters.'

'Long ago, I stood before this glass on my wedding morning,' the voice replied. 'I was beautiful then.' A sad sigh drifted from behind the mirror.

'What are you doing in No Man's Land?' Will asked. 'You're from our world, aren't you?'

'This is where I am bound. Like each of my sisters, I have a task to fulfil. I am not a ghost like them but the shade of a shadow.'

'Please, tell us what that means?' Oede came forward, his hands clasped across his chest in a gesture of peace.

'I am simply a reflection of what I once was. This glass was my betrothal gift, given to me the night before my wedding.'

James stepped up to the mirror, taking care not to look too closely at the reflection as Albert had once warned him. He thought he saw her from the corner of his eye, a ghostly form imprisoned within the glass.

'I knew one day you would come,' she murmured. 'He said you would.'

'*He?*' James felt his heart skip a beat.

'Arvad of course. My beloved Arvad.'

'Your beloved?' Dina tried and failed to conceal her surprise. 'Then he was the one you were going to marry.'

'Yes, I was betrothed to him. Only the night before our wedding our lives changed. He wished to cross between the worlds and take me with him to begin a new life. Only there were forces working against us and so we became caught here, in the land between. When Arvad died, his spirit returned home but my fate was to exist here as a reflection of my former self.'

James stared at the mirror in disbelief. There were so many questions to ask and so little time. 'How did Arvad know we would come?' he asked at last. 'He didn't know who would fulfil his quest. He didn't know they would be able to pass between worlds.'

'He knew there would be four, not one. Four gifts, four stones, four companions.'

'I've been here before,' James said. 'I didn't see you then.'

'It was not the time. All four of you needed to be here together and in a state of vulnerability, as you are now. You have dwelled too long in another realm and your bodies are becoming part of the in-between. Only when such an event occurs can the mirror's true purpose be revealed. Just remember, the longer you stay, the harder it will be to leave.'

James remembered Celaeno, Asterope's sister, offering a similar warning in Lover's Wood. 'We should go, then,' he concluded.

'Farewell,' Asterope whispered. 'I wish you safe passage back to the other realm.' There was a long silence but then her voice came again. 'What you seek is right before you. Just remember, all gifts come at a price.'

Looking into the mirror, James saw that the shadowy form had now vanished. 'What we seek is right before us,' he murmured aloud.

'What did she mean by that?' Dina asked.

James shrugged. 'I have no idea.'

Brushing past him, Aralia looked up at the mirror. She did not gaze into the glass but fixed her eyes upon the frame. 'It seems we came here for a reason after all,' she said quietly. 'Look.'

James raised his eyes to the gilded frame. Right in the centre, hidden amongst the intricately carved flowers and leaves, was a gem. Though the light in No Man's Land was dim, the stone glittered with flecks of yellow and gold.

'Is that what I think it is?' Will's voice shattered the stunned silence.

James couldn't tear his eyes away from the gem. It looked just like the drawing in the temple, only here it was gleaming and solid. He reached up to touch it. The surface was cold and smooth and sent a tingling sensation through his fingers. As the drawing had also shown, the middle section was engraved with an upside down triangle shot through with a line.

'The symbol for earth,' he murmured. '*This* is where Arvad left the gift. *This* is the talisman.'

'Why here?' Aralia queried. 'Why No Man's Land?'

'It all makes sense,' James continued. 'In bringing the talisman here, Arvad was protecting it from those who could not cross into this realm. If Arvad died here, as Asterope said, then it must have been the last gift in his possession before he died.'

'How do we release it?' Kaedon asked, bringing the conversation back to the task in hand.

'We have to look into the mirror.'

To do so was dangerous but James had a feeling that this was the only way to release the talisman. Asterope had said that only in a state of vulnerability would the true purpose of the mirror be revealed. If they looked into the mirror, they would all be in their most vulnerable state. He lowered his gaze to the glass and gazed into its depths. He sensed his friends gathering around him but he could not see them in the reflection. There was nothing behind him but swirling mist.

'Grab on to me,' he commanded. 'Hold on and don't let go.'

The reflection began to change. A shape appeared in the mist. It was not a human figure but the insubstantial form of a ghost. James gasped but his breath carried no sound. The spirit stared back at him for a moment before it opened its mouth and uttered a piercing scream. The air felt suddenly colder. James felt the hairs on the back of his neck prickling but didn't dare turn around. Glancing down at his body, he saw that it had completely disappeared.

'Will?' he whispered. 'Rai? Art? Are you there?'

He could no longer feel them holding onto him. Taking a deep breath, he slowly turned around. There was no one there. Not even the wailing ghost. He called out to his friends again but no one answered. Turning back to the mirror, he saw that the reflection had changed again. Within its depths, he could now see the distorted faces of his friends.

'Hey, what're you doing?' he called. 'Come back.'

The image vanished. He noticed that the mirror too was fading. The frame had become hazy and the glass rippled like liquid silver. He knew what he had to do. Closing his eyes, he pressed a hand against the molten glass and stepped into the mirror. Behind him, there came the sound of glass shattering.

'Another vestige of the boundary between worlds dies,' Asterope's voice whispered.

James turned back to the mirror. In a shower of shards, he saw the talisman falling. He reached out to catch it but the smooth gem slipped through his fingers and was lost. He knelt on the grass, searching desperately for it, but it was nowhere to be found. Even though it was cold, sweat pearled on his forehead. He knew he needed to leave this place but when he reached into his pocket for the clock, it was not there. His invisible fingers met with nothing but air. Trying not to panic, he sat back on his heels and looked into the mist. There was nothing for him to do, he realised, but wait for something to happen.

'Your friends are here.'

A voice startled him. It sounded close to his ear but was so faint he could hardly hear it.

'Who's there?' he asked. 'Show yourself.'

The mist parted and a figure appeared, dressed in a flowing white robe. James had only to glance at their face to know who it was.

'Sylvia!' He leapt to his feet and stood staring at her in disbelief.

She smiled and came towards him. 'James Fynch.' She stopped just in front of him and her cloak brushed against his hand.

'You seem real,' he observed with surprise, 'like you're actually here.'

'That is because I am,' she replied, 'though my body is no longer flesh and blood.'

'How is it that I can see your body but none of my own?' James asked.

'Your body is fading because you are no longer in the physical world. As your physical form ebbs away, so does your life.'

'Is that not the same for you?'

Her smile vanished. 'The ghosts of No Man's Land are the spirits of those who tried and failed to pass between worlds. I never chose to come.'

'Then why are you here?'

'I was sent here by those who wished to prevent me from fulfilling my role. A role that now belongs to you.'

'Arvad's quest,' James murmured. 'Our fates became twisted but I'm still not sure how.'

'Well you see, the same moment I entered No Man's Land, you did too.'

'When I was here with Albert, you mean?'

'Yes. In that moment, our lives and our fates entwined.'

'I don't understand. I dreamt of the Belladonna as a child. I found the clock. These things happened before I entered No Man's Land. I didn't even know about the other world.'

'There are many paths a person may take during their lifetime. Your potential to pass between worlds was always there but you had to choose to take that path. Imagine if your parents had not invited you on holiday or if the power cut hadn't happened or if you'd never found the clock shop. Your life would have been different.'

James nodded but was still not sure he really understood. 'Would yours have been different too? Are you trapped here because of me?'

'It is up to us to choose what path we wish to take but sometimes fate, or whatever you choose to call it, has other ideas. We can't be in control of everything but we can choose how to react.'

James frowned again. 'I'm not sure I understand.'

'I am not here because of you. The course of my life had already changed.'

James nodded and looked around at the thickening mist. 'My friends,' he began. 'You said they were here.'

Sylvia smiled. 'They stand on the other side of the Silver Lake.'

'How do I reach them?'

'You must now make a choice. You must decide which world you wish to belong in. Your friends know where they belong but you are not yet certain.'

James swallowed nervously. 'What happens when I choose?'

'I think you already know the answer, just as you know which choice is the right one to make.'

Already she was beginning to fade. James reached out to stop her but she slipped through his ghostly hands. As the mist began to close over her, she held out her hand to him. There on her palm rested the amber talisman.

'Take it,' she commanded. 'There is still time for you to leave this place and finish what you started.'

He reached out to her again. His fingers touched her palm and closed around the gem. As soon as the talisman was in his hands, Sylvia vanished altogether. James stood alone in the gloomy light, clutching the gift with both hands. He knew what he had to do but couldn't quite bring himself to act upon it. He thought of his parents, his friends and all the people he'd known and cared for in his own world. People he might never see or speak to again. Afraid as he was, he knew there was only one choice. He closed his eyes and the ground gave way beneath him. He was falling for a long time before his feet met the ground again and he opened his eyes.

'James!'

He sat up. His head was spinning, like he'd just stepped off a roller coaster. Something sharp pricked his eyebrow and reaching up, he felt a piece of glass wedged into his skin. He pulled it out and a drop of blood ran down the side of his nose. A reminder that he was flesh and blood after all. As the world settled around him, he rose to his feet. He had expected to see the Gulna Mountains rising around him but instead found himself standing on a rocky plateau shrouded in mist.

'James!'

He turned around. Will was behind him, his arms folded across his chest and his eyes wide with fear. For a moment, neither of them spoke.

'The mirror broke,' James then said.

'James, we're still in No Man's Land,' Will stated firmly. 'Why?'

'We can't be here,' Dina moaned. 'We must return to the mountains. We have to find Dara.'

James shook his head. 'No... no... we can't still be here.' He moved his hand and realised he was holding something.

'What's in your hand?' Will asked.

James opened his fingers. There on his palm was the talisman. Glittering, beautiful, a sign of hope. A golden gem set within a metal oval. In this light, the stone looked different. Dark swirls moved across the surface like clouds in an evening sky. Right in the centre was a black fleck, imprisoned within the ancient resin.

'How did you get it?' Aralia appeared at his side, closely followed by Arthur, Tala, Dina, Kaedon and Oede.

James handed the talisman to her. 'I found it in my hand.' He knew this was a half truth but he didn't want to tell them about his encounter with Sylvia, not for now at least.

'What's that black spot in the middle of the gem?' Arthur asked.

'It looks like a seed,' Dina observed. 'See how the edges curve around.'

'A seed from the Silver Tree,' Oede murmured, 'preserved for centuries inside this talisman. It is the way of nature to ensure the protection of its own species.'

'Of course!' James exclaimed. 'The preservation of the seed is what makes the tree's life eternal. In returning the seed to the site where the tree once stood, we will be releasing it from its eternal curse.' He took the talisman back from Aralia and held it up to the light. 'In return for this gift, we will receive the earthstone.'

'We must return to the Gulna Mountains,' Kaedon said. 'From there, we can find our way to the amber forests.'

James looked around at the misty landscape. 'There must be a reason why we're still in No Man's Land.'

The rocky terrain seemed out of place in this realm. He walked a little way ahead of their group to where the rocks dipped into a shallow basin. Standing on the rim of this basin, he found himself looking out over a changed scene. A plateau filled with trees stretched out before him; a dense forest of trunks and leafless limbs beneath a cream coloured sky. All were black, as if charred by fire. Each tree was spaced at an even distance from the next, making the forest look like the manicured setting of some horror film.

'It can't be,' he whispered to himself.

The forest looked just like the murals painted on the walls of the dryad dwelling. Only here the trees were dead and no dryads walked between the needled branches. The forest lay empty, a graveyard of blackened trunks inhabited only by ghosts.

# Chapter 27

THE scent of burning still lingered in the blackened forest. James felt the air moving as he walked between the lifeless trees, as if with the ghost of former flames. There was a sadness here too, the kind that clung to abandoned places.

'This isn't real,' Kaedon muttered, touching a tree stump to test its truth. 'It can't be.'

James ran his fingers along a blackened branch. It felt cold, like it was carved from stone. He'd heard of petrified wood but was sure the process took thousands of years. As far as he knew, this forest was not old enough for such an occurrence.

'It feels real,' he said aloud, 'even if we are still in No Man's Land.' He stopped between two trees that bent towards each other, forming an archway between their charred branches. 'Maybe places, like people, can become trapped here.'

Above the forest, the sky had taken on a yellow tinge. Sulphuric clouds scudded past and chased away the lingering trails of mist.

'The sky is darkening,' Oede observed. 'Something is changing.'

'It's the forest,' Tala suddenly said. 'Look. The roots are moving.'

Between the trees, the blackened roots had begun to writhe like angry snakes. They were not just twisting and turning but growing too, fattening by the second and blocking off the natural paths through the forest. Where one root came across another, the two twisted together in a strange mating dance.

'We should turn back.' Kaedon spun around full circle. 'We should go back to the rocks.'

'We can't!' Dina grabbed his arm. 'The roots are growing too quickly.'

'Then we climb over them.' Kaedon broke away from her and cleared the first knotted barrier in a single leap.

James looked from one side of the forest to the other. To his right, the rocks they had recently left behind lay dark under the thickening sky. To his left, a glimmer of light shone between the clouds and fell upon a swathe of grass.

'We shouldn't go back,' he called after his retreating friends. 'We should keep going.'

A shadow swept over the ground where he stood and he looked up. The branches above him were no longer stunted and bare. Silvery foliage sprang from every outstretched limb, gradually blocking out the light. Even though the air was still, the trees swayed of their own accord.

'James, come on!' Will paused between two knotted barriers and turned back to James. 'What're you doing still standing there?'

'We have to keep moving forward,' James shouted back. 'You're going the wrong way.' Some inexplicable instinct drove him to say this though he did not know why he wished to go in one direction rather than the other.

Will shrugged and turned back to his path only to find the way was blocked. Kaedon, Dina, Oede, Tala, Aralia and Arthur also stopped, their paths similarly cut off. They all turned back to James who stood facing the only remaining route.

'Head for the light,' Kaedon instructed. 'It's our only hope.'

The light at the edge of the forest became smaller with every step they took. After a short while, it disappeared altogether and an impenetrable darkness descended. A new light then flickered into being, held aloft by Oede.

'We must hurry,' he urged. 'We must run.'

They began to run, tripping over the roots which sought to hinder them. Someone cried out and turning, James saw Tala had fallen into a network of seething roots. Will was by her side in an instant, dragging her free from the coils that sought to choke her. Then they were running again, heading in what they hoped was the right direction.

'Stop!' Dina's voice suddenly rang through the silence. She stood stock still between two trees, her eyes fixed on something no one else could see.

'What is it?' James hissed. 'What can you see?'

She did not answer and simply pointed ahead of her. Something was moving just beyond the circle of light. A pale shape flitting through the trees like a ghost. The tangled roots were no obstacle to this insubstantial being and it darted through the forest with ease and grace.

'What is it?' James repeated. 'Does anyone know?'

'They are Lau,' Aralia answered. 'I've heard about them from folklore. They're keepers of the dryad forests. The tree spirits themselves. Each dryad is connected to a single tree. They are tasked to protect it for the rest of their lives. Dryads can speak to all trees. They can hear their whispers.'

'Do you have a tree?' Will asked.

Aralia shrugged. 'I don't know. I am half human so the rules are a little different for me, and for Art. The Lau aren't usually dangerous but these ones have been hurt. Try to stay calm. We must show them that we don't mean to harm them.'

She began walking again and everyone followed. The Lau slipped through the trees around them, absorbed in its own perpetual motion. Looking ahead through the gloom, James thought he saw light again. A tiny circle of daylight gleaming through the trees.

'Light ahead,' he announced and began to run.

This time the light did not vanish. The circle grew larger and larger until eventually it consumed everything. The forest came to an end and he burst out onto an open landscape. Here the ground was grassy and bathed in misty light. A weak sun hung behind the haze, offering only a little warmth. The air tasted fresh after the stagnancy of the forest and James breathed in great lungfuls of it.

'The ground is soft.' Kaedon materialised at his side. 'This must be marshland.' He pressed his feet into the grass and water seeped out around his shoes.

It was a different kind of marshland to the one where the Cutters lived. Here the ground was wetter and milky streams ran between grassy paths. Though the landscape itself was flat, thousands of tree stumps lay scattered across it creating an uneven effect. Many of the stumps were so worn away that they didn't even look like trees anymore but ashy coloured stones. The landscape felt prehistoric; a place that carried the secrets of a long forgotten past.

'Are we meant to cross these marshes?' Tala asked. 'What if the trees start to grow here too?'

'We have to move forward,' James answered. 'We can't exactly go back.'

He stepped onto a path between two streams. The grass

was spongy but did not give way beneath him. He walked slowly, testing each section as he went. His friends followed him silently, taking care to tread where he had already been. They crossed onto a second path and then a third and a fourth, heading deeper into the marshes. The forest faded away behind them; a nightmare shrouded in mist.

Pausing between two paths, James thought he saw a watery light on the landscape ahead. When he looked again, it was gone. It was with a sinking feeling that he found himself wondering if they had come full circle and were back by the shores of the Silver Lake.

'Does anyone else see water ahead?'

Glancing over his shoulder, he saw that his friends had joined another path which ran in the opposite direction to the one he was still on. Puzzled, he called out to them but no one turned around. He looked for the start of the path they were on but it was nowhere to be found. He chose another path but when he reached the end of it, he was further away than before. The shimmering light caught his attention again. Wondering if he could reach this instead, he began hurrying towards it.

The path he chose seemed to lead straight there but again, when he came to the end of it, he was further away than before. Now a path to his right looked like the better choice so he crossed onto it. For a third time, however, he found himself no closer to the lake than he had previously been. The grassy paths formed an impossible maze across the marshy landscape. He knew that if he could find the centre point, he could map the route backwards. Only there was no centre, just miles upon miles of grass and stubby tree trunks.

He began to walk away from the water. Glancing over his shoulder, he saw that the shimmering light was now closer.

Puzzled, he continued to walk forwards with frequent checks over his shoulder. The further away from the water he went, the closer it came. He was reminded of the seas surrounding the Isle of Opoc – home to Arvora. There, the only way to reach the shore had been to ignore all instinct and give in to the pull of the tide. Here, the illusion worked in the opposite way. He had to resist his directional instinct to reach his destination.

'Turn around,' he shouted to his friends. 'It's an illusion.'

He did not know if they could see the lake or not. They had passed into a place where he could not follow and he wondered if this was part of the illusion. Not knowing what else to do, he began to run, focusing all his attention on the shimmering water. He did not know why he desired to reach it but his instinct told him that was where he must go. He ran for a long time, dodging between the milky streams until his breath became ragged and a stitch gripped his side. Still, he pushed on, intent upon reaching the lake.

Suddenly, his feet struck harder ground and he stopped running. Looking down, he saw that he was standing on a strip of compacted sand. The landscape was completely flat, as if ironed by a tide, only the sand was completely dry. Freed from its misty prison, the sun glared down upon this desolate terrain. This dazzling light made the sand ripple with a watery mirage.

'We can't still be in No Man's Land,' James murmured to himself. 'This isn't real.'

Looking to his left, he noticed a shape rising from the sand. Stepping towards it, he saw it was a tree, its bark so pale that it was almost invisible against the white hot landscape. It stood alone on the sand without so much as a shadow to keep it company. The longer James looked at this tree, the more solid it became. From far away, it had looked like a sapling but up close, the trunk looked old and scarred. It was covered with sap filled blisters and the bark was grey and cracked. It looked like the tree was dying and had been for a long time. Under the bright sunlight however, the trunk and branches gleamed like silver.

'It can't be,' James said aloud.

He had expected the Silver Tree to be harder to find. Yet here it stood, proudly different from the calcified stumps scattered across the marshes. He reached out to touch the sickly bark. It flaked away beneath his fingers and left ashy marks behind. He placed both hands upon the trunk. His fingers tingled as if touched by a faint electric spark. This feeling spread to his arms and his chest and right down to his toes. An ancient power lingered here, one bound by eternity. He could feel it everywhere, even in the sun beating down from above.

He closed his eyes. Images danced across his inner vision. There was a girl dressed in white planting a seed in the folds of the earth. The seed sprouted into a sapling with white bark and sap the colour of silver.

The vision changed. The same girl stood gathering resin from the white tree. A circle of dryads stood around her, holding glowing orbs. She knelt by the tree, cupping the collected resin in both hands. There was a bright flash. The girl burst into flame and crumpled to the ground, lifeless. In her hands, the white sap turned the colour of amber. The dryads took the gem from her and vanished, leaving the body to deteriorate amongst the elements. As time passed, the tree grew old and died, but where the girl's body had been, a new shoot appeared.

Again, the vision changed. James saw the garden of the

Minha Mound where a green robed man stood apart from the temple Brothers. In his hand rested the amber talisman. Kneeling on the earth, he pressed the piece into the soft soil. Where it lay, a tree began to grow. Not white limbed but fresh and green. Watching this scene unfold, James realised that the man in green was Arvad.

Just as quickly as it had come, the vision faded and James opened his eyes. He knew now what he had to do. Taking the talisman from his pocket, he knelt beneath the tree. The object tingled with anticipation and he laid it upon the sand. Placing a finger on the gem, he pressed the piece downwards. Almost immediately, the ground began to shift and change. The metal surrounding the gem glowed hot and seared a deep channel in the sand. The amber melted like butter and flowed through the channel towards the tree. It climbed over the ashy roots and up the trunk, turning the bark gold.

All at once, a mighty crack split the air and the tree burst into flame. A rush of heat flung James backward and he fell onto the sand. The air danced with fire and he watched through slitted eyes as the Silver Tree burned.

## Chapter 28

FLAMES darted over the sand and licked at the edges of James' cloak. He watched, mesmerised, as the Silver Tree was consumed by fire. The branches crackled and hissed and ash fell like snow onto the sand. Soon nothing but a charred stump remained but still the fire burned. It devoured the trunk like some hungry animal and only when it was finished did it finally die out.

As the flames faded, James sat up and wiped the sweat from his face. He crawled towards the ashy pile on the sand but stopped when he saw something moving beneath it. He held his breath as whatever it was began pushing its way to the surface. When it broke through at last, he saw it was the tip of a new shoot. It was so fragile that it trembled even though there was no wind. The shoot did not stop here. It continued to grow, thickening at the waist and sprouting new leaves until it was the size of a small sapling. Still it grew, larger and larger until a small tree stood on the sand once more. The bark was no longer diseased and the branches gleamed silver.

'The living turns to ash and from the flames will be reborn.'

A voice startled him and he rolled over on the sand. Oede stood above him, with Dina, Kaedon, Arthur, Aralia, Tala and Will just behind. James leapt to his feet but found himself unable to speak.

'The seed has brought new life,' Aralia whispered, 'just as we thought it might.'

Another crack split the air. Turning back to the tree, James saw a great crack had formed down the centre of the trunk. From this split, a spring of water burst forth. It cooled the burning sand and filled the air with steam. The water found its way into the channel the talisman had left in the sand and flowed out towards the marshes. Everything the water touched turned pure white. First the sand, then the grass and the milky streams. From the petrified stumps, new life began to spring.

'With the return of the gift, the tree is no longer bound to Arvad's eternal curse,' James said, finding his voice at last.

'Phoenix tears,' Aralia murmured. 'The liquified amber is healing the forest. Like the phoenix, the forest and the Silver Tree ended in fire but from the flames and ash are now reborn.'

'Look,' Dina interrupted. 'Look at the trunk.'

Inside the split trunk, a small object now glittered. James reached inside the gap and closed his fingers around it. It felt cold and smooth in his hand and he drew it out into the light. As he did so, the split wood began to heal. The trunk sealed itself back together as if it had never been open at all. Turning to face his friends, James opened his hand. There on his palm rested a golden yellow crystal. The colour was rich but the surface was misted like ancient sea glass. He held the gem up to the light. It was not as heavy as the ruby and the sapphire had been and unlike them, was completely smooth. Deep in the centre, threads of resin spread outwards like veins to form the outline of a tree.

'Born from earth, fire, air and water,' he murmured, 'just

like the firestone and the seastone. The elements have set the earthstone free and in doing so have lifted Arvad's curse.'

He felt the gem's power coursing through him. It was an ancient power, like that which had pulsed around him when the dragon egg had been broken and when he had held the seastone on the island over Celaeno's lake. This magic was bound to the earth itself, wrapped up in the greater powers that existed beyond the physical world.

'We should not linger here.' Oede's voice broke the silence. 'We may admire the gem all we wish when we are safe.'

James reluctantly closed his palm over the stone before slipping it into his pocket. His fingers brushed against the cold surround of the clock and he drew it out in relief.

'Take hold of me,' he instructed. 'This time, we really are going home.'

He closed his eyes and filled his mind with images of Arissel. The sun cooled on his face and he felt the ground give way beneath him. Then he was falling, on and on until at last his feet struck solid ground again. The impact of this landing threw him to the ground where he lay winded for several minutes before daring to open his eyes.

The sky above him was a hazy blue, suggesting it was twilight. There was no mist and stars pricked through a clear atmosphere. The air was cool and fresh and he breathed in deeply before sitting up. He had hoped to see the cobbled grey streets of Arissel stretching out before him. Instead, he saw he was sitting upon a rocky outcrop of land overlooking the sea. The water was calm and grey and no boats rode the listless waves.

Twisting around, he saw Will, Arthur and Tala clambering to their feet behind him. A little further along the rocks,

Dina, Aralia and Kaedon sat huddled together. Something lay on the ground between them – someone. Heart leaping into his mouth, James stood up and hurried towards them. As he drew closer, he saw that it was Oede, lying on his back with his face turned to the sky. His eyes were closed and his breath was coming out in short gasps.

'What's wrong with him?' His voice wavered as he spoke. 'Is he alright?'

'We don't know,' Aralia replied in a choked voice. 'We just don't know.'

James noticed that unlike the rest of them, Oede's body was still faint around the edges. He was a half-ghost, caught somewhere between the worlds.

'We stayed too long,' James whispered. 'I don't know how to help him. I don't know what we should do.' He touched Oede's arm gently. 'I'm sorry. 'I'm really sorry.'

'It's not your fault, James,' Dina said sharply. 'We need to focus.' She bent over Oede and spoke close to his ear. 'Come on, Oede. Fight! Pull yourself back.'

Despite his own fear, James saw that hers was greater. She had already lost her sister and it would break her to lose a friend.

'We can't stay here,' Kaedon remarked. 'We have to find him a proper place to rest. A village perhaps.'

'We don't know where we are,' Will said. 'Clearly not the Gulna Mountains.' He looked towards the sea.

'Let's carry him down to the beach,' Dina suggested. 'There must be houses along the shore.' She stood up and took hold of Oede's arms. 'We must carry him gently.'

Kaedon and Will took a leg each while James and Tala supported his middle. Arthur and Aralia went on ahead to assess the route. Step by step, they edged towards the shore.

Fatigue made them weak but they managed to carry Oede all the way down to the sand. Here they laid him close to the rocks and spread a blanket over him. The twilight was disturbingly still. Even the waves were silent as they rolled gently onto the shore. James half expected the Shadows to appear in the hazy sky, but nothing happened. He felt like there should be a more significant ending to their journey, yet here they were in a place they didn't know with nothing but sea and sand surrounding them.

'It is because this is not the end,' said a voice in his mind. 'It is merely the beginning.'

He knew it was Sylvia speaking but her voice was far away. Already, their venture into No Man's Land seemed like a bad dream. The only thing reminding him that it had been real was the weight of the earthstone in his pocket. He looked along the dunes, trying to focus his tired eyes. Several huts rested between the rocks and the sand; simple buildings made from reddish stone. There were people standing out on the sand, he realised, huddled together in a close-knit group.

'Look,' he said quietly. 'There are people.'

Kaedon had seen them too. He took a step towards them, then stopped. 'I'll go and speak to them. Stay here with Oede.' He directed these words at all of them before striding away across the sand.

'Can someone please go with him?' Dina requested.

James, Arthur, Will, Tala and Aralia all stood up. Leaving Dina with Oede, they hurried after Kaedon. The group of people did not notice them as they approached. There was an uneasy hush in the air, the kind that usually signified death. Slipping around the edge of the group, James saw the reason for it. Three dead men lay on the sand, the waves lapping over their bloated bodies. They lay face down and all had large burn marks across their scalps. It was apparent that they had been dead for some time for their exposed skin was puffy and pale.

The woman closest to him started wailing. Her cry was taken up by others until the whole beach rang with melancholy voices. Several women tried to reach the bodies but others held them back, whispering words of comfort to ease their grief. A broken boat floated on the waves. It had been split through the middle, as if another boat had driven straight through it or something had plunged down from above. James glanced at Aralia who stood beside him, her face deathly pale.

'The Shadows found them,' she whispered.

James turned to the wailing woman and touched her on the arm. She looked at him as if he was an alien species before opening her mouth to begin weeping again.

'Please, wait,' James pleaded. 'Can you tell us what has happened here?'

The woman continued to stare at him. She muttered a few words in her own tongue and drew a circle on her chest with one hand.

'She draws the sign of protection,' Aralia warned. 'She does not trust us.'

James turned back to the woman. 'Where are we?' he asked. 'Are we in Outici?'

'Nnta Outici,' the woman croaked with sudden understanding. 'Nnta Outici,' she repeated with a shake of her head. 'Eeron. Ila Eeron.' She pointed to the sky and plunged one hand towards the other, crashing them together and spreading her fingers to mimic something shattering.

'We're not on the eastern continent anymore,' Aralia said quietly. 'We are on the island of Eeron, close to Henlos and

Arvora.'

James looked at her sharply. 'Arvora?'

'The people tremble like the devil is in them.' Kaedon suddenly appeared behind them. 'They are afraid but they do not understand the true scale of what has happened here. We are not safe here.'

James turned his gaze towards the horizon beyond the sea. It felt like a long way between these shores and home.

'We're not safe anywhere now,' Will said as he, Tala and Arthur joined them. 'They're targeting the innocent.'

'What does that make us?' Arthur asked.

'The deaths here are a message,' Kaedon replied gravely. 'There is only one reason why the innocent die without cause and that is war. This is a clear sign that the war we've all been waiting for has now begun.'

## Chapter 29

OEDE lay on the sand, barely breathing. His skin at least was warm, a sign that he was still alive even though he was unconscious. Several of the villagers noticed his predicament but made no effort to help, too consumed by their own grief.

Hardly knowing what he was doing, James hurried up the beach to where a woman stood outside her hut, watching the proceedings. He pointed desperately to Oede and her hard expression softened a little. She darted inside, only to return a moment later with a water gourd and a loaf of bread. Rather than invite James inside, she pressed these offerings into his hands with a flat smile. Thanking her, James ran back down the beach to Oede. Uncorking the gourd, he poured a drop of water between his lips but still he did not stir.

'He can't,' Dina said. 'We should share the bread between the rest of us.'

In No Man's Land, their insubstantial bodies had not required sustenance but here they realised the full extent of their starvation. They devoured the bread in one sitting, too tired to think about saving any for the remainder of their journey home.

'The people here must keep boats,' Will pondered. 'If we could reach the coast of Henlos, we wouldn't be so far from home.'

'Oede is weak,' Kaedon reminded him. 'He won't be able

to travel for days. Plus it's far too dangerous. There will be Shadows everywhere.'

'The people here may also be unwilling to lend us a boat,' Arthur added.

'Surely it's more dangerous to stay here, so close to Arvora?' James said. 'If we were on a boat, we would at least be travelling towards safer shores.'

'Why are we even here?' Dina asked. 'Why not the Gulna Mountains or even *Arissel*?'

James pressed his fingers into his eyes until the colours danced. He had been asking himself the same question. He had tried to return them all safely to Arissel and not once had that intention wavered.

'If they won't lend us a boat, we'll just have to borrow one,' Tala suggested and everyone turned to look at her with surprise. 'I said borrow, not steal,' she added with a roll of her eyes. 'What other choice do we have? If the Shadows really are close to these shores then time isn't on our side.'

'We have a skilled navigator amongst us after all.' Aralia gestured towards Kaedon. 'If you think we could make it safely across the Eeron Sea, shouldn't we at least try?'

With great reluctance, Kaedon bowed his head. 'Five against two, it seems,' he replied with a faint smile.

'Actually, six,' Dina said apologetically. 'We can't help Oede here. We need skilled healers who can understand what affliction he suffers from.'

Kaedon was silent for a long time but at last he spoke. 'We just need to keep him alive while we travel. The journey won't be easy.' He cast his eyes along the beach. 'There's a boathouse just below the dunes. At least, I think that's what it is. James, Arthur, you come with me. The rest of you stay with Oede. If there is a boat, we'll drag it down here.'

He jumped to his feet and strode away, leaving James and Arthur to follow. They reached the shack which passed as a boathouse and Kaedon tried the door. It was stiff but unlocked and he pulled it open. It was dark inside but he created a light before slipping through. Three boats lay side by side on the sandy floor. The vessels were simply built with slim frames and shallow bottoms. They didn't look strong enough to hold eight passengers, let alone sail the Eeron Sea.

'Moonboats,' Kaedon said. 'I've only ever heard of such vessels.'

The ends of each boat curved upwards, making them look like crescent moons. There were no oars, nor any rowlocks fixed along the gunwales. Each vessel was however equipped with a folded sail and worm eaten rudder.

'Come on,' Kaedon urged, 'let's get one of these boats moving. I'll pull one end and both of you push the other. Somehow we have to drag the boat across the beach without being seen.'

Between them, they slid the boat out of the door and onto the sand. The grieving people on the beach had not yet dispersed but were oblivious to the activities taking place by the boathouse. Kaedon, James and Arthur pushed the Moonboat along the base of the dunes before changing direction and heading down the beach to the sea.

'Ry nta?'

A voice hailed them. Turning, they saw an old man hurrying down the beach towards them. His face was contorted with anger and his fists were clenched into tight balls.

'I think we might be in trouble,' Kaedon muttered. 'Hold the boat.'

James and Arthur held the vessel still while Kaedon

jumped aboard. Close by, Will, Aralia, Tala and Dina lifted Oede's body between them. They carried him to the boat and helped Kaedon to lay him gently inside. The old man continued his steady progress towards them, his voice growing louder and more agitated.

'He doesn't look happy at all,' James said under his breath.

Dina, Will, Aralia and Tala clambered into the boat and James jumped in after them. The old man's shouting had now caught the attention of several others. Three younger men were running down the beach, flailing their arms and yelling. One even raised a hand and sent a beam of light towards the boat. It fortunately missed and fizzled out amongst the waves. Kaedon hoisted the sail without delay. There was no wind and the white triangles did not fill. Kaedon hopped out into the water and pushed the vessel away from the shore. Another beam of light shot towards them. This time it hit the mast which splintered but did not snap.

Two of the young men were now wading into the water, trying to catch up with the slow moving vessel. Kaedon raised a hand and a shower of sparks burst over the sails. He turned his hands in a circular motion so that the light particles swirled around the mast. This movement began to stir up an artificial wind. The sails filled and the boat began to pick up speed. Dina grabbed the tiller and steered the vessel away from the beach. Behind them, the men floundered in the deeper water and were forced to end their pursuit.

'The last part of the journey is often the hardest,' Dina said but a sense of relief had already settled over them.

Sitting in the bow of the boat, James took the earthstone from his pocket and cupped it in his hands. It was warm to the touch and glowed faintly in the gathering dusk. It was not as intricately formed as the firestone or the seastone but was still beautiful.

'May I hold it again?'

Aralia held out her hand and he passed it to her. Its inner light illuminated her pale face, giving it the likeness of a Renaissance painting. James found himself staring at her but looked away when she smiled at him, suddenly embarrassed. He closed his eyes. Perhaps it was best, he thought, to sleep and not allow the fear of being out in the middle of the ocean to haunt him. The gentle motion of the boat had already lulled him into a more relaxed state and he felt his body moving with the rhythm of the waves.

Suddenly, the boat lurched in the water. James opened his eyes again. Eeron was still visible on the horizon, the land a shade darker than the sea. The boat lurched again and he instinctively looked to the sky. No Shadows swooped across the cloudless blue and relief washed over him. His second thought was that perhaps the water was infested with monstrous sea creatures, like those written about in Greek myths. He didn't think they were real, not even in this world, but his fatigued brain was unable to escape his fears.

'Did everyone else feel that?' he asked.

He peered over the side of the boat. Although it was dark, his eyes came to rest on two glowing balls of light that had fixed themselves to the bow. They were bright and round and twinkled gently like stars.

'Astrels!' Will exclaimed. 'In other words, starfish. They're just saying hello.' He reached out to tickle one and it twinkled at him.

James sat back and smiled. 'I thought we'd been attacked by Shadows!'

Aralia passed the earthstone back to him and he tucked it

in his pocket. His eyes were burning from the salt spray and he closed them again. Sleep however eluded him and after a while he simply sat gazing up at the stars. The boat shook again. He smiled to himself and looked over the side once more at the twinkling Astrels. It was amazing, he thought, how such small and boneless fish could cause such a disturbance. Suddenly, the boat jerked with such force that he was thrown against Aralia. There was the sound of splintering wood and looking up, he saw the fractured mast snapping in two.

'That wasn't starfish,' Aralia said tremulously.

'There's something else out there,' Kaedon warned. 'Stay low.'

They cowered in the base of the boat, huddled around Oede. Peering over the gunwale, James saw something moving on the water. At first he thought it was a large wave but he soon realised it was another boat.

'There's a boat out there,' he hissed. 'It's on our tail!'

A soft gasp escaped Aralia's lips. 'It's not the only one. There's a whole fleet out there!'

More boats had materialised behind the first, black shapes sliding through the water.

James thought there were nine or ten of them but a precise number was impossible to calculate. The fleet kept a clear distance between themselves and the Moonboat. All at once the sky was illuminated by a blinding light. Dazzling beams burst forth from every vessel in the fleet, merging to forge a gleaming dome. After just a few seconds, the dome exploded in a shower of white hot sparks.

'Stay low!' Dina repeated Kaedon's instruction. 'Don't let the sparks touch you.'

Shoulder to shoulder, they cowered in the base of the boat.

Dina raised a hand and sent her own stream of light into the sky. It struck a cluster of sparks and a screeching sound filled the air like that of metal on glass.

'Fight back if you can!' Dina now called. 'Disperse the sparks.'

She stood up and the boat wobbled precariously. Holding her hand up high, she sent stream after stream of light into the sky. James, Will, Arthur, Aralia, Tala and Kaedon joined her, fighting with all the strength they had. Undeterred, their attackers fought back and the sky rained with fire. It was then that the Shadows came. They swooped down from above in great numbers, the wind from their wings whipping the waves into a frenzy. The ocean rose to meet the fiery sky and a poisonous steam began to fill the air.

A wayward spark struck Dina on the arm and she cried out. It burned a hole straight through her clothes and fizzled against her flesh. There was no blood but the wound was open and raw. Aralia leaned across to help her but Dina pushed her away.

'Don't tend to me, keep fighting,' she gasped.

'You have to put something on it,' Aralia insisted.

'Nothing will help.' Dina's tone was harsh. The spark continued to fizzle against her skin, burning a hole through her flesh. 'I need treatment with more than just medicine,' she snapped. 'If it spreads to my heart, it will burn that too.' She tore a strip of fabric from her cloak and bound it around her arm.

The sparks released an ashy powder that settled on everything like snow. It coated the boat and everyone in it with a fine, sticky layer that could not easily be wiped away. The sky was alight with fire and dust. Sick and exhausted, James sat down next to Dina who had knelt to check on

Oede. Her face was grey but not just from the ash.

'Are you alright?' he asked. She turned to look at him but didn't speak. 'Is it your wound?' he continued.

She shook her head and tears sprang into her eyes. 'It's not me,' she whispered. 'It's Oede.'

James looked at Oede's sleeping form. 'He'll be alright,' he said with false assurance. 'He has to be.' He could see Oede's breathing had become more ragged and his chest hardly moved at all. In his mind, he called for Sylvia. He repeated her name over and over but she did not answer.

'I think it might be too late to help him,' Dina gulped. She ducked away from a bolt of light and raised herself again with great effort.

Noticing that something was wrong, Kaedon stopped fighting and sat down. He wrapped an arm around Dina and she hissed in pain as he brushed against her scalded arm. Arthur, Will, Aralia and Tala knelt beside him.

'We're outnumbered,' Arthur observed. 'We can't keep this up for much longer.'

The companions looked at one another, wondering if this was the end. Time stood still. Sparks continued to rain down around them but they were oblivious. All eyes rested on Oede. They watched his breath coming out in shorter and shorter gasps and his body slowly failing. His eyes flickered but did not open and Dina gripped his hand tightly in her own.

'We couldn't have done any of this without you,' she murmured. 'Come on, Oede. Live. Fight. We've already lost Dara. Don't let us lose you too.'

Raising her hand one more time, she cast a sheen of light into the air. It formed a dome over the boat, protecting them from the fiery rain.

'We'll never forget you, old friend,' Kaedon croaked.

'I must have something to help him.' Aralia began rummaging in her bag but Kaedon placed a hand on her arm to hold her back.

'There's nothing you can do, no medicine to help. People aren't meant to be caught between this world and No Man's Land.'

'What happens if he becomes trapped there?' Will asked. 'Will he become a lost spirit too?'

'His body is here,' Dina said with a reassuring nod. 'His spirit will be here too.'

She held onto Oede with one hand and Kaedon with the other. James put his arms around Aralia and Will, Will held onto Tala and Arthur and Kaedon also linked arms to form a tight circle around Oede. They sat in silence, watching his chest rise and fall like the waves. Here in the middle of the Eeron Sea so far from home, Oede breathed his last breath. It left his lips like a whisper of wind and vanished into the ether.

A howl of grief escaped Dina's lips. Kaedon tried to hold her but she fought him off.

Looking over the side of the boat through stinging eyes, James saw the beginning of the end. More ships were sliding through the darkness towards them. Ancient battleships with white sails. Light filled the sky and for a moment it shone as bright as day. The air filled with screams and the sound of wood splintering. He realised then that the battleships were not here for them. They had come to fight against the attacking fleet and little by little, the darkness began to fall back.

# Chapter 30

JAMES stood up in the boat. He watched as the enemy fleet began to retreat, their vessels unable to withstand their attackers' torment. The sky was alight with sparks and the Shadows screamed as their eyes were burnt by the brightness. They vanished from the skies in great numbers, leaving the ocean fleet to fight alone.

The new battleships did not move forward unscathed. Several small vessels capsized and their sailors drowned. The scene was horrifying to watch and yet James could not tear his eyes away. His ears rang with the sound of cracking wood and human screams. He knew he ought to feel hopeful that the enemy was falling back but his chest was still tight with anger and fear. This battle wasn't over yet. In the grand scheme of things, it was just the beginning of the war.

Someone reached for his hand and turning, he saw Aralia standing beside him. Her ash covered cheeks were streaked with tears. She didn't speak and stood with her hand in his watching the battle unfold. One of the white sailed battleships broke from the main fleet and came towards them. It was smaller than the rest and filled with green cloaked warriors. At the helm stood a woman. Her cropped cloak was stained with blood and her hair was grey with ash. Her expression was fierce but it softened a little as the ship drew parallel with the Moonboat.

'Who are you?' James asked in a cracked voice. 'Who sent you to help us?'

'My name is Reed,' the woman replied. 'My fleet acts under the command of the Twelfth Messenger.'

'Albert?' James rubbed the dirt from his eyes with trembling hands, hardly able to believe what he'd just heard. 'Albert,' he repeated. 'How did he know where we'd be?'

'He has his ways,' Reed replied gently. 'Now, I must urge you all to climb aboard my vessel. The enemy may be gone for now but they will return with renewed forces.'

Something struck the side of the Moonboat. One last stream of light, sent by a retreating enemy ship. The Moonboat splintered in the centre and water began flooding in. Reed held out her hand to Tala who leapt across to safety first, followed by James, Will, Aralia and Arthur. Hardly aware of what was happening, Dina allowed herself to be prised from Oede's side and passed over to the larger vessel. Kaedon lifted Oede' body over the gunwale into the arms of several waiting warriors.

'Does he live?' Reed asked bluntly.

Kaedon shook his head. 'He is dead.'

Safely aboard Reed's ship, the companions watched as their flooded boat sank beneath the waves. Too tired to do anything more they sank to the floor, finally undone.

'Where are you taking us?' Will asked heavily.

'Back to the north,' Reed replied. 'Albert will be watching for your safe return.'

James rested his head against the gunwale. Someone offered him water and he drank. Bread was pushed between his lips but he couldn't eat. There was a pain between his ribs and every time he swallowed a lump came into his throat. He was unfamiliar with the feeling of grief that now held him in its grasp. He had been sad when his grandmother had died but he'd only been young. He still felt pangs of sadness for his sister even though she had died before he was born. When Dina's sister Daphne had died on the cliffs above Celaeno's Lake he had felt deep regret. The pain of losing someone he'd known well, even if only for a short while, was all consuming. He closed his eyes but all he could see behind his lids were images of Oede.

The ship slid through the waves, flanked by the rest of Reed's fleet. The companions slipped in and out of consciousness, sometimes sleeping and at other times delirious with fatigue. None of the warriors spoke to them, leaving them to rest and grieve alone. The sky changed above them, first the grey light of dawn then the bright blue of day. Soon enough the sun was gone again and the sky darkened with the coming of night. James saw these changes through feverish eyes but could not tell how much time had passed.

Somewhere in those long hours he must have slept for he awoke to find that the boat had stopped moving. The sky was light again but whether it was morning or afternoon he no longer knew. A shadow fell across his chest. Looking up, he saw one of the warriors standing above him with his hand outstretched. Taking the hand, James allowed himself to be pulled to his feet. He saw that the boat had come to rest in a small cove. The tide was low and the salt prints left by the waves ran all the way up the sand. The beach was bordered by low cliffs and sealed off at the top by trees. Jumping from the boat onto the sand, James felt his legs buckle beneath him. His whole body felt like it was still moving with the rhythm of the waves.

'How long have we been at sea?' he heard Tala ask.

'Two days and one night,' Reed answered, 'but the journey

isn't over yet.' She pointed to the trees. A group of ferastia now stood beneath the branches, stamping their hooves with evident impatience.

'Where are we?' Will asked. 'Is this the northern continent?'

'We are in Mellandore, the most southerly region of the northern continent.' Reed held up a hand for silence. 'There will be time for questions when you are safe. For now, we must keep going.'

The companions allowed themselves to be led towards the ferastia. Several attendants stepped from between the trees to take their bags while several others guided them to the waiting ferastia. James found himself allocated to the same beast as Will. They mounted with the help of their assigned attendant. The young man was not much older than themselves and offered a sympathetic smile as he helped them onto the ferastia's back.

'Where is Oede?' Dina's voice rang through the trees.

James turned to look at her. She sat hunched behind Kaedon, her face still grey with ash. Reed trotted over on her own ferastia, a large beast with a white mane and tail.

'Your friend is safe,' she reassured. 'He has been sent on ahead with several of my warriors.'

'Sent on where?' Kaedon asked as if anticipating Dina's next question.

'You will see.' Wheeling her ferastia around, she rode back down the beach. The remainder of her fleet lay waiting beyond the cove. Raising a hand, she cast a stream of green sparks into the air. Almost immediately, the ships began to move, sailing away from the northern shores.

The waiting ferastia stepped aside as she rode through their midst to the head of the group. Several warriors remained on the beach to tend the ship while six accompanied the companions on ferastia. Though James felt safe in their company, he kept tight hold over the earthstone in his pocket. Its smooth surface gave him some comfort when all else was failing. Part of him wished he could exchange the earthstone for Oede's life but he knew the laws of nature did not work in this way.

The ferastia began to walk, following Reed's command. They soon left the beach and the trees behind and broke out into open fields. After a while, the ground began to rise in a gentle slope that eventually levelled out to form a clifftop. The sea appeared again on the horizon, the waves sparkling in the dying light of another day. The air was colder on the northern continent, as if here winter had come early.

Though the afternoon was warm, James shivered. He thought not only of Oede as they rode but also of Dara. Their search for her had only led them further away and he doubted they would ever see her again. Amongst the slave traders, she would not survive. Even if she made it to womanhood, she would become a target for experimentation like the rest of her wrongly imprisoned sex. Her loss, like Oede's death, was a sign of things to come. There could be no world without cruelty and no war without death. All anyone could do was wait for the inevitable hardship that was to come.

The late sun was just setting when James caught sight of their destination in the distance. At least, he assumed it was where they were going for it was the only place they had come across all day. A gleaming tower rose from the landscape. It was built almost entirely from glass; hundreds of windows placed on top of one another to reflect the light of the sun. At this hour, the many colours of the sunset made the tower look like it was made from stained glass. A circular trench divided the building from the surrounding landscape; the site of an ancient moat perhaps. Seven bridges curved across it, gateways to this magical place.

'The Glass Tower,' Reed announced.

'It looks like a palace,' Aralia said in awe.

The ferastia reached the first bridge and began to cross it. On the other side was a circular courtyard paved with white stones. A man in a white robe stood waiting for them. He was young and had a mere haze of stubble on his chin. James thought he looked familiar but could not for the moment place him. The young man greeted Reed with a bow and she dismounted. Following her lead, the companions also slid down from the ferastia. James' legs ached unbearably but there was no time to stand still. The young man began to lead their party across the courtyard towards the tower.

The glass doors opened of their own accord. Beyond them was a small entrance hall and a freestanding staircase spiralled upwards through a hole in the ceiling to another floor. In fact, a hole had been cut around the stairs on every level meaning it was possible to look right up through the centre of the tower to the top. Emerging onto the first floor, the companions found themselves in a corridor made entirely from glass. Only the floor was made of more solid materials for which everyone was grateful. Catching sight of his reflection in one of the windows, James stopped to stare. His face was so coated in ash and salt that he almost didn't recognise himself. In such a pristine place, he felt subconscious of his grubbiness.

The young man led them up the next flight of steps and into another glass corridor. Looking out through the windows, James caught a glimpse of the sea glistening in the light of a newly risen moon. Mounting the third flight of steps, the companions now found themselves in a corridor lined with doors. The young man opened the first without ceremony to reveal a twin bedroom on the other side.

'You must be tired,' he said, speaking for the first time. 'I have been told of your journey and of your loss for which I am sorry. Here you may rest, eat and cleanse yourselves. For now, your journey is over.'

Leaving this room to Kaedon and Dina, he proceeded to open two more doors. He sent Tala and Aralia into one and Arthur, Will and James into the other. As James passed through the doorway, the young man caught him by the arm.

'Not you,' he instructed. 'I'm afraid you must come with me.'

James stared at the young man in disbelief. 'Why?' he managed to ask.

'You must follow me. I'm afraid your presence is required as a matter of urgency.' He glanced down at James' pocket as if he could see the gem lying there.

James cast a longing glance at the beds inside the room before reluctantly turning away. He allowed the young man to guide him down the corridor and up another section of the spiralled steps. They arrived outside another door and the young man opened it before standing aside to let James through. The room beyond was devoid of furniture. Three walls were however decorated with gold flowers which gleamed under the light of a single orb. A row of windows formed a fourth wall through which James could see the star spattered sky. A figure stood in front of the central window. Under the light from the orb, his gingery hair looked gold like the flowers.

'Albert,' James said.

The Twelfth Messenger turned around. His face was grey

and drawn and he didn't step forward with his usual cheerful greeting. At first, James thought the older man simply had not seen him. His eyes looked haunted and were unable to focus on anything.

'I know you are tired,' Albert murmured, 'but I'm afraid we must speak.' His voice was dry, as if he too had gone without water for hours.

He gestured to a chair hidden behind the door and James sat, aware more than ever of the earthstone in his pocket. Albert did not ask about the gem, however. Instead, he began pacing the length of the room and did not speak again for a long time.

'The boundary between worlds is thinning, James,' he said at last. 'You know that more than anyone. Therefore, it is time that I told you about the Elemental Prophesy.'

# Chapter 31

JAMES stared at Albert, wondering what on earth he was talking about. He had never heard of the Elemental Prophesy and it was clear that Albert had planned it this way. For a moment, as he looked into the Messenger's expressionless eyes, he felt a spark of curiosity ignite in his mind.

'What's the Elemental Prophesy?' he asked.

'I am about to tell you.' Albert stopped pacing and came to stand in the middle of the room. His answer was, as ever, infuriatingly ambiguous. James opened his mouth to speak again but the Messenger held up a hand for silence. 'The universe is changing, James,' he uttered. 'The boundary between worlds is thinning and already the darkness spreads to your world.'

James said nothing. He already knew this. The clockmaker, Sylvia and even the Belladonna had told him much the same.

'War is coming,' Albert continued. 'I hoped I would never have to speak those words but it seems I must. When war becomes inevitable, all anyone can do is prepare. And prepare we must. The war waged by the darkness will touch both worlds and the outcome will decide the fate of the universe. One day soon, the barrier between worlds will break and then you must make a choice.'

'I must choose which world I wish to stay in,' James

interrupted. 'Whether the light or the dark prevails, I will still have to choose.'

Albert looked surprised but this expression quickly faded. 'I suppose it was obvious that you would find out before you were told.'

'I *was* told,' James revealed, 'by the clockmaker.' The old man had spoken about more than just this but James did not have the energy to impart what he knew just yet.

'Ah, yes,' Albert began. 'The clockmaker.'

The way he said this made James suddenly wonder if he knew about everything anyway. He was about to ask Albert if this was true when the Messenger spoke again.

'Those who watch for disturbances between the worlds know when someone enters No Man's Land,' Albert explained. 'They know too when someone passes from one world to the other and back again. All crossings are known to them, regardless of the purpose or the outcome.'

The memory of Oede lying lifelessly in the Moonboat sent a spear of pain through James' chest. 'You know about Oede, don't you?' he managed to say. 'Is there any way we could have saved him?'

Albert inclined his head but it was not obvious which question he was answering. 'All magic comes at a cost,' he said. 'It is the way.'

James remembered Asterope saying the same words in No Man's Land. She had warned there might be a price for taking the talisman and the earthstone. A price paid by Oede's life.

'Few enter No Man's Land and survive,' Albert continued. 'Fewer still have a body to return to like Oede. He did not die because he was weaker than anyone else. He died because he was far stronger.'

James thought of Sylvia. She had died a different kind of

death to Oede, one where she lived on as a ghost with a half-life. He felt suddenly glad that Oede at least had been spared that fate.

'How is it that you've passed through No Man's Land?' he said aloud. 'You've been to my world. I saw you at the airport. Why did nothing happen to you?'

'I was never really there. I was merely a projection of my real self. It is how I survived. I can reach into your world in the same way the Belladonna can. You, who have a place in both worlds, can see the projections of those who pass momentarily between.'

'How is it that my friends passed between worlds alongside me?' James asked. 'Were they projections too?'

Albert shook his head. 'I'm afraid it is more complicated than that.' He did not elaborate and instead returned to James' original question. 'Oede could not have been saved. Not by you or anyone else. The condition he suffered from is known as Ne-Tema. The state of prolonged in betweenness. Such an occurrence has only been recorded once in history. Some people believed that Arvad suffered such a fate.'

James fiddled with the corner of his robe and let a flake of ash float to the floor. His shoes were filled with holes, he noticed, and the hems of his trousers were crusted with salt and sand. A prolonged silence fell over the room. He could hear the beating of his own heart and the ticking of the clock in his pocket.

'Now,' Albert spoke at last. 'Let me return to the Elemental Prophesy.'

James sat up a little straighter, wondering what Albert was about to reveal.

'The prophesy refers to the occurrences set in motion at the exact moment the crystals were formed,' he began. 'It does not predict or refer to the fate of any one person. It simply prophesies the event that will bring the crystals together again and all that such an occurrence signifies. Arvad understood the power of the crystals and foresaw the completion of his quest. He knew that if the crystals were brought together by the right person at the right time, they could create an extraordinary force for good.'

James nodded. Albert had told him of the crystals and their power the first time they'd met formerly in No Man's Land. He'd known right from the start that the whole purpose of this quest was to bring the crystals together again. He watched as Albert raised a hand and traced a row of letters in the air to spell out the words: 'The Elemental Prophesy.'

'I always thought prophecy was spelled with a C,' James said, noting Albert's use of an 'S' in the final word.

Albert couldn't help but smile. 'Well observed, James Fynch. You are of course right. In the old language, this word is neither spelt with a C or an S, however. The modern spelling uses an S to make pronunciation easier.' He drew another letter in the air. It was formed of two curves and two straight lines; much like an S only the lines and curves were not connected. 'This is an ancient letter, used to symbolise eternity and great power,' he explained.

'What kind of power?' James asked.

'It represents many things in different cultures. However, see how the letter has four parts to it. Two lines and two curves. The lines represent the strength of fire and earth while the curves represent the free flowing natures of water and air. The four lines also represent the four quarters of Arvad's tale, a tale kept secret for generations by…'

'The Quartet Keepers,' James finished for him, 'known as Lekkaro in the old language.'

Albert inclined his head. 'Arvad's tale was divided into quarters to protect it. Written records are rare for the simple reason that no one really knows the story save for the Keepers. For centuries, the Keepers have given up their lives to keep the secret. Now however, three crystals have been found and three quarters of the story revealed.'

James looked at his feet. 'You know who they are, don't you?'

Albert looked away and a sliver of moonlight fell across his tired face. 'I know of two, just as you do. Nuria, the Chinjoka dragon keeper, and Tala.'

'Tala!' James exclaimed. 'She's one of the seven sisters, not a Quartet Keeper.'

'She is both, just as Nuria is both and just as the remaining two Keepers shall be.'

'Why did Tala never say anything before?' James demanded.

'Because I asked her not to.'

James narrowed his eyes. 'How is it that you know her? When I spoke to you about her before, not long after I met her, you feigned ignorance. Why?'

'I thought you might have worked it out,' Albert replied.

James rubbed his stinging eyes. Several times on their journey, he had wondered why Tala spoke of Albert as if she knew him. He had never asked her and she had never said.

'I don't know,' he replied. 'Why would I?'

Albert did not answer immediately. 'I thought it might change things if you knew,' he eventually said. 'You see, Tala is my daughter.'

James gaped at him, not knowing what to say. Of all the possible reasons for Albert and Tala to know each other, father and daughter had not crossed his mind. He opened his mouth to say something but no words came.

'One thing you must understand, James, is that all of us are here to help you,' Albert said. 'Yes, the workings of this world are complex but together we are finding a way to understand it. I would not put you in the company of those I do not trust.'

'Your daughter?' James spoke at last. 'Why didn't you say anything? Why didn't she say anything? I would never have guessed.'

'She looks like her mother,' Albert murmured with a smile. 'Her mother came from Yth, a desert region on the southern continent. She was an oracle and the wisest individual I have ever known. Oracles do not have symbols. For them it is not seen as a curse but a blessing. While I have a symbol, Tala, like her mother, does not. I met her mother while I was travelling the south in search of a temple. The same temple where I first met Oede.'

'How long have you known Oede?' James asked. 'How long did you know him for, I mean,' he added hurriedly.

'I knew him as a young boy there. He was a Brother before moving to the Hidden City in answer to another calling. The green necklace he wore at his throat was a symbol of the temple.'

James swallowed the lump in his throat. 'What happened to your… to Tala's mother?'

'She died soon after Tala was born. I brought the child here with me to the north where she grew up in Idessa. It is why you saw her there in the streets. I wanted you to meet her but I did not want you to know who she was. It was not the time. Had she told you her quarter of Arvad's tale, you would not have been able to complete the quest.' James opened his mouth to ask why not but Albert held up a hand. 'Some things will have to wait.'

He moved across the room and opened a door at the far end. He went through it without a word, leaving James to follow. Rising from his chair, James dragged himself over to the doorway but stopped when he saw the room beyond was not empty. Five people stood at the far end: three men and two women. All of them were watching him expectantly. Staring back at them, he realised that they weren't all strangers. The woman in the centre was Isla, Albert's Messenger sister who had come to the village of Muir to take the seastone from him. Seeing that he recognised her, she smiled and came towards him.

'Greetings, James Fynch.'

'These men and women are fellow Messengers,' Albert said as James entered the room. 'Five out of twelve. You have of course already met Isla.'

James nodded and allowed Isla to take his hand. She was dressed in a pure white cloak and he once again felt self-conscious of his own dirty appearance. When she stepped back, the other Messengers came forward in turn to take his hand. He nodded politely at them as they introduced themselves but was too tired to engage with anything they said.

'The Messengers are here because they believe in our cause,' Albert said in his ear. 'They believe in the light, in the prophesy and in you. With their support, the light strengthens. It is time for you to show them the crystal.'

With all eyes upon him, James felt a rush of nerves. He wished his friends were with him to take credit for their part but they were not and he had to face the room alone. With trembling fingers, he reached for the crystal. Part of him wanted to keep it hidden, to lock it away where only he could see it. It had filled his mind for many months and he almost didn't want to share it.

'Show them,' Albert urged again.

James drew the crystal from his pocket and slowly opened his hand. The amber gem glittered fiercely in the light of the many orbs hovering above him. He could feel the stone pulsating with power and knew that the other crystals must also be here. A hush fell over the room. It was the silence of those consumed by awe. Isla came towards him again and he saw that this time she held a box in her hands. The same box with the imprinted cushion inside where he had placed the ruby and the sapphire before.

The power of the earthstone filled him, pounding through his veins with such force that he felt suddenly dizzy. The light in the room began to spin and everything became a colourful blur. He stumbled backwards and felt someone catch him before losing consciousness.

# Chapter 32

JAMES woke up with a start. He sat up abruptly, wondering where he was. Holding out his hand, he filled his palm with a ball of light and sent it floating above his bed. It illuminated a small, white painted bedroom, different to the one he'd entered with Will and Arthur several hours before. The bed he was in was soft and warm. Another bed stood against the opposite wall but this one was unoccupied.

Reaching up to touch his face, he found that his skin was smooth and clean. He vaguely remembered bathing in a deep bath but couldn't recall any more than that. Looking to his left, he saw that a breakfast tray had been laid on his bedside table. The meal comprised of oatmeal, bread and fruit and he began to eat hungrily. As he bit into an apple, memories began flooding back to him. A lump rose in his throat but he swallowed the piece of apple, forcing it back down. Before he could take another bite, a knock sounded on the door.

'Come in,' he called.

Will entered. 'He wakes, the hero of the hour,' he said with false cheeriness.

James rolled his eyes but instantly regretted it as pain seared his head. 'I'm no more a hero than anyone else. How long have I been asleep?'

'Almost a day. We've all were.'

'Have you seen the others, then?' James asked.

'I can't quite believe we're here.' Will ignored the question and opened the curtains at the end of James' bed. 'Every time I close my eyes I'm still sweating on a mountainside or lost in some mist.'

James blinked in the evening sunlight streaming through the windows but said nothing. Another knock sounded on the door. Will opened it to reveal Arthur on the other side.

'We've been summoned downstairs,' he announced. His eyes wandered over to James'. 'What happened to you last night? We thought you were sharing a room with us?'

'Albert,' James replied but did not elaborate.

He leapt out of bed. Arthur and Will left the room so that he could change into the fresh clothes that had been laid out for him. He re-joined them in the corridor moments later, still rubbing sleep from his eyes. Though he still felt exhausted, his limbs did not ache as much as before and some of the woolliness had cleared from his mind. A woman stood waiting for them at the end of the corridor. She smiled at them and proceeded to guide them upstairs to the next floor. The same floor James had been led to the evening before for his meeting with Albert. Sure enough, the woman opened the door to the same room and stood aside to let the boys through.

They were not the first to arrive. Dina and Kaedon stood by the central window, wrapped in one another's arms. Tala and Aralia hovered on either side of them. The only other individual present was Albert. He stood gazing out of the window but turned around as James, Will and Arthur entered.

'Welcome,' he said. 'Thank you all for joining me.' The formality he had lacked when speaking to James the night before was no longer absent from his voice. 'There are things that must be done,' he continued. 'Tonight there are to be two celebrations. We come together to remember the life of our friend Oede and to observe the Binding of two who still stand among us.' He glanced towards Kaedon and Dina who smiled tiredly at each other.

'What's a Binding?' James whispered to Will.

'It means they're committing to each other forever. Like a marriage but without the paperwork. A Binding Ceremony joins two people together using magic and is therefore unbreakable.'

Dina detached herself from Kaedon and came to stand in the centre of the room. She was dressed in a flowing blue robe against which her red hair looked striking. Her expression was softer than James had ever seen it, even though it was still sad.

'We never know when life will end, as it did for our friend,' she said quietly. 'Kaedon and I wish to be Bound before the world is consumed by war.'

'And so you will be,' Albert reassured, 'but first we have some farewelling to do.'

He gestured for everyone to follow him out of the room and down the stairs to the entrance hall. From here, he led the way across the courtyard and over the empty moat to the twilight fields that led down to the sea. A boat rested on the narrow strip of sand by the water's edge. Inside it lay Oede, dressed in a green cloak with his arms crossed over his chest like a Viking warrior. His face was peaceful and his lips even bore the memory of a smile. He was attended by two women in white who stood respectfully aside as the mourners approached.

'He always wanted to be sent off this way,' Dina said. 'Not buried beneath the earth but free beneath the sky.'

Albert laid a hand on her arm. 'Are you ready?'

Dina nodded. 'It is time.'

'Once there were eight, now there are seven,' Kaedon murmured. 'Farewell Oede from the Arco family. It was a privilege to have known you.'

James had never heard Oede's family name mentioned before and wondered where he had really come from. He joined his friends in a semicircle on the upper shore. Albert left them and wandered down to the boat. The white clad women pushed it out onto the water and set it afloat. Raising his hand, Albert cast a stream of light over the vessel and it burst into flame. James had never attended a funeral before, let alone a boat burning. A send off such as this seemed more natural and more moving than simply placing a body in a coffin, singing sad songs and dressing in black.

Between the fire and waves and under the open sky, Oede was returned to the elements. His burial vessel carried him forth over the ocean towards unknown shores. The companions stood on the beach watching his departure. Even after the boat had vanished into the twilight, they stood gazing out to sea with heavy hearts. Only when it became darker and colder did Albert suggest they return to the tower. They crossed back over the fields in a close knit group, feeling like they were leaving a part of themselves behind on the shore.

Orbs had been lit inside the Glass City. From the outside, the windows were dark but all was ablaze within. Albert led his heartsore troop up several flights of stairs and through several corridors to an unfamiliar room. A long table stood in the centre, covered with a white cloth and piled high with food. Platters of meat, vegetables, bread, cakes and fruit; enough to feed hundreds. The room had been decorated with paper streamers and an excess of orbs gave the space a palatial glow.

'Now it is time for our second celebration,' Albert announced.

Dina looked suddenly doubtful but Kaedon took her face in his hands. 'Oede would have been happy for us. We have not forgotten him so soon. We could never do that. Let's celebrate and in doing so remember our friend and his sacrifice.'

Albert bade them come and stand before him. He raised his hands and streams of white light burst from his fingertips. These glowing trails wrapped themselves around Kaedon and Dina's wrists before surrounding them entirely. They drew together in a kiss and Will uttered a cheer that was swiftly echoed by James, Aralia, Tala and Arthur. The doors of the room swung open. In came the Messengers James had already met, followed by more people, those who had been on the fighting fleet and those who seemed to work here. Dina and Kaedon sat at the head of the table and everyone else settled around them.

The night was long and filled with much celebration. Peeling away from his friends, James went to stand by the central window. The night was dark but tiny stars pricked through the velvety sky. Less than two days ago, he and his friends had been navigating the Eeron Sea and now they were here, revelling in relative luxury. He was surprised to find himself missing the fresh air and the strange simplicity that came from taking life one hour at a time.

He turned back to the room. Everyone was laughing and smiling, forcing themselves to celebrate when deep down they all knew what was coming. This might be the last chance for festivities and people were making the most of it. James looked around for the faces he knew. Albert still sat at the table with Isla and the happy couple, deep in conversation. Aralia and Arthur stood talking with one of the Messengers whose name he could not remember but Will and Tala were nowhere to be found. He scanned the room again and spotted them standing in the far corner. Their faces were close together and their lips just touching. He grinned despite himself. Will had evidently forgiven Tala for her curse though he clearly didn't know about Albert being her father yet.

James looked again at Aralia. Catching his glance, she stood up and came towards him with Arthur just behind. Will and Tala also tore themselves apart and came to join him by the window. The conversation was light, masking any hidden pain and fear. They all felt a mutual desire to forget what lay beyond the windows of this magical place, to pretend there was no Belladonna and no war.

As he stood amongst his friends, James heard a voice deep within his mind. It did not sound like Sylvia or anyone else he knew.

'Rest now,' it whispered. 'The world will soon be consumed by darkness but for now the light still shines.'

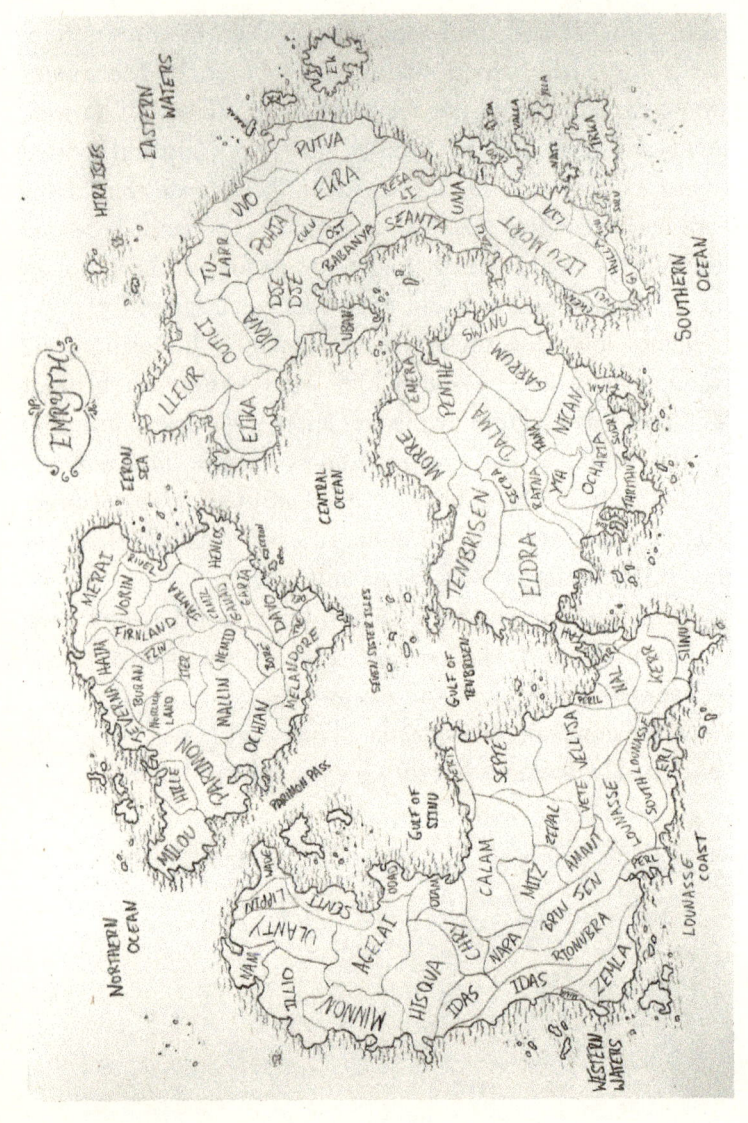

# ACKNOWLEDGEMENTS

To see this series coming to life has been a lifelong dream. As ever, I'd like to thank several people for helping me take this next instalment across the finishing line: Rhodri for standing by my side through all the ups and downs of being an author and for his steady logic, my mum for her insightful edits and continual encouragement, and my grandma and Sandra for their support and excellent feedback. I'd also like to thank Maureen Vincent-Northam for her professional edits and Gina Dickerson of RoseWolf Design for the cover and interior formatting. My thanks also go to Authors Reach for publishing my books and to all my fellow authors for their continual support. Lastly, I would like to thank my readers. Without you, there would be no one to write for and I am, as ever, grateful to each and every one of you.

# ABOUT THE AUTHOR

Francesca Tyer is a Salisbury-based young adult fantasy author and founder of the Untold Stories Academy which offers creative writing workshops and editorial/mentoring support to writers of all ages and abilities. Her mission is to inspire readers and writers through stories.

Francesca studied English Literature at Royal Holloway, University of London. As well as writing books and running her academy, she works as a freelance editor, content writer and English tutor.

You can find Francesca at www.francescatyer.com and on Facebook and Instagram. You can also read about her books at www.authorsreach.com.

If you'd like to learn all about the Untold Stories Academy, you can do so at www.untoldstoriesacademy.com.

# ALSO BY THIS AUTHOR

## *THE FIRESTONE*

Don't miss Book One in *The Elemental Prophesy* series!

*'It was thirteen minutes past midnight when the airport screens went black ...'*

In the early hours, just after midnight, a power cut strikes and in an abandoned street, a broken clock starts ticking. The clock, held in the hands of a teenage boy, has the power to change his fate and the course of history. James Fynch doesn't believe in magic, but his discovery of a coexisting world changes his destiny. The barrier between worlds hasn't been broken for centuries, but with dark powers rising, it is more fragile than ever before. In this magical world, James becomes bound to a quest for the firestone, one of four mythical crystals able to destroy the rising darkness. Although James doesn't believe in magic, he must find the firestone or else both worlds may fall...

*'To think this is Tyer's first novel is mind-blowing - for this is the work of a seasoned writer whose attention to detail, character development and world-building, galvanises her as a most accomplished author.'*
– Dr Who Online

**What readers are saying:**

'An exciting book from beginning to end. I didn't want to put it down and think anyone between the ages of 8 to 80+ will love it.'

'It is no good trying to read one chapter at a time, as every chapter ends with a sentence that spurs you on to the next.'

'One of those books you don't want to put down.'
'Well thought out and imaginatively written.'
'An excellent YA adventure.'
'Fast-paced and exciting.'
'A page turner.'
'Great debut book.'
'A roller-coaster of a story.'
'Gripping. Magical. Stunning.'
'Fantastic! I was gripped from word 1!'

**Available online and in bookshops.**
**Now also available on Audible, narrated by Clive Mantle.**

## *THE SEASTONE*

Don't miss Book Two in *The Elemental Prophesy* series!

***"No tale is ever complete. Stories go on forever and it is only we who end them ... "***

Several months have passed since James Fynch returned to his world, but not a day goes by when he doesn't think about his extraordinary adventure. Turning the dials of the clock, he finds himself once again in Arissel. Reunited with Will, Arthur and Aralia, the quest for Arvad's crystals begins again. The task ahead is daunting and the companions must use every skill they possess to fight against the rising darkness. Danger lurks everywhere, but the journey is far from over. Following nothing but a myth about the mystical island of Arvora, they face enslavement and death in their race to find the seastone...

### What readers are saying:

'Francesca weaves a story that keeps the reader entranced from beginning to end. We visit new lands and watch the four friends face more dangers as they race to reach the next crystal.'

'This is the second book in Francesca Tyer's series, and every bit as good as the first. Packed full of mystery and adventure, it is a great read for children of nine or ten upwards.'

'Perfect for everyone who believes in magic.'
'Plenty of thrills, twists and turns.'
'I didn't want to put it down.'
'Thrilling from start to finish.'
'The description of the scenery is brilliant.'
'Such a well-written book with an enticing story line.'
'Suitable for fans of *His Dark Materials* or *Harry Potter*.'
'A super novel—I'm looking forward to the next instalment.'

### Available online and in bookshops.

# LEAVE A REVIEW

One of the easiest ways you can help an author is by leaving a positive review.

If you enjoyed *The Earthstone* or any other book by Francesca Tyer, a review on Amazon, Goodreads or Waterstones would be much appreciated. Alternatively, you can send a message directly to Francesca via her website: www.francescatyer.com

# BOOKS FOR ALL AGES

ADVENTURE
FANTASY
HISTORY
HORROR
MYSTERY
PARANORMAL
ROMANCE
THRILLERS

Visit us at: www.authorsreach.com
Join us on Facebook
Join us on Instagram

LET THE MAGIC BEGIN!